Praise for the **Kate Jones Thriller Series**:

"...an unrelenting thriller of a tension-filled novel... *Yucatan Dead* is the stuff of which blockbuster movies are made...very highly recommended..." ~ ***Midwest Book Review***

"...*Yucatan Dead* ratchets up the tension from the start as Kate deals with hit women, warring Mexican drug cartels, and unofficial paramilitary organizations. Survival is never a given..." ~ ***Big Al's Books 'n Pals***

"DV Berkom's latest Kate Jones novel is absolutely superb! I was hooked from the first page and had to be ejected from my aeroplane seat by a member of staff because I was so engrossed in the book, I had not realised we had landed..." ~ (*A One Way Ticket to Dead*) **Carol Wyer**, *bestselling author*

"...Fast moving intrigue [and] adventure. I would highly recommend this book to readers who enjoy a fast-paced book with strong, interesting characters." ~ (*A One Way Ticket to Dead*) **Barbara Rauch**, *Amazon Reviewer*

"As a stereotypical guy, I usually don't enjoy, or read much of, fiction that has a female as the main character - mainly because I can't relate to them. However, D.V. Berkom is one good storyteller and I am looking forward to reading the continuing saga of Kate Jones..." ~ (*Bad Spirits*) **Michael Gallagher,** *Top 10 Amazon Reviewer*

VIGILANTE DEAD

D.V. BERKOM

Cover by Deranged Doctor Designs

This book is a work of fiction and any resemblance to any person, living or dead, any place, event or occurrence, is purely coincidental. The characters and story lines are created from the author's imagination and are used fictitiously.

ISBN-13: 978-0-9979708-4-5
ISBN-10: 0997970847

For the NaWo

ONE

Lisa

THE PULSING MUSIC made the excruciating pain worse.

Lisa closed her eyes for a moment, trying to block the spearing ache in her left temple. Silver flashing pinwheels erupted in her periphery and were getting worse, a sure sign that a whopper of a migraine was on its way.

She had to find Momo. Ian had said he'd be there. She would have waited until Ian showed up after work to make the buy, but the headache had become too severe and she needed relief, now.

Making her way through the shifting crowd in the living room, Lisa pushed past a massive guy with shoulders the size of a building bobbing his head up and down to the strains of Nicki Minaj's *Super Bass*. The room smelled of sweat and booze and weed, and it was all she could do to stay on task. With so many bodies in such close proximity the air was thick and warm. And suffocating. If Lisa hadn't been feeling so shitty she'd have been dancing and singing along with everyone else. Instead she was fighting to concentrate.

She spotted the evening's host, Althea, across the room, and by sheer force of will caught up to her before she could disappear into the crowd. Althea smiled at Lisa and bent over to hear her. She still had to yell to be heard above the booming bass.

"I'm looking for Momo."

With a raised eyebrow, Althea straightened and scanned the crowd. Apparently not finding what she was looking for, she said something to a man standing next to her. He replied and nodded toward the stairs leading to the second floor.

"Momo left about an hour ago."

Lisa groaned. "Ahh, God, no." *I'll never make it back home. Not like this.*

"Looks like you need something now," Althea said, her warm breath tickling Lisa's ear. She smelled of wine and cigarettes. "Momo's boy, Bobby, is upstairs, first door on the right."

A small flame of hope flared in Lisa's chest. She managed a smile and nodded her thanks before making her way around the perimeter of the room to the stairway. Halfway up the stairs she stopped to take a deep breath to fight a wave of nausea.

Once the sick feeling receded, she continued to the second-floor landing. Beige carpeting stretched in both directions, punctuated by white trim and closed doors. The overhead lights spiked into her brain and Lisa shaded her eyes. Two people stood at the end of the hall to the left, sharing a blunt and waiting for the bathroom. The sharp, acrid scent of marijuana made her headache worse. Holding her breath, Lisa went right and knocked on the first closed door.

There was a pause and the door opened. A thin young woman with translucent skin and dishwater blond hair beckoned her inside and closed the door behind her. Although the pain didn't diminish, relief came as the muffled music receded to a manageable thump.

She was in someone's bedroom. To her left stood a bed, two night stands, and a large dresser. Prints on the wall depicted bucolic settings in some European country, a world away from the Seattle neighborhood in which Lisa found herself. A slight, wiry guy with sandy brown hair and brown eyes sat on the queen-size bed and regarded her with mild curiosity.

"Are you Bobby?" Lisa asked, working hard to maintain against the alarming throb spiking through her head.

He nodded. "Yo. And who are you?"

Lisa winced at the loudness of his voice.

"Lisa. I was supposed to meet up with Momo, but Althea said that you're the guy to talk to. I'm looking for something to help with my pain." She kept her voice low and tried to keep the words to a minimum, but the act of speaking still lanced through her like a thousand blaring horns.

"Yeah, I'm taking over for Momo." Bobby leaned forward, a smug expression on his face. "What are you looking for?"

Lisa rubbed her temples and closed her eyes for a moment, willing the pain to lessen enough so she could hold a conversation with the man.

"Anything. I usually take oxy, but my doctor—"

Bobby waved her explanation away. "Say no more. I got just the thing." He reached into his coat pocket and brought out a plastic baggie. He picked out half a dozen pills, which he handed to her.

"What are these?" she asked, suddenly apprehensive. She didn't know the guy. Were they safe? Then she remembered Ian assuring her that Momo only dealt in what were considered the best counterfeits around, and she relaxed a little.

"I think you'll like them," he said with a smile. "They're strong, but they'll do the trick. Just take one to start."

She dry-swallowed one and put the other five in a metal case in her purse. "How much do I owe you?"

Bobby shook his head. "On the house."

Lisa glanced at him in surprise. "I can pay."

"Any friend of Momo's is a friend of mine. Besides, you like them, you come back and only deal with me."

Lisa nodded. "Bobby, if these work, I'll come back and buy everything you've got, believe me."

Bobby smiled as he stood. "I gotta bounce." He stuffed the baggie back in his pocket and picked up his coat from the bed. The other woman slipped her arm through his and they walked to the door.

"Do you think it would be all right if I just lay down here for a minute?" The thought of heading back downstairs into all that movement and heat and suffocating noise made Lisa want to hide in a dark corner and assume the fetal position.

He shrugged. "Don't see why not."

As soon as Bobby and the woman were gone, Lisa turned off the bedside lamp and crawled onto the bed with a heavy sigh. Tears of pain rolled down her cheeks, wetting her neck and hair. The discomfort was so intense she thought her skull would literally explode.

Come on, little pill. Start working your magic.

With oxy, relief usually came within minutes, although it wasn't working as well as it used to. She hoped Bobby's concoction would be as fast or faster. During her last visit to the clinic, her doctor had told her he couldn't in good conscience write another prescription for oxycodone, even though it was working to alleviate the migraines. He suggested trying various over the counter remedies or possibly some herbs.

She patiently explained that she had tried everything, from naproxen sodium to warm baths to diet to alcohol, but nothing worked. Still, the doctor had resisted.

Lisa checked her watch. Twelve minutes had elapsed. She took a deep breath and waited, hoping for blessed relief. Closing her eyes she tried the visualizations the pain therapist had taught her, but the tropical beach and cool blue water weren't cutting it this time.

The minutes ticked by and Lisa was about to get up from the bed when a warm flush started low in her belly and flowed outward to her arms and legs. The sensation rushed through her, bringing with it a feeling of immense relief and well-being. The migraine receded into the background and for the first time that evening, she smiled.

Damn, if that's what these little pills do, I'm going to buy stock in Bobby's company. Lisa giggled at the thought of a drug dealer going public and selling stock to shareholders.

Why not? I've heard of stranger things.

Lisa's arms and legs grew heavy, and she tried to move. Too much effort was involved, so she gave up. She felt like she was soaring in space, and she heard herself giggle again. A euphoric, floaty feeling replaced all other sensation and she gave herself over to it, enjoying the relief the pills offered. She'd never felt this good, ever.

But then the floating sensation changed—subtly at first. The welcome lightheaded feeling soon turned to dizziness. She struggled to stand and the vertigo hit her, knocking her back onto the bed. Nausea churned her stomach. Something wet and warm spread across her legs and she looked down. She'd vomited and hadn't realized it.

Alarm swept through her and she fought to move off the bed to get to the door, but her legs wouldn't support her and she fell onto the carpet with a thud. The euphoric feeling receded, replaced by dread. Breathing became difficult and she opened and closed her mouth, trying to get enough oxygen into her lungs.

It didn't work.

The bedroom door opened and excited voices joined in with the driving bass of the music below. Hands gripped her under the arms and she was pulled to a sitting position. She closed her eyes and sank toward the darkness, not knowing how long she'd been there and not caring, either.

The last thing she heard were the sirens.

Two

Kate

THE CROWD MILLING around the front of the nightclub obscured my view of our target. Bright streetlights cast an artificial glow across the partygoers taking advantage of the unseasonably warm spring evening. I checked my watch: it was after ten.

The multitude parted briefly and I caught a glimpse of green fabric and greasy brown hair. Dressed in an army field jacket, dirty cargo pants, and heavy combat boots, Charlie Krueger, the guy Sam and I were following, looked more like a down-on-his-luck vet than a high-level informant. Krueger glanced furtively at his surroundings. An instant later he disappeared into an alley leading through the bowels of Pioneer Square. Sam motioned for me to follow.

"Let me know which way he goes and I'll bring the Tahoe around the other side."

I nodded and hurried past the club, working my way between two twenty-something women with multiple piercings and a group of selfie-addicted tourists wearing Hello Kitty T-shirts. I made it to the alley and turned left in time to catch a glimpse of our slippery target. Charlie Krueger blended with the shadows and I did the same, staying close to the wall. At the end of the alley he stopped to look over his shoulder. I froze in place, thankful for the darkness. Apparently satisfied that he wasn't being followed, he disappeared around the corner of the building. I upped my pace to keep him in sight.

My name is Kate Jones, newly minted private investigator for Akiaq Investigations. Jones is just one of several last names I've had over the years. Changing names, addresses, and hair color becomes second nature when you're on the run, and keeping track of who I was supposed to be ended up being too much like a full-time job. Now that the bad spirits from my past were gone, I'd settled on Jones. It was easy to remember.

"He's headed east on King Street," I said into the whisper mic pinned to the inside of my collar.

"On my way," Sam replied.

I'd gone full Seattle tonight, tucking my now-blond hair up under a dark blue ball cap and wearing a quarter-zip sweatshirt over a pair of jeans and a gray tee that read "Nirvana," a hidden tribute to the '90s grunge band. The ensemble was topped off with an unremarkable-looking waterproof slicker in case the weather went to crap. Since moving to Western Washington from Arizona, I'd given up guessing at appropriate attire and resorted to the Seattle-native standby of layering against the elements. Spring in Western Washington was like that; what might be an epic downpour one minute could morph into a balmy evening like tonight, but might just as quickly flex into freezing cold, with black ice on the sidewalks.

We were tailing Krueger because he was somebody's informant, and were keeping tabs on him for a friend of Sam's in the Seattle Police Department. We'd both thought it would be a routine stakeout, but then Charlie went rogue.

Krueger was on a mission. Without a glance to either side, he turned right off of King Street and disappeared. I hurried to the corner, but he was already halfway down the next block.

"He's headed south on Occidental," I murmured into the mic.

"Copy that. Stay with him. Maintain discreet so you don't get burned."

"On it." I slowed my pace enough so I didn't look like I was chasing him but still kept Krueger in sight. At the next intersection he paused and checked both ways before he crossed the street and continued south. Sam's SUV appeared down the block to my left and pulled to the curb. I took out my phone and pretended to check the screen while I continued along the same sidewalk.

A cop turned private eye, Sam Akiaq was a long-distance runner, martial arts master, and the most accurate marksman I'd ever met. He was also an enigma who lived by a spiritual code I couldn't begin to understand. It probably had something to do with his Native Alaskan heritage. Either that, or it was all a ruse to get me into bed.

If so, it worked.

I hung back and crossed the street. There'd been a concert at the Wamu Theater earlier, and there were still plenty of people around. Krueger wouldn't think anything of my being there. I glanced behind me to see Sam and the Tahoe less than a block away. My subject entered a parking lot and upped his pace when a dark green van pulled next to him and stopped. I ducked behind a vehicle, keeping Krueger and the van in sight.

"He's got company," I said to Sam.

The van's door slid open and two men exited. Krueger pivoted like he intended to run, but they were too quick. There was a brief scuffle before the two larger men managed to drag him inside the vehicle. They slammed the door closed and the van sped off.

"Shit." I turned and sprinted back to the SUV, threw the door open, and climbed in.

"Did you get the plates?" Sam asked as the Tahoe squealed away from the curb.

"Yeah." I grabbed a pen from the console and wrote it on my hand while Sam speed-dialed the friend we were working for and put him on speaker.

"Hey, Mac. We're in pursuit. Our guy was apprehended by two thugs in a dark green van and they're headed south on Occidental."

"Copy that, Sam. Keep on him. I'll see which one of our units is available. Do not make yourselves known. This is a high-level informant. We don't want him compromised."

"Hi Mac, Kate here. I have the plate number."

"Go ahead."

I recited the information and then Sam ended the call. We both fell silent as he concentrated on tracking Krueger.

The van turned off Occidental and headed toward the warehouse district. Sam hung back as much as he could without losing them. Several blocks later, they pulled into a dirt lot next to an older brick building and parked. Sam drove past, turned around in a nearby parking lot, and pulled to the curb on the other side of the street.

"I'll keep an eye on where they're taking him," I said, and exited the SUV.

Phone to his ear, Sam leaned across the console and said, "Wait for me at the door. Do not go inside the building. Mac's sending backup."

"No problem." I grabbed my 9mm from underneath the seat, slid it into the holster in my waistband, and closed the door.

I slipped past the chain link fence that surrounded the lot just as the two thugs from the van dragged Krueger inside the building. Head hanging limply between his shoulders, his face was all different shades of bloody.

The four-story structure looked like it hadn't been used in decades. Along with a boatload of chipped and missing mortar, major cracks ran up its brick façade giving the impression that the last earthquake had almost finished it off. Several of the windows boasted plywood instead of glass.

Sam joined me a couple of minutes later.

"It's not looking good for Mac's guy," I said, and told him what I'd seen.

"Backup is fifteen minutes out, maybe twenty." He scanned the outside of the building.

"I say we go in and find out where they're keeping him, and relay the info. That way, Mac's guys can get to him sooner."

Sam nodded. "Don't take any chances. If they think he's been followed, things will escalate, fast."

We stopped at the door they'd used, and Sam tried the handle. It was locked.

"Here, let me." Stepping in front of him, I slid my slender case of lock picking tools from my pocket and pulled out a turning tool and rake. I learned how to use them by watching YouTube videos. Amazing what a person could find on the Internet. Sam kept an eye out for passersby while I worked my magic.

There's a little larceny in all of us. I just tended to use mine more often than most.

Private investigator work suited me, especially when I was on a case with Sam. After the hell I'd been through dealing with Mexican drug cartels, rogue commandoes, and dirty Drug Enforcement agents, working as an investigator was a cakewalk.

A few minutes later, we were inside. My initial assessment had been correct: the place had cobwebs hanging off of cobwebs, and dust motes that could swallow a Volkswagen. My eyes watered and I stifled a sneeze. A lone bulb flickered above our heads. We stood in the middle of a long hallway. Cold, amorphous shadows obscured corners where rats and other nasty occupants could hide, while a rickety staircase led upward into the gloom. The smell of old-building mildew hit me hard and I reminded myself to breathe through my mouth.

"I'll take right," Sam said as he pulled out a flashlight and disappeared down the hallway.

I glanced to my left, but there wasn't much to see aside from old cobwebs, battered fir-plank flooring, and nineteenth-century brick walls. Sliding a mini Maglite from my pocket, I twisted it on and picked my way along the moldy corridor.

Several yards later, the hallway took a turn to the right. A bare bulb hung from the high ceiling, illuminating a small section of floor, but the light soon dropped off, leaving the rest of the corridor in darkness. Obsolete gas lines that had long ago fueled lamps ran high up along one wall, and steam pipes originally used to carry warmth to the upper levels hung cold and immobile from the ceiling. Something skittered across the floor in front of me and I stopped, my breath catching in my throat. The squeak of a rat echoed in the darkness. Shaking off an involuntary shiver, I continued.

Another turn, another corridor. I'd about given up when a murmur of voices floated toward me. I couldn't judge how far away they were. Cold, dark, and musty places are disorienting that way. I turned off the Maglite and edged closer. Just down the hallway, a glimmer of light from an open door speared through the gloom. I inched toward it and stopped to listen.

"Hit him again." The man's voice was hard-edged and raspy.

"No—don't—"

There was a sickening thud, followed by an *ooph*.

"Tell me who you're working for."

"Like I said—" The speaker, obviously Krueger, gasped between sentences. "I'm not working for anyone. I don't know where the fuck you got the idea—"

Another thud, this time followed by a retching sound.

"Where *the fuck* I got the idea, as you so elegantly put it, was from our mutual friend, Chacon."

"How the hell would Chacon know anything?" Krueger asked. A loud crack echoed against the walls. Krueger groaned.

I edged out of earshot so I could call Sam.

"I'm near the room where they've got Krueger," I said, my voice low. "They're beating the hell out of him."

"Stay there. I'm on my way."

"I'm going to try to get a visual."

"Don't. Just hold on. I'll be right there." The exasperation in his voice chafed. Like I didn't know how to stay hidden and not blow my cover.

I'd had a lot of experience in that department.

I returned to my position near where they were beating on Krueger. The door had been left ajar, and I chanced a peek into the room. The cavernous space was empty except for a pile of broken-down pallets in one corner. A wire-cage light hung from the high ceiling, directly overhead. Four men stood in a circle around Krueger, who was secured to a chair with duct tape that covered his chest, arms, and ankles. His face had taken the brunt of the hits. He looked like a washed-up prizefighter at the losing end of twelve rounds. Blood trailed down his shirt and both of his eyes had swollen shut. I slipped my phone out of my pocket, and after making sure the sound and flash were both off, crouched near the floor and aimed the camera up at the group.

"I swear, Morrie, I'm not working for anybody but you." Krueger's voice cracked.

Dressed in a blue and white tracksuit, one of the men leaned in close and smiled. I assumed it was Morrie. "You see, Charlie, I just don't believe you. Now, Chacon? He don't lie. Understands the way things work, you know?" The guy in the tracksuit stepped away, pointing at Charlie's shoes.

"Shoot him in the foot."

One of the other men pulled a gun and fired. Krueger screamed and rocked back in his chair. A gunman standing behind him put his hand out to keep him from toppling over. Blood pooled on the floor near Krueger's foot.

My heart beat double time as I continued to record the scene, wondering when in the hell Mac or Sam or somebody was going to show up and stop them.

Morrie stepped closer to the now-sobbing Krueger and grabbed his chin, jerking his face up so he could look him in the eyes. "Who are you working for?" he demanded, his voice low.

"I'm telling you the truth. Please, just…let me go." Krueger was whimpering now.

Morrie let go of Krueger's chin and stepped back. "Fuck him."

He turned away as the man behind Krueger fired two rounds into the back of his head. Krueger slumped forward, the tape holding him upright in the chair. I must have gasped, because Morrie's head snapped up.

"What was that?" he asked.

Heart in my throat, I jerked the phone away from the door and sprang to my feet.

"Over there—by the door," Morrie yelled.

I could have qualified for the Olympic track team with how fast I ran.

"Krueger's dead. Get out of the building now, Sam," I muttered into my collar as I raced toward him. I tried to keep my voice even, but the adrenaline dump kicked my vocal cords up an octave.

I sprinted down the hallway, blew around the corner, and almost knocked Sam over. His flashlight skittered across the floor, coming to rest near the base of the wall. Sam picked it up and gave me the once-over. The alarm on my face must have registered, because he pushed me behind him, switched off the light, and drew his gun, flattening his back against the wall. The glow of a bulb down the hall behind us gave off scant light, but I was able to make out Sam's form in the darkness.

"How many?" he asked.

"Four. All armed."

Sam dropped to one knee and raised his gun. I slid the 9mm from my holster. Footsteps echoed toward us along the hallway. Sam peered around the corner and fired. Someone shouted and the footsteps scrambled. A second later, gunshots cracked through the air, pinging off the bricks.

Too close. Sam snapped back, out of the line of fire, and indicated I should go high. I nodded and took the position above him.

Sam rocked forward and back, and on the next rock forward we rotated as one around the corner and fired. Muzzle flashes lit the dark hallway like a strobe. They returned fire and we fell back.

Neither of us had been hit. A soft moan erupted from around the corner, followed by urgent whispers.

Sam stood and fired again. He slipped back, ejected his magazine, and jacked in another one.

"Mac's guys have to be here by now. Run for the entrance and give them a heads-up."

"I don't want to leave you," I said, irritated that my voice caught. I'd almost lost Sam in Alaska when I left him by the side of the road so I could lure an assassin into the woods.

This is different, Kate.

"I'll be fine. Go!"

Shoving memories of Alaska aside, I sprinted down the hall and skidded around the next corner before running flat-out again. I was almost to the entrance when the front door slammed open. Officers wearing jackets that read Seattle PD spilled through the entryway. I skidded to a stop and raised my hands.

"Drop your weapon," bellowed the man standing in front. His gun was aimed at center mass, as were the other six. I held my semiauto out to the side and let it fall to the floor.

"Hands behind your head."

Not a great time to argue. I did what he said.

"My name is Kate Jones. I'm a private investigator with Akiaq Investigations." The words tumbled out in a rush. "My partner, Sam Akiaq, is armed and down that hallway." I nodded behind me. "He's holding off four gunmen and needs help, now. One of them just killed Charlie Krueger."

As if to punctuate my words, a *pop! pop! pop!* reverberated through the cavernous building. My heart rate skyrocketed.

Still covering me with his weapon, the man in front barked orders and a stream of officers raced past me toward the gunfire. Thankful that Sam would have backup, I let out the breath I didn't know I'd been holding.

The guy in charge kept his gun trained on me. I wasn't sure what I could say to make him believe I was on his side. At that moment a tall, muscular man strode through the doorway.

Mac. Relief flooded through me. "You can confirm my identity with him." I nodded at the man who'd just joined us.

"I'll take care of this, Jim," Mac said. "They need you." Jim nodded and lowered his weapon. He hurried past me to join the others.

"Sam's in there," I said, picking up my gun. "I need to go." More shots were fired, followed by shouting.

"Sam's going to be fine. My people are good, Kate. You know that."

"But—"

"No buts." He stood aside and gestured toward the door. "Let's get you out of here." You didn't argue with Mac.

We walked outside and crossed the street. Officers were posted at strategic locations around the perimeter of the building. Yellow tape blocked the entrance to the parking lot and part of the sidewalk. Several unmarked sedans, two patrol cars, and a panel van blocked the street, keeping traffic at bay. An ambulance idled nearby.

"They killed Krueger," I said.

He nodded. The lines under his eyes had deepened since I'd seen him last, and he looked as though he should sleep for a month.

I stared at the door across the street, willing Sam and the others to appear. What was taking so long?

A small crowd had gathered behind the yellow tape, and passersby were trying to get a look at what was going on. Some were using their cell phones to film the scene. Two cops worked the crowd, telling them to move along.

"Here. You'll want to see this." I dug my phone out of my pocket and brought up the video of Charlie Krueger's execution. Mac watched it in silence, his jaw set.

"Can you shoot me a copy?"

"Of course." I entered his phone number and pressed send.

"He was about to give up the name of his source." Mac crossed his arms and stared into the distance. "We were so close."

"Do you guys know the Chacon person mentioned in the video?"

Mac shook his head. "No, but you can be sure we'll follow up."

Just then, a group of agents came through the door, their faces grim as they escorted three handcuffed men to a waiting van. The man in the track suit, Morrie, walked with a bad limp and had bloodstains on his pant leg. The agent supporting him peeled off and led him to the ambulance. I strained to see if Sam was among the exodus. He wasn't.

As two paramedics rolled a gurney into the building, the lead agent and Sam walked out. Sam looked like he was all right.

I took a step into the street, but Mac held me back.

"Wait until they give us the all-clear."

The bloody scene on the side of an Alaskan highway over a decade before came rushing back with full force: Sam lying on a gurney after being shot by Angie McKenna, a freelance assassin hired by the cartel to kill me; the heart-wrenching belief that he'd given his life to keep me safe; the unbelievable joy at the realization he was still alive; the rollercoaster of emotions capped by knowing I had to leave Alaska and Sam behind if either of us were going to survive.

Now that my ex, Roberto Salazar, and his boss, Vincent Anaya, were both dead, and Angie had crawled back to whatever hole she'd been living in, it looked like Sam and I would finally have a chance at a normal life.

I resisted the urge to run to Sam and folded my arms across my chest. He said something to the agent before crossing the street to join us.

"About time you showed up," Sam quipped.

"Hell, if I'd known you two were going commando, I'd have left you to it," Mac replied.

I'd first met Mac Trundle two years before, after I'd moved to Seattle. Mac's affable, laid-back manner belied a turbulent and often violent upbringing, having spent his formative years as a member of one of Seattle's most notorious street gangs. At the age of eighteen, he was shot and almost killed by a rival gang member. The near-death experience got his attention, and he turned to mentoring inner city kids, working with local law enforcement to keep them engaged in more positive pursuits. Eventually, he took the next logical step and applied to and was accepted by the police academy. He now supervised a group of undercover narcotics agents working with dozens of informants trying to stem the flow of drugs into what he affectionately referred to as "his town."

I turned to Mac. "Sorry about your informant, Mac. I wish we could have saved him."

"Yeah. Me too."

"What's next? Any other good leads?" Sam asked.

Mac nodded. "They said something about a guy named Chacon on the cell phone video Kate got. We'll follow up on that. I've got a couple of possible informants, but they're going to take time to bring into the fold." He held out his hand. "Good work tonight, guys. Sorry it didn't go to plan."

"Good luck," I said. The three of us shook hands, and Sam and I walked to the Tahoe. We were almost there when my phone rang. I slid it out of my pocket and answered.

"Kate Jones."

"Ms. Jones, this is Marietta Cranston, the head nurse at Harborview Medical Center."

"What can I do for you?"

"Your number displays as the contact number on one of our patient's phones. A Lisa Schroeder?"

Lisa? A chill ran through me and I stopped dead in my tracks. "Is my sister all right?"

"I'm so sorry to tell you this, but she was found unresponsive at a residence in the Green Lake neighborhood. She's in a coma."

THREE

I T WAS AFTER two in the morning when Sam and I
made it to the emergency room. Lisa's boyfriend, Ian,
was in the waiting area, along with several other
people. Early Sunday morning was obviously prime time
for emergencies. There were only four chairs available in
the room: two to Ian's right and two to his left.

The fluorescent lighting gave Ian's skin and streaked
blond hair a yellow-gray cast, accentuating the worry
etched on his face. He looked up and motioned us over. I
sat in one of the chairs next to him, and he gave us the
latest update, which didn't sound encouraging.

"When the paramedics found her, they immediately
suspected an overdose. They pumped Lisa's stomach and
gave her Narcan to try to stop any further damage.
They're monitoring her closely, but so far she isn't
responding."

"But how did this happen? Lisa doesn't do drugs." I
shook my head. "I mean, don't you think we would have
noticed? She's been living with us for months."

"Was she taking pain medication for anything?" Sam asked. "Maybe she forgot how many she'd had."

Ian nodded. "She was taking oxycodone for her migraines, but she's taken it before without any problems."

"Oxy?" I asked. "I didn't know opioids worked on them." How did I not know my own baby sister was taking narcotics? I'd known about the migraines, of course. She'd had them since she was a teenager. But she'd never let on that they'd gotten that debilitating.

Ian rubbed his eyes. "It was the only thing that helped. And she tried it all."

I leaned back and stared out the window at the darkness beyond, trying to make sense of what happened. The memory of a few days ago came rushing back, when I'd helped her and Ian paint the space they'd secured for their new wine bar in a funky Seattle neighborhood. An older building, the high ceilings had proven a challenge when it came to renovations—and Lisa had almost fallen off the scaffolding they'd rented. Luckily, Ian had been nearby and caught her before she did.

Had she been taking oxy then? Why hadn't I noticed? The medication could have made her unsteady. I'd never have let her climb the scaffolding if that had been the case.

A well-dressed couple somewhere in their late thirties came through the emergency room double doors and walked wearily into the waiting room. The woman, her hair disheveled and eyes rimmed red from crying, walked to the two chairs on the other side of Ian. The man plodded in her wake, a blank stare on his face.

I knew how he felt.

I nodded at them as they sat down. The woman looked away. The man's gaze passed over us as the woman leaned against him. His body rigid, he put his arm around her as she began to cry quietly.

"How did this happen to our baby?" she moaned. The man just stared into space without replying.

A doctor appeared at the nurses' station. Slender, with jet-black, shoulder-length hair, she stood maybe five-six and had an intense air about her. The nurse nodded in my direction and said something as she handed the woman a clipboard. The doctor glanced over her shoulder and gave me a brief nod. She finished writing on the clipboard and handed it to the nurse. I was out of my chair and standing beside her before she turned around.

"I'm Lisa's sister, Kate." I stuck out my hand and the doctor shook it. Her nametag read Dr. Trish Patel.

"Trish Patel, attending physician."

"Is my sister going to make it?"

Dr. Patel's expression gave no clues as to how Lisa was doing. Why didn't doctors ever show any emotion? At least then people could gauge the severity of the problem. It's like they were taught how to present themselves in medical school—the bland, unemotional expression—all to manage overwrought family members. A little bit of humanity would have gone a long way toward helping me deal with my sister's overdose.

"We're cautiously optimistic."

Optimistic. I could work with that.

"Unfortunately, your sister had fentanyl in her system. Are you familiar with the drug?"

Fentanyl? My mind raced for context. How did she get fentanyl? "Isn't that the drug that killed Prince?" Dr. Patel nodded. "She was taking oxycodone for her migraines. How would she get fentanyl?"

"That's the question, isn't it?" Dr. Patel shifted her weight. "Has your sister ever used cocaine or heroin?"

"Never. She's afraid of hard drugs. Thought if she took them that she'd be hooked immediately. I was surprised to find out she was taking oxycodone."

Dr. Patel nodded, weariness plain on her face. The skin around her eyes sagged, and it looked like she hadn't slept in days. "The reason I ask is that we've seen an increase in overdoses involving an especially potent form of fentanyl.

"According to the families, none of these patients had a prior history of illicit drug use. And it's not just younger people. Last night we admitted a sixty-seven-year-old male with a similar concentration of the drug in his bloodstream. He'd been the picture of health except for some arthritis." She sighed. "Drug dealers use fentanyl to cut heroin—it's cheaper and delivers an intense high, and most illicit drug users are aware of the risks. But ingesting it in any form is dangerous, and overdosing isn't unusual."

"Was there oxycodone in my sister's system?"

Dr. Patel shook her head. "Not that we detected. We're sending a sample to the lab for further testing. We've discovered some disturbing chemical abnormalities in recent cases."

"Such as?"

"A high percentage of lead and mercury. Trace evidence of banned industrial chemicals."

"Which could have been introduced at any point in the manufacturing process," I finished for her.

"I'm afraid we'll see more cases unless and until someone figures out where the drugs are coming from." The nurse at the station motioned for the doctor. Patel turned to leave. "I need to get back to my patients. If you'd like to see her, you can go in now. Just don't stay too long. Give your cell phone number to the on-duty nurse, and I'll call you if there's any change."

I nodded and we shook hands.

"I'll do everything I can to help Lisa," Patel said. The impassive expression was gone, replaced by obvious concern.

"Thank you. I believe you will."

Dr. Patel gave me a brief, weary smile and then returned to the nurses' station. I walked back to where Sam and Ian were sitting.

"The doctor says I can go in to see her for a few minutes." I glanced at my watch. It was three a.m.

"What caused the overdose?"

"Fentanyl."

The man sitting next to Ian stiffened and turned. "My son—" he started to say, but was obviously overcome with emotion. The woman lifted her head and glanced at him, then turned to us.

"Our son is in the ER because of fentanyl." She wiped the tears from her cheeks. "I don't understand where he got it. He doesn't take hard drugs."

"It's the same with my sister, Lisa," I replied, adding, "I'm Kate."

"John and Ellen Whitmore." The pronounced shadows under John Whitmore's eyes spoke to the severity of his son's condition. Ellen Whitmore gave me a brief nod.

Sam narrowed his eyes. "I thought Lisa was taking oxy."

"She was. How on earth did she get the fentanyl? It's not like doctors prescribe it like they do oxy." I shook my head. "The doctor mentioned that there's been an increase in overdoses from contaminated fentanyl, but no one knows where the stuff's coming from. And none of the patients have a prior history of serious drug use."

"Sounds like it might be related to your son's overdose," Sam said to the couple.

I turned to Ian. "Where was Lisa tonight?"

"She went to a party in Green Lake." He clenched and unclenched his fists, as though trying to control his emotions. "I had to work late, so I told her to meet me at home when it was over." Tears sprang to his eyes, and he wiped at them angrily. "I should never have let her go alone."

"If you don't mind my asking," I said, leaning across Sam to speak to John Whitmore, "where was your son when they found him?"

"At a party."

"Was it in Green Lake by any chance?"

John Whitmore's eyes widened. "Yes. Don't tell me. Your sister?"

I nodded. Bingo. I looked at Sam.

Sam leaned forward and was about to say something when Dr. Patel reappeared at the nurses' station. We all turned to watch her make her way through the waiting room. The air stilled as the five of us collectively held our breath, waiting to see who she was coming for.

She stopped in front of the Whitmores. Ellen stood first, and John did the same. They held each other, waiting for the doctor to speak. The weariness in Patel's eyes delivered the news even before she spoke. Jason Whitmore had died. As John stiffened, Ellen Whitmore sobbed, the sound seemingly ripped from deep within her chest. Dr. Patel put her arm around Ellen Whitmore and walked them both through the waiting room and past the double doors leading to the emergency room.

Sam pulled out his phone and nodded toward the nurses' station. "Go see your sister. I'll find out what my buddies at Seattle PD can tell me about the rash of overdoses."

"Thanks." As I stood, a wave of exhaustion passed through me. I took a deep breath, shook it off, and went to see my sister.

A nurse led me to the intensive care unit, where they'd moved Lisa. The door whispered closed behind me, isolating all sound except for a monitor beeping in the background. Lisa lay immobile on the hospital bed, translucent skin only a shade or two darker than the white bedsheets.

My younger sister had our father's blue eyes and jet black hair and grandmother's willowy build. A slight widow's peak punctuated her heart-shaped face, which matched her sweet, forgiving nature. I, on the other hand, was my mother's daughter all the way: tall and athletic with green eyes and blond hair. At least when I wasn't trying to hide my identity. Unfortunately, I also inherited her nature: impulsive and impatient.

Too bad Mom wasn't around to see it. My biological mother died when I and my older sisters were young, and Maureen, my father's second wife, had come along soon after to take her place. Dad professed to be happy, but I'd never gotten along with her.

I moved to the side of the bed and put my hand over hers. Her fingers were cold to the touch, like pebbles on a beach. Tears pricked my lids and I stifled a sob. My baby sister was in a coma and there was nothing I could do.

As soon as Sam and I got home from the hospital, we fell into bed, exhausted. I woke up hours later, disoriented. As if someone alerted him, Sam appeared at the bedroom door with a cup of coffee and a plate of scrambled eggs and toast. He was spooky like that. He sensed things normal people didn't and rarely talked about it. I assumed it was because of his training as a shaman growing up in Alaska, but when I asked him, he shrugged the training off and said he learned more being a long-haul truck driver and a cop than he ever did from the village shaman. I didn't push him to explain.

"I thought you could use some breakfast." He set the plate on the nightstand and handed me the coffee.

"Thank you." I breathed in the rich aroma before taking a sip and then glanced at my phone, which I'd left next to the bed. No messages. I decided the lack of contact from the hospital was a good thing.

"No news?" Sam sat on the edge of the mattress.

"Not yet." I scooped up a forkful of eggs, but my stomach lurched at the smell. I changed my mind and set it down. "Sorry, I'm not very hungry."

Sam smiled and took the plate back, placing it on the nightstand with my coffee. "No worries. Let me know when you get your appetite back." He caressed my cheek with his hand. A wave of despair washed through me.

My baby sister was in a coma. I couldn't help wondering if there was something I could have done to protect her. How did she even get the fentanyl? The drug wasn't easy to find unless you were acquainted with the street or knew someone who was. Lisa definitely didn't fit into the street-savvy category.

"What did your friends at the police department say?"

"Like the doc said, there's been a huge spike in fentanyl overdoses. SPD's investigating multiple cases." He leaned over to give me a kiss before he rose from the bed. "I was just going in to work. Thought you might want to take the day off, spend some time with your sister."

"Thanks. I will."

Sam left and I brought my breakfast dishes downstairs to the kitchen and put them in the sink. Unable to shake off my worries about Lisa, I wandered into the extra bedroom where she'd been staying, hoping to find something that would explain what happened. I rummaged through her dresser, the closet, and under her bed, looking for something, anything that would make the puzzle pieces fall into place.

Nothing unusual popped out at me. I went into her bathroom and checked the medicine cabinet. The usual stuff lined the shelves: toothpaste, mouthwash, cleanser. I closed the cabinet and glanced at the garbage. A brown prescription bottle peeked through a cloud of tissues. I pulled out the empty container and read the label. Lisa's oxycodone prescription.

Using the date the prescription was filled and counting the days on my fingers, I concluded that she'd run out the week before. I checked the label. No refills.

I thought back to how she'd acted in the days before her overdose. She'd been happy, although not any more so than usual. And she hadn't been out of it, leading me to believe that she didn't have to take painkillers every day.

Oxycodone hadn't been the cause of the overdose. That was fentanyl's doing. But if she'd become dependent on painkillers, why use fentanyl? She could have just gone back and gotten another prescription from the doctor who was treating her. I assumed he would have given her at least one more refill, if she'd asked.

I checked the linen closet for evidence but only found sheets and towels and toilet paper. Wouldn't there be something that would point to where she got the fentanyl? A pill bottle, a phone number, something? Returning to her bedroom, I went through her things again. I didn't have any better luck than the first time.

Then it hit me. Where was her purse? The pumpkin-colored leather satchel hadn't been in the locker at the hospital. With new purpose, I searched the rest of the house and came up empty. I called Sam to find out if he'd seen it recently.

"Not that I can recall. The hospital had her driver's license and insurance card, though. Why don't you check with Ian? He might know where it is," Sam suggested.

I hung up and scrolled through my contacts for Ian's number. When I called, there was no answer. He was either at work or still sleeping—like Sam and me, he'd had a late night at the hospital. I grabbed my bag and headed out the door to find him.

Ian wasn't at work, so I drove to his apartment on Capitol Hill and scored a parking place across the street from his building. The front entry had a call box, and I pressed the buzzer for his apartment.

"Yes?" Ian's groggy voice floated through the speaker.

"Ian, it's Kate. Can we talk?"

"Oh. Sure. Give me a sec and I'll buzz you up."

The buzzer sounded and the door clicked open. I pushed through and took the elevator to his floor. I'd obviously woken him up, but my sister was in a coma. Being polite wasn't an option.

He was waiting for me in the doorway to his apartment. Dark circles rimmed his bloodshot eyes, giving him a haggard appearance.

"Looks like you're doing about as well as I am."

"Has there been any change?" Ian stepped aside so I could enter.

"No. But at least she's stable." Small victories, I thought.

He closed his eyes. "I can't believe she's in a coma. She's just lying there, all alone…" His voice cracked.

"I tried to call you, but there was no answer." I walked to the couch and sat down. A narrow shaft of sunlight spilled through blackout curtains and sliced across the floor in the otherwise darkened room. A lone lamp on a side table emitted a soft glow. The place smelled of his distinctive cologne and burned toast.

"Sorry. I shut off my phone. I didn't get home until six and needed sleep."

"I won't keep you long. Earlier today I went through Lisa's things, looking for something that might give me a clue about where she got the fentanyl, but there wasn't anything. And then I realized I hadn't seen her purse at the hospital."

"Maybe the police have it."

I shook my head. "Sam checked. Do you remember the last time you saw it?"

Ian closed his eyes again as he thought. A few moments later he opened them. "Sorry. I can't remember."

A sigh escaped me and I leaned my head back. "Do you have any idea how she might have gotten the stuff?"

"Not that I can think of. All I know is what I told you last night—that she was taking oxycodone for the pain."

"I couldn't remember her acting like she'd taken anything during the day. Do you two have any friends that use?"

Ian shook his head. "None."

"Well, that's it then." I rose from the couch to leave. "Do you mind if I use your bathroom? I had way too much coffee this morning."

"Sure. Down the hall, last door on your left."

I followed the hallway past two bedrooms and a linen closet to the bathroom. Ian had always struck me as a nice guy with a tendency toward order and cleanliness. He'd be a good match for my sister, who we were certain was allergic to cleaning. My mood plummeted at the thought that they may never have the chance to be a "match." What if Lisa never came out of the coma? Or, what if she did and suffered brain damage?

When I was finished, I went to the sink to wash my hands. Being the nosy sort, not to mention fiercely protective of my little sister, I eased the door to his medicine cabinet open. Aside from shaving cream, toothpaste, and aftershave, there were two prescription bottles and an herbal remedy for pain. I rotated the bottles so I could read the labels. One of the prescriptions was a muscle relaxant, and the other was oxycodone. The fill dates were over two years old. Turning on the water to mask the sound, I opened first one and then the other to check the contents. The bottle with the muscle relaxers was half full, and the oxy bottle only had three pills left.

Screwing the caps back on, I replaced the bottles, closed the cabinet, and shut off the water before walking into the brightly lit hallway. One of the bedroom doors was ajar. A band of light shone across the floor and onto the bed. Something in that beam of light caught my eye, and I stepped into the room for a better view.

It was Lisa's purse.

FOUR

FLICKING ON THE overhead light, I stood at the side of the bed and stared down at Lisa's satchel. Anger welled in my chest as I rummaged through the compartments. Her checkbook and credit cards were all there, along with her phone. Digging through the rest of the bag, I found the usual suspects: business cards, a hairbrush, mascara, lip gloss, tissues, and a tin of mints. Frustrated, I dumped the purse upside down on the bedspread. When I did, the cover on the mints flipped open, spilling its contents.

Funny looking mints.

Squinting, I stared at the imprint on the side of the pills. 6767. The number wasn't familiar. My anger at Ian's lie at a full burn, I gathered the five tablets in my hand and shoved the rest of Lisa's things back inside the satchel before carrying everything into the living room. Ian was in the kitchen, making a pot of coffee. Blood pounded in my ears. I dropped the bag onto the coffee table.

Take it easy, Kate. Ian might have a good explanation.

But then again…

"Why did you lie to me?" My voice serrated the air in the quiet apartment.

Ian turned around with a puzzled look on his face. His gaze dropped to the purse, and he opened his mouth to respond. Then his eyes moved to my open hand. He clamped his lips shut.

"Where did she get these?" I held out the pills. My hand shook. I took a deep breath, trying to calm myself.

"I'm not sure. I—I didn't lie to you." Ian set down the bag of coffee he was holding. "Isn't that Lisa's purse?"

"You know damn well it is." My anger spiked. I hated lies. There'd been too many in my life, including mine. "Why did you tell me you didn't know where it was?"

"Because I didn't." Ian frowned and stepped toward me. "Where did you find it?"

"In one of the bedrooms."

"Which one?"

"The first one on the right."

Ian's frown cleared and he said, "That's the guest room. I hardly ever go in there." He shrugged. "Maybe she left it when she went to the party."

Although leaving her purse anywhere didn't sound like Lisa, my conviction that Ian had known about the purse lessened slightly and I backed off. He could have been telling the truth. She might have left it, preferring to just keep her identification with her rather than being a target for a mugging. But that didn't explain what I'd found in the tin.

"What are those?" He nodded at the pills in my hand.

"I'm not sure. I thought you'd be able to tell me."

Some kind of emotion flashed across Ian's face that I couldn't read. My fingers curled around the pills, and I slid them into my pocket.

"Do you think they might be what put Lisa in a coma?" Ian's frown was back again. This time I caught the emotion that flickered in his eyes. It was fear. Alarm bells went off in my head as I studied him closely. Little beads of perspiration had formed on his upper lip and his breathing was faster than normal.

Not exactly relaxed.

"Okay." I crossed my arms. "This is how it's going to work. You're going to tell me again how her purse ended up in your guest bedroom, and then you're going to tell me where these pills came from."

"But I told you—"

I cut him off. "Stop. Just stop. You're a bad liar." I sighed. "Please, just tell me the truth."

Ian crossed his arms, matching my stance. "I am telling you the truth. That room is my guest bedroom. I hardly ever use it." He waved at the open living room and kitchen. "As you can see, my laptop is out here on the kitchen table, so obviously I don't use the room as an office." He narrowed his eyes. "And why were you snooping around my apartment? It's not like you can see the bed from the hallway." He took a step forward.

"How did you know the purse was on the bed?"

Ian froze. He closed his eyes and bowed his head.

"I didn't know." His voice was so soft I barely heard him.

Cold dread gripped me. "Didn't know what? About her purse being on the bed or something else?"

Ian opened his eyes and blinked back tears.

"I was too late. He was supposed to be there." His voice cracking, Ian collapsed into a nearby chair.

"He?"

Ian nodded, misery plain on his face. "Momo. The guy I get my painkillers from."

I stepped closer. "This Momo is a friend of yours?"

Ian shook his head. "No—yes, I mean, kind of. He's a customer. Hangs out at the wine bar where I work. About a year ago, I mentioned I had lower back pain and that I had to wait another month before my doctor would prescribe any more painkillers. He told me he could hook me up—made it sound like he did runs into Canada for cheap meds. I've been using his stuff for months. Nothing like this has ever happened."

"And?"

"Lisa ran out of oxy, and she asked me if I had anything to take care of the pain."

I finished the sentence. "And you sent her to the party to buy some."

A sob escaped him and he buried his face in his hands. "Oh, God. I did. I'm the one, and now she's—"

"Why didn't you give her some from the bottle in the medicine cabinet?"

He shook his head as he wiped at his eyes. "I was low on oxy and didn't want to give any away, so I told her to meet me at this party and I'd help her buy from Momo."

"Only she didn't wait."

Ian shook his head. "I got there as the paramedics were rolling her out on a gurney." He leaned back and stared at the ceiling. "I took her purse in case she'd already scored, and followed them to the hospital."

"That's bleak, Ian." When he didn't respond, I added, "I'm going to need Momo's contact information."

Ian nodded again, his gaze unfocused. He recited the number from memory.

Swallowing a retort about memorizing his drug dealer's number, I plugged the information into my phone. "Have you ever thought about quitting? Because, you know, you might have a teensy problem."

His eyes met mine. Misery and pain gazed out at me from their depths. I didn't have to do anything to make him understand the magnitude of what he'd done. He was already there.

My compassion was in short supply that morning. Lisa was in a coma because she trusted Ian, and Ian had let her down. Fresh anger boiled in my chest as I grabbed Lisa's purse and walked to the door. All of this could have been avoided if Ian had been honest about his oxy supply, and if Lisa would have been honest with me about her addiction to painkillers. But I supposed that was the nature of addiction. Honesty rarely enters into things.

I opened the door and left.

When I arrived back home, I cleaned the house. Which told me I was avoiding something, since I *hate* to clean.

I started with the bedrooms, worked my way to the living room, and was scouring the toilets when it hit me. I hadn't called my family back in Minnesota to let them know what happened to Lisa. My dad and his wife, Maureen, had made reservations to fly out to visit Lisa and me, and were due in a few weeks.

The thought of telling them that Lisa was clinging to life by a thread made me clean like the possessed. They'd blame me, of course.

The black sheep of the family, I was the brunt of my stepmother and two older sisters' no-holds-barred judgment. I was the one who had left my safe, successful little life in the Midwest for a last hurrah in Mexico and fallen for a drug lord. It didn't matter that in the beginning I had no idea what Roberto Salazar did for a living, or that when I did find out I chose the only path of escape available. That much was clear when I asked for help and none came. Every time I called them, they harangued me for my poor choices, as if they alone were the moral equivalent of judge and jury. According to them, the mere fact that I wanted more out of life than what they deemed an appropriate path, a.k.a. marriage, family, career, and a safe life in the suburbs, threw suspicion on any choices I made.

The house clean, I'd run out of obstacles to the dreaded phone call. Maybe I'd be lucky and my father would answer. Holding on to that flimsy hope, I grabbed my cell and hit speed dial.

"Hello?"

My heart squeezed at my stepmother's crisp, efficient voice. I took a deep breath.

"Hey, Maureen—it's Kate."

"Kate, dear. How nice to hear from you. Hold on and let me get your father. I'm sure he'll want to speak to you."

As I waited, I imagined Maureen wearing the proper attire with just the right amount of makeup, recently manicured nails in an acceptable color, not too outrageous of course, and her hair smartly coiffed in some new but not too trendy style for whatever function was being held that afternoon at the country club. Her heels would be comfortable, yet stylish, and would click smartly along the hardwood floors of my parents' home. Later, despite her perfect attire, she'd joke with her country club sisters about how she desperately needed a shopping trip to New York.

On the other hand, my father, George, was content puttering in his workshop in the backyard, inventing new ways to make life easier for Maureen, or reading a good book in his hammock, strung between two old oak trees. He'd be wearing his favorite cardigan, patched wherever holes had formed—the one my stepmother ceaselessly nagged him about, telling him that it was time to retire the old thing. I loved that he ignored her and wore it anyway.

His own little mutiny.

"What's up, love bug?"

The warmth in my father's voice as he called me his pet name melted my heart, and I instantly regretted thinking uncharitable thoughts about my stepmother. "Minnesota nice," or the instinct to be polite no matter what, is tough to overcome. Just ask anyone from the Midwest.

"There's been an accident."

I flinched at Maureen's sharp intake of breath. Apparently, she'd remained on the line when my father got on.

"Is everything all right?" The concern in my father's voice counteracted the tirade I knew would come from Maureen as soon as I explained.

Clearing my throat, I said, "Lisa had a bad reaction to a painkiller. She's in a coma."

"*What?*" My stepmother's tone ratcheted up, and I held the phone away from my ear. "What do you mean, Lisa's in a coma?" Her voice dripped disbelief mixed with accusation.

"She had a bad reaction to a painkiller," I repeated. I took another deep breath and let it go. *You just have to get through the initial shock, Kate. Things will settle down after that.*

"How did it happen?"

"She ran out of painkillers the doctor prescribed for her migraines, and instead of going back to ask for a refill, she decided to take someone else's medication." I wasn't about to tell her the "someone else" was Ian's drug dealer. Maureen would somehow link Ian's behavior with my past—the information would only give my stepmother more ammunition in her War Against Kate.

"What's the prognosis?" My father's calm, rational tone had a soothing effect.

"Her vitals are stable and there's brain activity, but she's unresponsive."

"When did this happen?"

"Late last night."

"And you didn't think to notify us until now?" The indignation in Maureen's voice set my teeth on edge. "Isn't that just like you, Kate? Only thinking of yourself."

"Now, Maureen. Don't be so hard on her. It can't have been easy for her to call with such bad news."

Maureen huffed. "I assume you haven't told your sisters yet?"

"They were next on my list," I lied. I figured Maureen would want to call them so that she could whip them into an indignant froth and the three of them could partake in some juicy Kate-bashing.

"As soon as we end this call, I'm going to change our reservations." Maureen's tone brooked no argument. "We'll fly out tomorrow instead of our original date."

"There's not much you can do for her at the moment, I'm afraid."

"Oh, I think there is. I'm sure you haven't vetted her doctors properly. There's an art to dealing with medical personnel. But then you probably wouldn't know that, what with your sordid past consorting with drug dealers and thieves."

"Maureen." My father's tone held a warning.

"What? I'm just being truthful."

"Can you get a cab at the airport?" I asked, changing the subject. "Sam has to use the Tahoe for a case," I lied. Again. "I could pick you up, but the Jeep is a little small for your luggage." Maureen never traveled light. I pitied the poor taxi driver who ended up driving my parents to their hotel.

"Don't you worry about it, love bug. We'll manage."

"You're sure you don't want to stay at Sam's and my place?" Not that I wanted Maureen under my roof, but Minnesota nice was interfering once again.

I'd have to work on that.

"Why on earth would we want to stay with you and be party to your…illicit relationship?"

My father sighed and I almost laughed. It wasn't like George and Maureen had waited to consummate their love until *they* were married.

Hypocrites tended to rub me the wrong way. Before uttering something I'd regret, I said, "Why don't you two plan on coming to the house for an early dinner tomorrow night? We can head over to the hospital afterward to see Lisa."

"That sounds fine." My father added, "Doesn't it, Maureen?"

"If that's what you both want. But I insist on bringing the wine. I doubt you have anything even remotely acceptable in your wine cellar."

I almost told her we didn't have a wine cellar, but that would have only baited her into haranguing me about all the mistakes I'd made in my life, the worst of which would be not having developed a discerning palate.

Instead, I said, "That would be perfect, Maureen. Give me a call when you get settled."

We ended the call and I closed my eyes.

That went well.

FIVE

MAUREEN AND DAD arrived late Monday afternoon. After checking into their hotel, Maureen made noises about not being hungry and could she take a raincheck on dinner? Relieved she wouldn't be joining us, Sam and I met Dad at a local oyster bar and had a classic Pacific Northwest dinner of wild salmon and assorted shellfish, accompanied by a bottle of Washington wine. Afterward, we went to see Lisa. According to the nurse, Maureen had been there already, and gone back to the hotel, pleading a terrible headache. The look on Dad's face as he sat by his youngest daughter's bedside broke my heart, and I resolved to step up my game in the hunt for the tainted med supplier.

The next morning, the Whitmores called and made an appointment to meet Sam and me later that afternoon to discuss the death of their son, Jason. When the Whitmores had expressed an interest in reconnecting, Dr.

Patel had given them the number I'd left for Akiaq Investigations.

"What do they think we can do that the police won't?" I asked Sam as I brewed a pot of tea for our potential clients. I'd just gotten back from visiting Lisa in the ICU. She was breathing on her own but was still unresponsive.

"That's just it. Seattle PD won't pursue their specific case to the detriment of all the others on file."

"So what do they want us to do?"

"Find out who sold the drugs to their son."

"And then what, somehow they're going to bring that person to justice? Or are they planning to deliver their own?" I wanted to know who had sold those drugs to my sister, too, but Mac had assured me they were working on finding the source. I'd let them do their job.

"They didn't specify. They've lost their only child. I'm pretty sure it's a case of needing to do something, anything, to make sense of the tragedy." He turned his attention back to me. "I think we should work with them. Maybe we can help them find closure and expose some bad actors at the same time."

"Not to mention help SPD discover who sold my sister contaminated drugs." That would satisfy my need to help bring the dirtbags to justice. "You're thinking of passing along any information we uncover to Mac, right?"

He nodded.

"You do realize that the source is likely to be cartel related, at least peripherally."

Sam leveled his gaze at me. "I'm counting on it."

The five-room suite that made up Akiaq Investigations was situated over a popular deli in downtown Seattle, close to the waterfront and Pike Place Market. The space worked well for our needs. Sam avoided paying the exorbitant rents normally charged so close to the city center by choosing a building with steep stairs and no elevator, and a front door that opened onto an alley. Clients didn't seem to have a hard time finding the place—some even preferred the discreet entrance. Climbing the stairs was another matter.

At the top of the stairs a short hallway led to the suite, the front door of which opened onto a decent-size waiting room. A two-tiered reception desk fronted an area with a worktable, an all-in-one copier-printer-fax, and several file cabinets. Sam's photographs of Alaskan wildlife populated the walls, while woven baskets and other Inuit artifacts from Sam's heritage took up residence on the side tables. Two offices were accessed down another short hallway, with a cozy conference room in between them.

It was there that Sam and I met with Ellen and John Whitmore to talk about their son.

"More?" I asked, indicating the pot of white peach tea on the well-used conference table.
John Whitmore and Sam declined. Ellen nodded and held out her cup.

John Whitmore's haggard expression belied his well-toned physique—as though he'd kept up his exercise regimen but hadn't been sleeping well.

Ellen Whitmore displayed the toll their son's death had taken the most. Her sallow complexion exaggerated red, puffy eyes, and two deep, vertical creases between her eyebrows gave her the look of someone perpetually concerned. She had the habit of continually picking at her cuticles, although her nails were freshly manicured. I poured her another cup of tea and topped off my own. The four of us had been discussing Lisa's prognosis, and getting comfortable with each other before settling down to business.

"How can Akiaq Investigations help you?" Sam leaned back in his chair. "I understand you've already spoken with police."

Ellen glanced at her husband and nodded for him to go ahead. John cleared his throat and moved to the edge of his chair, leaning his forearms on the table.

"I'm going to be blunt." He shot a look at me and then turned his attention to Sam. "We want justice for our son's death."

Sam nodded, keeping an open expression on his face. "I understand you and your wife are hurting from the tragic loss of your only child. It's normal to be angry, to want to make someone pay. I don't fault you for that. But"—he shifted slightly in his chair—"be aware that if we do discover the identity of the person or persons responsible for providing narcotics to your son and you decide to act on that information, you will be entirely on your own. Kate and I cannot condone vigilante justice. We're also obligated to turn over the information to the authorities."

John Whitmore's expression darkened and he gave a short nod. "Of course. I understand." His words came out clipped. Ellen Whitmore placed a hand on her husband's arm.

"What he's trying to say is that we want to prevent this from happening to another family. Anything that we can do to bring those animals to justice will help bring us peace. And hopefully spare someone else this pain." Ellen blinked back tears as John patted her hand.

I set my cup down and leaned forward in my chair. "There's nothing I'd like more than to find out the source of the fentanyl. My sister's in a coma because of them. The dealers deserve to be brought to justice."

"But?" John Whitmore gave me an angry look.

"But. You do realize that this investigation will most likely lead to organized crime? Fentanyl and heroin are big money-makers for them. Fentanyl is cheap to produce and easy to sell." I let the information sink in. "If it turns out to be organized crime, I would urge you to rethink payback. That's not a group you want to get involved with, believe me."

"She knows what she's talking about," Sam added. "Kate has extensive experience dealing with these organizations. Particularly drug cartels."

John and Ellen Whitmore both looked at me with renewed interest. I kept my expression as neutral as possible. Inside, I was thinking they were nuts to even consider trying to delve into the dark underbelly of the drug trade. It took eleven years and the deaths of two of the major players to extricate myself from that world because of one stupid mistake. Granted, it was a big mistake, but still. Why would they risk being gunned down in the street? Especially two suburbanites who likely had never crossed paths with a criminal.

John cleared his throat again. "Understood. We're willing to pay whatever it takes. The police think my son is—was a junkie. He wasn't. As far as I know, he never touched the hard stuff. Sure, he smoked a little pot and drank a few beers, but at that age, who doesn't? Besides, last time I checked, marijuana is legal in the state of Washington."

"Is it possible you didn't know your son as well as you thought?" Sam asked.

I added, "Lisa kept her oxy habit a secret from both Sam and me, so that's why he's asking."

John nodded. "That's a fair question. Jason was our only child, and the three of us were very close. We talked candidly about everything, including sex, drugs, and alcohol. In fact, his mother and I were lenient when it came to alcohol and soft drugs. As long as he and his friends imbibed responsibly and did so in our home, then he was free to experiment as long as no one got behind the wheel until the effects had worn off."

"We believed that a more liberal approach removed the 'forbidden fruit' aspect of drugs and alcohol, reducing the lure by making them commonplace."

The earnestness in Ellen Whitmore's voice told me that she was clinging to the correctness of her decision. I couldn't argue with her—her stance seemed logical. Thing was, people didn't always act logically. I glanced at Sam. His expression was unreadable, as usual.

"Do you have a copy of the autopsy report?" he asked.

Ellen nodded and slid a large envelope across the table toward him. Sam pulled out the report and began to read.

A moment later he said, "This says there wasn't any heroin in your son's system and no puncture wounds were found."

"Exactly." John Whitmore crossed his arms and leaned back in his chair, a satisfied look on his face.

"We told the authorities that Jason had never used heroin, but they didn't believe us, even when we assured them he had a phobia about hard drugs," Ellen Whitmore added. "They assumed he'd switched to fentanyl because of the high and had taken it orally instead of shooting up in order to hide his addiction."

The officers who responded to Lisa's overdose had thought the same thing until we contacted Mac to explain our concerns. They added our information to the report.

"Do you have a list of Jason's friends and their contact information? Maybe a girlfriend?" I asked.

"Yes, of course." Ellen rummaged through her purse and pulled out a handwritten list on a piece of paper, which she slid across the table. "I copied the contact list on his phone and checked the online accounts on his tablet, too." She took a deep breath and tried to smile while blinking back tears. "I'm sorry. It was difficult to scroll through our son's virtual life. Like a lot of young people his age, he was an open book. He posted everything."

"Would it be possible for us to have access to those social media sites? There might be useful information there." Sam's gentle tone had the right effect. Both Ellen and John nodded their assent.

"Please. Anything that will help."

"Well, then, if we're in agreement," Sam said, rising to his feet, "I'll print up the contract for the hours and fee that we discussed on the phone, and we'll get started."

Between visits to the hospital to see Lisa, and working our other cases, Sam and I spent the next two days combing through Jason Whitmore's social media accounts, gaining a more complete picture of the twenty-year-old. Jason had taken a "gap year" after he graduated high school to backpack across Eastern Europe with a buddy before enrolling in college. Along with the usual cat videos and political posts, his feeds were filled with photographs of his travels. He also had hundreds of friends from all over the world, many of whom he apparently met while overseas.

Ellen Whitmore had been right—Jason was an open book. He'd posted several times a day and kept a blog while traveling. Sam and I divvied up his posts and the comments from his friends and gleaned a couple of promising leads. But it was when we started cross-referencing his phone contacts with his online friends that we hit pay dirt.

Bobby "the Barracuda" Branford was by far the main responder to Jason's posts, across all accounts. I would have categorized his activity as stalking. The guy inserted himself into Jason's life in every way possible—likes, smiley faces, comments, shares—he was like a specter on every post. Like many insecure people, in his comments he alluded to knowing dangerous players in the criminal underworld and bragged that he derived much of his income by doing things for them. I say insecure because if Bobby had actually been as deeply involved with organized crime as he claimed, he'd have been warned to knock off the public posts, or they would have stopped it for him. No way would he have been allowed to continue hinting at his connections. Not unless his "friends" were as new to the game as he appeared to be.

Sam put the phone down and leaned back in his chair. "That was Ellen Whitmore. She says Jason never mentioned anyone by the name of Bobby, and she definitely didn't remember anything about a barracuda person. Her words."

"That's odd, given how close they say they were to Jason."

There'd been dozens of calls and text messages logged between Bobby's phone number and Jason's.

Interestingly, a long gap appeared where his contact with Jason abruptly ended and re-started just prior to Jason's death. The same gap showed up across each of Jason's accounts.

I had a theory about Bobby's sudden absence.

"I'll lay odds that our friend Bobby was experiencing our fine prison system from the less desirable side of the bars."

It made sense. According to his posts, Bobby held criminals in high regard. It was a matter of time before his bragging caught up with him, whether by someone calling his bluff, or by attracting the attention of an actual criminal. Either way, to save face Bobby would have to put up or shut up.

"Possibly. Or, Jason could have deleted the exchanges between them. I called Jax. He'll be here tomorrow morning. Maybe he can tease more information from the phone or the tablet."

One of the best in the business, Jax was our go-to high-tech guy in a city where you couldn't throw a rock without hitting an IT expert. Lucky for us he preferred smaller, freelance jobs, shunning the giant high-tech colossi that dominated the Pacific Northwest. Not that the big corporations hadn't tried to hire him. He just wasn't interested in what they had to offer.

Money had never been Jax's raison d'être. Freedom, women, and hacking were.

Sam asked a contact in the Washington Department of Corrections to run a search for Bobby Branford, and I hunted down his place of residence. The closest I got was an older sister living across Puget Sound in the city of Bremerton. When I called, she told me she'd be home that evening and to come between six and seven.

"I think I'll take a trip to Bremerton to talk to the sister." I checked the ferry schedule online. The 4:20 would get me there with plenty of time to do reconnaissance. "Don't hold dinner for me."

"Take the rig. I can catch a ride home."

Sam tossed me the keys to the Tahoe. "See you tonight."

Six

I BARELY MADE the busy commuter ferry—mine was the last vehicle loaded. The boat got under way and an hour later I was headed to Bobby Branford's sister's house.

A city of roughly 40,000 people situated on the Kitsap Peninsula, Bremerton is surrounded by salt water and towering trees. Home to the Puget Sound Naval Shipyard, the town's heyday was during the Second World War when it boasted a population of over 100,000 shipbuilders, support personnel, and their families. Now a major hub for retired as well as active-duty Navy personnel and highly skilled tradesmen and women, whenever a ship pulled in for repairs or retrofitting, Bremerton's population swelled for the duration of the assignment.

I pulled into the driveway of a well-kept, World War II-era cottage—a square, one-story house with a hipped roof, clapboard siding, and shallow eaves. The single-car garage took up a third of the lower level directly below a large picture window. An added carport shaded the driveway and currently sheltered an older model Chevy Malibu. The front yard was a riot of pink and purple blossoms adorning the mature rhododendrons ringing the perimeter.

I climbed the front stoop and rang the doorbell. A minute later, the door opened and a woman holding a sleeping baby on her hip appeared. She had cornflower blue eyes and hair the color of weak tea pulled back in a messy ponytail, and wore a bubblegum pink T-shirt under a loose pair of overalls. Her expression was a cross between curious and wary.

"Dora Trask?" I smiled and held up my business card. She nodded. "I'm Kate Jones. We spoke on the phone earlier?"

Dora squinted at the card. Recognition registered in her eyes and she opened the door.

"You're here about my brother. C'mon in." She stepped back to let me pass and closed the door behind us. "Go ahead an' sit anywhere there's space."

The house smelled of mothballs, cats, and pepperoni, and the living room looked like a cat five hurricane had recently blown through. Magazines, newspapers, dirty dishes, and children's toys splayed across the floor, with more scattered on top of a blue velour couch, matching recliner, and tweed loveseat. The lone coffee table practically groaned under the weight of unopened mail. Brightly colored sippy cups and empty beer cans really pulled the place together. After the meticulous yard, the hoarder's paradise was a surprise.

I picked my way past the precarious stacks of celebrity magazines, old newspapers, and tabloids to the couch and shoved aside a plastic laundry basket filled with what I assumed were dirty clothes. Dora walked over to one of the recliners and with her free hand shoved a stack of papers to the floor before taking a seat. The baby didn't stir.

"Whad'ya want to know about Bobby?"

My eyes watered and I cleared my throat. The inch-thick cat hair on every surface and epic stench of a dirty litterbox combined with the unseasonably high pollen count of an early spring, was threatening my oxygen habit.

"The firm I work for has been hired by the parents of a friend of Bobby's to investigate their son's death. Your brother was one of the last people he communicated with before he died, and I'm following up to see if Bobby might have information we could use."

"What's the friend's name?"

"Jason Whitmore."

"I don't think I ever heard Bobby mention him. How'd he die?"

"It's been ruled an overdose. They found fentanyl in his bloodstream."

Dora's wary expression returned. "I'm pretty sure my brother wasn't close friends with this Jason character. Bobby ain't into drugs."

"By the looks of Jason's online accounts, they knew each other pretty well."

She shrugged. "Well, whatever. I ain't seen Bobby in months. Not since he got popped for jacking Cookies Tavern. For all I know, he could be dead."

Not exactly what she'd told me on the phone, but I let it pass. It did, however, explain Bobby's online absence.

"When's the last time you saw him?"

She gazed at the ceiling and cocked her head as she thought. "End of February." She stared at me without blinking, as if challenging me to contradict her.

"I'm sorry." I leaned forward, careful not to bump the stack of papers next to me. "This morning you said he owed you money."

Dora gave a harsh laugh and then replied, "He does. His ass was usually in trouble, and I *always* bailed him out. He couldn't keep his mouth shut, for one thing. Always braggin' on himself. That didn't set too well with his boys."

"His boys?"

"He hung out with a couple'a gangsta types. You know, hardcore wannabes." She shrugged. "This ain't LA, that's for sure."

The baby roused, gurgling and kicking her tiny legs as she stretched her arms above her head, miniature fists testing the air. Dora rocked her gently and dipped her head. The kid burst into a delighted smile and reached for her mother's hair. Dora shook the strands out of reach and smiled. "Well, look who's awake. Li'l happy baby." She glanced down at the child with obvious affection and cooed, "Are you my happy Missy? Yes you are."

A black and white cat wandered in and wound itself around my ankles. Purring filled the room. I reached down to scratch it behind the ears and noticed something small and white peeking out from under the couch. I quickly palmed the oblong pill and sat upright. "Do you know the friends' names?"

"One guy called himself The Terminator." She rolled her eyes. "And the other one went by Bruce Wayne."

"Like Batman?"

Dora nodded. "Pretty stupid, huh?" She shrugged. "Anyway, they ain't been around since Bobby bailed."

"Why do people refer to him as the Barracuda?" I asked.

She waved the question away. "Oh, that was just Bobby trying to be a badass. No one called him that. He was pissed when the name didn't take off."

A maple hutch covered with framed photographs caught my attention.

"Looks like you and your brother were close."

"Only when he needed something."

Time to change tactics. "Is it just you and the baby?"

Dora stiffened and her eyes narrowed. "Yeah. Just me and Missy."

"I didn't mean to pry. I assumed with the last name of Trask…"

"You're wondering when my *husband* gets home?" Dora scoffed and shook her head as she pushed herself to her feet. "Six o'clock last year, that's when he gets home."

Apparently the interview was over. I stood, stifling the urge to brush off my pants. Just then, there was a clank from inside the kitchen. Dora hesitated for a moment before continuing toward the door.

She waved at the kitchen. "My other cat." There was another clank, quieter than the first.

"Can I take a peek?" I asked, feigning excitement and heading for the kitchen. "I used to have a tabby and really miss her."

"I don't think that's a good idea. She doesn't like strangers." Dora's expression floated somewhere between alarm and annoyance. When I didn't stop, she came up behind me and grabbed my elbow, bringing me up short.

"I said, that's not a good idea." Her tone instantly morphed from fake-friendly to threatening. The baby looked as though she was going to burst into tears.

A shadow darkened the entrance to the kitchen as a man matching Bobby "the Barracuda" Branford's description walked into the living room.

Eyes wide, Dora opened her mouth to say something, but Bobby gave her a quick shake of his head.

"It's okay, Dora. Let her go."

Reluctantly, Dora released my elbow and stepped back.

"Don't be mad at my sister. She was just trying to protect me. Ain't that right, Dora?"

"You know it, Bobby." Dora didn't look like she felt one bit guilty about lying. In fact, her nonchalant expression told me her dishonesty came naturally.

"What do you want?" Bobby asked, a surly look on his face.

"I'm looking into the death of an acquaintance of yours—a Jason Whitmore."

Bobby frowned and his mouth curled downward. "Yeah, I heard about that. What a waste." His body tense, he moved across the room to sit on the edge of the recliner that Dora had vacated earlier. "Drugs, right?"

"Overdose." I studied his reaction. There was something off about the guy. His body language was too considered, too precise, like he was trying to be careful not to say too much.

"Ah, man, that blows. I didn't even know Jase liked the hard stuff."

"I'm not sure that he did." I leaned forward and placed my hands on the back of the couch. "What kind of relationship did you and Jason have?"

He shrugged. "Pretty casual, you know? Lots of banter." Bobby picked at the velour armrest. "No big deal."

"Did you guys do anything other than interact online?"

Averting his eyes, Bobby shook his head. "No. He lived in Bellevue. Kinda far to go to party, you know?"

"When did you see him last?" I asked.

"I don't remem—" Bobby stopped himself and he narrowed his eyes for a second. "Like I said, we never met. He lived in Bellevue. That's a different world over there."

"Right." I pushed back off the couch. Dora took that as her cue. She and Missy the Happy Baby started for the door.

"Sorry to cut this short, but Missy gets cranky if I don't feed her on time." She gave me a fake apologetic smile.

"Of course." I fake-smiled back at her and handed her my card. "If either of you hear of anything else that might be useful to our case, I'd appreciate it if you'd give us a call."

Dora took the card and slid it into her front pocket. "Sure," she said, her voice dripping with insincerity as she ushered me out the door.

Well, that was pleasant.

I glanced up at the picture window and waved at Dora, who was watching me leave. After navigating the steep driveway, I unlocked the SUV and got in. Remembering what I'd found on the floor in the house, I reached in my pocket for the white, oblong pill and studied it in my palm. The numbers 6767 were stamped on the side. The same numbers that were on the pills I found in Lisa's purse. After handing over three of Lisa's pills to Seattle PD, Sam had dropped off the remaining ones at an independent lab. They didn't have the backlog that SPD did, and it was possible that we'd find out the chemical makeup sooner than the police lab. He could do the same with this one. I dropped the pill inside a small baggie I kept in the console and stuffed it back in my pocket, then started the engine and backed onto the street.

Looked like I had a long night of surveillance ahead of me.

On my way to meet Dora I'd passed a crowded park situated on a hill with a great view of her place. I drove to it and parked in the lot facing the house far enough away from the other cars so that I wouldn't attract attention. My stomach rumbled, reminding me I hadn't eaten in a while, so I checked the nearby restaurants on my phone and decided on Thai food, since the place wasn't too far from the park. Stakeouts were generally long, drawn-out affairs, and I was always game to compensate myself with a good meal.

I called the Thai place to ask if they delivered. When they found out I was calling from a park, the woman on the phone balked, but after a couple minutes of cajoling she relented and said her driver would be there in twenty minutes or less.

I reached behind the front seat and brought out a large, waterproof case. Inside was a laser microphone. Making sure there was no one nearby who could see what I was up to, I attached the receiver and the transmitter to mini tripods and aimed the laser beam at the big picture window. The mic worked by directing the beam at the glass to capture sound vibrations within the room. The beam then bounced back to the receiver, which converted the vibrations into an audio signal. It took a few tries to line things up, but soon the audio signal from inside the house came across in my headphones as clearly as if I was standing a few feet away.

Then I grabbed my camera out of the console and trained the long lens on the house while I waited for my food.

"I don't think you should go with them," Dora was saying, her voice strained.

"I'll be fine," Bobby replied. "They're my boys. They got my back. Ain't nothin' gonna happen to me."

"What if you don't come back? What do I do then? Me and Missy can't make it on my salary alone."

There was a brief pause. "Glad to know you're so concerned about me, sis." Bobby's voice dripped sarcasm.

"You know I care, Bobby. But you shouldn't have come out when that woman was here."

"I had to—"

"No, you didn't. I had it handled." Dora's voice rose an octave. "She was almost out the door when you decided to make your entrance."

"Whatever," he said, shutting her down. "What's done is done. I'll explain it to Chacon—he'll understand. I didn't give her anything she could use."

Chacon. Now where did I know that name?

"You believe what you want to believe. That man is trouble." Dora's tone indicated their little spat was over. A long silence ensued, punctuated by the baby's fussing. I settled back in my seat to wait.

Five minutes later, the driver from the restaurant showed up with my order of Pad Thai. I had my headphones off and was out the door to pay him before he could get a good look inside my car. He grinned at the big tip and was soon on his way.

The mouth-watering aroma of chicken Pad Thai emanating from the container could not be resisted and I dug in.

I'd just finished eating when a tricked-out Honda Civic with low profile tires and an aftermarket spoiler and hood scoop boiled into the driveway and two men got out. Both wore hooded sweatshirts and baggy jeans, and one sported a tattoo on the side of his neck. The Terminator and Bruce Wayne? I peered through the camera and took a number of pictures, zeroing in on the tat. His sweatshirt covered a good portion of the ink, but something about the design struck a familiar chord.

With my history, you pay attention to details like that.

The two men climbed the front steps and rang the doorbell. Bobby opened the door and let them inside.

At first, there was some friendly banter, with the men's voices dominating. Then came a pause in the conversation.

"We gotta bounce, brah." The husky voice belonged to the guy I'd dubbed Bruce Wayne.

"Yeah. I know." Bobby sounded resigned.

"I won't let you take him." Dora's voice was higher than usual. The baby fussed in the background.

"Take it easy, Dora," Bobby assured her. "It'll be all right, once I explain things."

"Yeah. Don't you worry, Dora. Li'l bro here's gonna be just fine," the one I thought of as The Terminator said. "We gotta take him to the man and get this shit straightened out or it's bye-bye Bobby."

"Call me when the meeting's over, okay, Bobby?" Dora said, worry thick in her voice.

"Sure. See you later. Bye, little Missy-girl." The baby erupted in giggles.

A moment later the front door opened, and Bobby and the two gangsters walked outside, headed for the Civic.

SEVEN

THE THREE MEN walked to the Honda and climbed in—one of them sat behind Bobby, who was in the front passenger seat, and the other drove. The taillights blinked on, and the Civic backed down the driveway. Tires chirped on the pavement, spitting rocks as the low profile hot rod zoomed away.

I quickly stashed the mic and called Sam to give him the plate number as I followed at a discreet distance. The Honda sped along surface streets, heading toward the highway. Luckily, traffic was light and I was able to stay behind a couple of cars while at the same time keeping them in view. I had no idea if any of them were trained in spotting tails. Like Sam always said, never underestimate the target.

My guess was that both of Bobby's "friends" were packing. In the cartel world weapons were the first items on a wannabee's list of must-haves. One-upmanship between rival factions was the norm, and it often devolved into a pissing match over whose gun was bigger.

The Honda turned south on the highway heading toward Tacoma. I kept a couple of car lengths back, but from what I could see the occupants weren't especially concerned with the vehicles around them. Not once did either of the gangbangers turn in his seat to check behind them, and the driver wasn't overly enamored of the rearview mirror.

I followed them across the Tacoma Narrows Bridge and merged south onto I-5. Traffic was uncharacteristically light, so I could still hang back far enough that they'd never suspect they were being followed. The sun had set and the shadows worked in my favor.

A few minutes later, Sam called back with information on the car. I fed the call through the car's speakers.

"Your Civic belongs to a John Hastings of Lacey, Washington."

"Is there anything in the database?" I asked.

"Nope. He's clean. You want his info?"

"Sure. Text it to me."

Sam sent John Hastings's address, birthdate, and other particulars to my phone. Having contacts with access to the Department of Motor Vehicles was helpful in our line of work.

"Got anything else on him?"

"I did a search, but there's more than one John Hastings. None of them fit what you're looking for. It's like the guy doesn't exist."

"What about Kitsap County civil and criminal cases?"

There was a pause while Sam looked up the information. "Nada. And I checked surrounding counties. Want me to keep going?"

"No reason. There probably isn't anything to find."

The Honda continued on the interstate past Tacoma. A few miles out from the city of Olympia, they exited the freeway and took a left, headed toward a rest area at the top of a hill.

"Hey, looks like they're pulling off. I'm going to have to call you back."

"Be careful, Kate."

"Will do." I ended the call and followed them to the rest stop.

A number of big rigs took up space in the truck lot, acting as a temporary hotel for long-haul drivers. There weren't many vehicles in the car lot.

The Honda continued past the building that housed the restrooms to the back of the truck lot where shadow overruled light. Only a couple of semis had opted for the dark side of the rest area. I assumed load safety took precedence over sleeping in total darkness for most.

The Civic rolled up to a white van parked at the far end. The doors to the Civic opened and the three men got out. The driver walked to the van and knocked on the side door. I cut the lights and parked next to an idling semi.

A short time later, the door slid open and a dark-haired man who looked like he'd just woken up climbed out. In his hand was a hood, which he pulled over Bobby's head. Bobby didn't struggle, which led me to believe he expected it. Then the guy with the tattoo on his neck zip-tied Bobby's wrists together behind him and helped him into the back of the van before the driver rolled the door shut.

One of the men from the Honda handed the driver an envelope. He opened it, glanced at the contents, and slid it into his back pocket with a nod. Then he circled the van to the drivers' side and got in.

Was there money in the envelope? I couldn't be sure, even with the camera's long lens. Bobby didn't act scared, so I doubted the driver was being paid to kill him. Assuming the envelope contained cash, it was possible they were delivering a payment for something else.

I decided to follow Bobby and let the two in the Civic go. Something told me Bruce Wayne and The Terminator were minor players. The van driver struck me as a pro. I'd have to be more careful tailing him.

The two gangbangers got into the Honda and sped off, while the van waited a few minutes before hooking a U-turn and heading for the on-ramp to the freeway. I pulled out and followed at a healthy distance.

Half an hour later, the white van exited and drove through a residential area. The homes in the neighborhood were larger than average, and the lawns looked finely manicured, as though a service handled the upkeep. Here and there a higher-end car or SUV was parked in the driveway.

A block ahead, brake lights flashed and the van slowed, pulling into the driveway of one of the houses. I continued past and turned left at the next intersection, then circled back from the opposite direction. Slowing, I doused the headlights and pulled to the curb across the street and slightly down from the house.

The van was no longer in the driveway. My first thought was that the driver had spotted me and used the house as a decoy, but after checking, I noticed a detached garage. The back of a white van was visible on the far side. I breathed a sigh of relief.

It took less time to set up the mic since I'd left things partially intact from surveilling Dora's place, and I pointed the beam at the large picture window near the front. The receiver picked up some ambient noise but no vocals. I repositioned the transmitter, targeting another window, but didn't have any luck there, either.

If I wanted to find out what was happening to Bobby, I had to get closer. I quickly broke down the mic and put it in the case before grabbing my semiauto from the console. Scanning for a better place to set up, I zeroed in on a thin stream of light coming from a window on the far side of the house. A hedge of hydrangea bushes marked the edge of the lot, providing good cover, though I'd have to leave the safety of the Tahoe in order to get in position.

What if there are dogs?

Being mauled by a pack of angry pit bulls was not my idea of fun. Even a yappy Chihuahua could spell trouble if the neighbors investigated. If the owners had dogs, wouldn't they be outside by now? Or at least barking their heads off? I decided to chance it.

I parked the SUV in the driveway of a darkened, uninhabited-looking residence on the opposite side of the street. Grabbing two tripods and the case with the mic, I scanned the street for cars. The neighborhood was quiet. It was late enough that most folks had settled in for the evening.

A few minutes later, I was in position behind a massive hydrangea bush and had the equipment set up with the beam pointed at a window on the side of the house. Luckily, there were no dogs in sight. I zipped my jacket closed against the cool spring evening, glad that rain wasn't in the forecast.

The mic picked up a faint murmur that resembled conversation, but it wasn't clear. I adjusted the beam, moving it back and forth across the window surface like I was tuning a radio station until I could make out the words. A man whose voice I didn't recognize was speaking.

"I hear a PI came to visit you today. Is that right, Bobby?" The question was followed by the sound of ice clinking in a glass.

"I told them I didn't know anything."

"Of course. But still the woman found you. How do you think she managed to do that?" More ice clinking.

There was a brief pause. "I think she logged into Jason's online accounts and was following up with his friends. Look." Bobby's voice held a hint of desperation. "It's nothing. I was just one of a bunch of Jason's contacts. He had, like, thousands of online friends."

"Yes, but how many of them went to prison for robbing a bar?" Another pause. "Or have a connection to us?"

Who is this guy?

"Like I told you, the bar thing was a mistake. One I promised to never make again." Bobby's voice had gone into pleading mode.

"I think that's wise." The man paused. In the background, a door opened and closed. "I also think it's wise that you are no longer part of our operation."

"What're *you* doing here?" Bobby's voice wavered. He sounded surprised.

Instead of an answer, two *thuds* burst in rapid succession followed by the sound of something falling to the floor. Pulse racing, I froze.

"Get him out of here. And clean this mess up," the man said. There was a deep sigh and another clink of ice cubes hitting the sides of a glass. "This doesn't make me happy."

"What should I do with the body?" a third voice grumbled.

"I don't care, but take him far away where no one will be able to connect us to his death."

I'd heard enough. I yanked off my headphones, grabbed the equipment, and ran.

EIGHT

HEART HAMMERING, I made it to the SUV in record time and tossed the case with the mic in the passenger seat. I shoved the keys in the ignition, started the engine, and backed down the driveway, trying to act like a normal suburbanite going to the store.

Possibilities raced through my mind, but I kept coming back to what I thought Sam would do in this situation. He'd keep the killer in sight and call his buddies in law enforcement with his location. That way, at least the body would have a chance of being recovered and hopefully provide some clue to the killer.

Dora may have lied to me, but she'd likely done it to protect her brother. I might have done the same thing. If I could just keep tabs on the body, there was a possibility that the authorities would recover something they could use against Bobby's killer. The physical evidence from the burial site along with the location of the murder might be enough to kick off an official investigation into Bobby's death.

If the killer even stuck around. It had been my experience with Salazar's thugs that killers usually skipped the country until things cooled down.

I idled near the end of the block next to a small stand of cedars with a good view of the driveway, waiting for a vehicle to exit the house. I fired off a quick text to Sam giving him my location and telling him I'd call him in a few minutes. A short time later, the white van drove out of the driveway, turned left, and headed in my direction. I'd parked so that the Tahoe was well hidden, but I slid down in my seat nonetheless, allowing myself just enough of a visual to see who was in the driver's seat and which way they were going. The van passed by heading north. Two people occupied the front seats—the same guy from the truck stop was driving. I couldn't make out any features of the person in the passenger seat.

I waited to make sure no one else followed from the house. After a few beats, I pulled into the street behind them with my headlights off, then flicked them on once we turned onto the main thoroughfare.

The van merged onto I-5 and then took 101 North, heading toward the town of Shelton. City lights faded to the occasional street lamp, and I dropped back even farther. The taillights on the van were distinctive and easy to track from a distance, but I still didn't take my eyes off of them.

I called Sam. He answered on the first ring.

"I'm on 101 headed north just outside of Shelton in pursuit of a white van with a possible dead body inside. The driver and passenger are prime suspects and most likely armed."

There was a long pause before Sam replied.

"When you left this afternoon you said you were going to talk to Bobby Branford's sister. How did a simple interview turn into chasing a killer and a dead body?"

I explained about Bobby and the two gangbangers and how they delivered Bobby to the guy in the van. Then I told him what I'd heard at the house outside of Olympia.

He took a deep breath and let it out in a slow exhale. "And you thought that following the killer was a good idea because…?"

Ignoring the question, I said, "Can you run the plates for me?"

"What the hell were you thinking?"

"I'm only doing what I thought you would do in a situation like this."

"You what—never mind." He let out a deep sigh. "Kate, I'm trained to respond in this kind of situation. You aren't."

"How else am I going to learn? Seriously, Sam. Can't you just help me?"

There was another pause. Impatient, I tapped my fingers on the steering wheel.

"Fine. Give me the number."

I rattled off the license plate and waited, listening to the one-sided conversation he had with his guy. A few minutes later he got back on the line.

"The plates are unregistered. You need to stand down, Kate. I'll contact the sheriff and they can take over."

"If I stop now I'll lose the van and they might not be able to recover the body. I don't want these guys to get away with murder."

"Are you to Shelton yet?"

"About five minutes out. If the body is in the van, and I'm 99.9 percent certain that it is, sooner or later they're going to pull off the highway and look for a place to dump it."

"All righty then." Sam's tone had pissed off written all over it. "I'll relay your position and the location of the possible homicide. And I'll give them the description of the suspects, victim, and van. But I'm also going to let them know you're alone, without backup, without a radio, and that I told you to ABORT, to get the fuck out, now—"

"Sam, I've got this. Don't worry."

"—and that you're incapable of listening to reason."

Silence.

I waited, imagining him struggling to control his anger. Sam rarely got angry. In fact if I really thought about it, he only got pissed off when I did something he deemed dangerous.

He sighed again, long and loud. "If they turn off, make a note of the location. With any luck, the sheriff will catch up to you and take over the tail before the killer gets to where he's going. Just don't follow the guy off road." Sam paused for emphasis. "Okay?"

"Okay. And, thank you. I just didn't want to let this one go."

"No kidding." There was another long pause before he spoke again. "If you make it through this alive, I may very possibly kill you myself."

We ended the call in détente.

The van blew past Shelton and continued along Highway 101 to the Skokomish Indian Reservation on the Hood Canal. I dropped back even farther, as there was little to no traffic on the road and I didn't want them to figure out I was tailing them.

Just past the small town of Brinnon, the van slowed and turned right down a gravel drive, toward the water. I drove past to see where they were going before hooking a U-turn to head back. A short distance from the driveway I killed the lights and pulled to the side of the road. Grabbing a penlight and my black coat, I slid my phone into a side pocket and the semiauto into the holster underneath my shirt, and exited the vehicle.

Careful to keep away from the ditch but remain close enough to the woods to hide, I picked my way through the darkness, silently cursing when a clutch of blackberry vines snagged my coat. Keeping my fingers clear of the brambles I released the vines and continued on. I stopped for a moment to let my eyes adjust to the lack of light and made a mental note to store a pair of night vision goggles in the console. Luckily, the moon was full so I had its blue-white glow to guide my way.

The air was cool and damp with the distinct aroma of cedar mixed with briny salt water. Gravel crunched underfoot as I followed the road down a slope toward the canal, all while staying alert for signs of the white van.

It wasn't long before I spotted it parked next to a small cabin on the shore of the canal. There weren't any lights on, so I skirted the building, staying in the shadows in case one of the van's occupants decided to take a stroll.

The sound of low voices floated through the night air as I crept toward the water. A long wooden dock stretched into the canal. The two men were on the dock, struggling to carry a large bundle between them. Moonlight glinted off the plastic they'd used to conceal what I assumed was Bobby's body. They made it to the end of the dock and dropped the bundle at their feet. One of the men broke away and headed back toward shore. I ducked behind the thick trunk of a fir tree as he walked to the van and climbed inside.

A few minutes later he reappeared with a coil of rope and something heavy in his hands and retraced his steps to the end of the dock. One of the men half-lifted the body, while the other secured the heavy object to its chest with the rope. Finished, the man let go of his half of the body, and they rolled it over the end of the dock into a small skiff. Water lapped at the sides of the boat from the impact. The shorter of the two jumped in behind it and started the motor. The rpms increased, humming through the quiet night air as he drove away from the dock. The second man watched him go for a moment and then turned back toward the van.

Just then, my cell vibrated against some loose change in my pocket.

Shit.

The man on the dock froze for an instant before he turned. Heart in my throat, I slipped farther behind the tree and silenced my phone. Then I eased my gun out of the holster.

"Who's there?" The man reached behind him. The silhouette of a gun appeared in his hand. He started walking toward me.

My finger curled around the trigger, but then I thought better of it and released the pressure. If I shot at him from this distance in the dark, I'd likely miss and give up my position. On the other hand, hitting me while moving would be a lot harder to do, especially since I was dressed in all black. Besides, the sound of the gun going off would carry farther since we were near the water. I didn't think he'd want to wake up the neighbors.

I decided to chance it.

Pivoting, I sprinted back the way I'd come, ramping into a flat-out run by the time I cleared the cabin. A round splintered a tree next to me, spraying bark, while another thudded into the dirt a couple of feet away. Adrenaline mixed with fear spurred me on. I crested the drive, and a sharp stitch wracked my side. Gasping, I clutched at my ribcage and slowed to catch my breath. I didn't hear any footsteps behind me.

Then the van's engine turned over.

The stitch eased enough so that I covered the rest of the ground between me and the Tahoe in a matter of seconds. I jumped in, turned the key, and roared onto the highway.

It wasn't long before the van's headlights appeared behind me. Casting furtive glances in the rearview mirror, I shoved the accelerator to the floor and the SUV shot forward.

The lights of the van grew smaller, and I breathed a sigh of relief. I kept up my speed and scanned the road ahead.

My headlights illuminated a curve in the road. I eased off the accelerator with a glance in my rearview.

Lights. And they looked close.

Accelerating out of the curve, the Tahoe screamed past mailboxes and darkened waterfront cabins. No one was out this time of night.

Where the hell was the sheriff?

I dug in my coat pocket and brought out my cell. I pressed the first number, but there was a loud *crash* as the van slammed into the Tahoe's tailgate. The SUV juddered forward. I lost my grip on the phone, and it launched onto the passenger floor.

The van rammed me again. Struggling to keep hold of the steering wheel, I floored it and the gap between us widened.

And then closed.

There was only one thing I could think of to do. I checked that my seatbelt was secure, and took a deep breath.

And hit the brakes.

The tires squealed in protest, filling the cab with the acrid scent of burning rubber. My arms, legs, and head shot forward, while the rest of my body stayed put. Everything that wasn't secured in the cargo area took flight, slamming into the windshield and pelting the back of my seat.

Then the van plowed headlong into the back of the SUV and my head snapped into the headrest. Metal twisted and groaned and splinters of shattered glass flew through the air. The crunch of metal drowned out my moans as the joined vehicles shuddered to a stop.

Heart galloping in my chest I did a quick inventory, feeling for broken bones and lacerations. A lot of body parts promised to ache for days, but nothing seemed broken, just a bunch of little cuts and soon-to-be bruises. Fighting back a wave of nausea I pivoted in my seat to survey the damage.

The Tahoe's cargo compartment had been replaced by the front end of the white van. What was left of the driver lay across my back seat, having entered the Tahoe through the van's broken windshield. The grisly scene would have been a good poster for what could happen when you didn't use a seatbelt. The van's one remaining headlight lit up the blood and brain mixed with shards of glass lacing his dark, matted hair. Swallowing the bile rising in my throat, I waited to see if he moved, but he didn't. Reality hit and another wave of nausea roiled through me. I unbuckled my seatbelt and tried to take a deep breath. Sharp pain lanced across my ribcage.

Shallow breaths, Kate.

Shouldering open the door, I fell out of the SUV onto the blacktop and groaned, my right hand gripping the doorframe to stay upright. I felt my torso but the gun wasn't there. After a quick search, I found it underneath the steering column. I staggered around the Tahoe to better assess the damage. The result was a crudely smashed together SUV-van hybrid.

I wasn't going anywhere.

Unable to open the passenger door, I climbed into the driver's side and gingerly leaned over the back seat, careful not to graze the tender areas on my chest and abdomen. Even though I knew the gesture was futile, I wedged myself in between the two front seats and felt the man's neck for a pulse. Warm, sticky blood from his head wound covered my fingers. I'd been right—there wasn't a beat.

Satisfied that he wouldn't come to life á la some bad teenage horror film, and still fighting the nausea, I wiped my hand off on his jacket and turned around to search for my phone. It was still on the front passenger side, wedged underneath the floor mat. I grabbed it and looked at the screen.

Sam had sent a text.

Come home. It's Lisa.

Stomach twisting into knots, I hit speed dial. The call didn't connect and I checked reception. No bars.

I slammed my hand on the steering wheel, tears of frustration pricking my eyes. "Dammit!"

Walking up the road didn't help. I was in cell phone hell. I texted Sam my location and a cryptic description of the accident and crossed my fingers that the message would make it through.

Sam got the message, and half an hour later two deputies from the Jefferson County Sheriff's Department arrived, followed by a tow truck and an ambulance. After the paramedic checked me for injuries and cleaned and patched the cuts on my hands and face, I gave a detailed statement to the detective who arrived shortly afterward. Once the detective cleared me to leave, I hitched a ride back to Hoodsport with the tow truck driver.

As soon as I had bars on my cell phone, I called Sam.

"Lisa's had a turn for the worse. You need to get to the hospital, now."

"Can you come and pick me up? I had to have the rig towed."

"I'll be there as soon as I can."

When we arrived at the hospital, a nurse took me straight back to Lisa's room. Dad and Maureen were already there. Dad gave me a hug, but Maureen turned away when I walked in.

Nice.

Dr. Patel was off that evening, and the attending physician in the ICU was busy with other patients. By the looks of my sister, it was obvious that things weren't good. Lisa's blood pressure had dropped significantly, and they'd had to intubate her to help her breathe.

"What happened to you, love bug?" my dad asked, referring to the bandages on my face.

"Nothing to worry about. Just a fender bender." I didn't feel like going into my harrowing evening. I was still processing.

We sat silently. With her eyes closed, Lisa looked peaceful, even though a machine was breathing for her.

Feeling helpless and unable to take any more of Maureen's glares, I walked back out into the waiting room where Sam was reading a magazine. I sat down next to him and leaned my head on his shoulder. He put his arm around me.

"Lisa's stable, at least." I sighed, holding back tears. The adrenaline from the evening had dissipated, leaving me weak and empty.

Sam turned me to face him. He ran his finger lightly over one of the bandages on my face. "How are *you* doing?"

The concern in his eyes was comforting. I clung to it like a drowning woman would a breath of air.

"I'm fine. Sorry about the rig. I'll pay for a new one."

"Don't worry about it. Insurance will probably take care of most of the damage." Sam raised an eyebrow. "You mentioned a 'minor' accident when you called. Imagine my surprise when I show up to find a hunk of twisted metal." He shook his head. "I'm just glad you're all right."

I gave him my best rendition of a smile. Remembering the pill I'd found on Dora's living room floor, I pulled the baggie out of my pocket. "I found this at Dora's. Looks like the same kind that was in Lisa's purse."

He raised his eyebrows. "I'll drop it off at the lab first thing. What happened to Bobby?"

"Somewhere in the Hood Canal. I don't think the guy driving the van was the killer. Another man helped weigh down the body and roll it into a skiff. Then he got in and motored away. Obviously, he was going to dump it somewhere. I think there's a good chance that he was the killer. I told the detective, but without the body, what can they do? It's six hundred feet deep in places."

"I imagine there's more than just Bobby's corpse floating around out there. It's a good place to dump someone."

I gave him a look. "Since when did you start thinking about good places to hide a body?"

He shrugged. "Police work. You have to think like the bad guy."

I stared at him. Of course. I'd been going about this all wrong. I needed to think like a criminal. I had a lot of experience in that department. Why not use it?

An idea began to form in my mind, but I didn't want to share it with Sam. Unless and until I'd thought it through and could present a coherent argument for doing what I was thinking of doing, I'd have to keep quiet.

I just hoped I had enough time.

NINE

THE NEXT AFTERNOON, Sam's contact at the lab called with the preliminary test results for the pills I found in Lisa's purse. Not only did the screening identify an excessively large dose of poor-quality fentanyl, but the lab picked up significant amounts of lead and other contaminants, including arsenic, matching what Dr. Patel said.

"We have to find out who manufactured these counterfeit meds, and where they got their ingredients." Sam tossed the Whitmore file on the desk. Earlier in the day Jax, our IT guy, had emailed a report on whatever information he could recover from Jason's laptop. There wasn't much that looked promising.

We'd regrouped at the office after the harrowing night at the hospital. Lisa was still hooked up to a machine and she still hadn't recovered from the earlier blood pressure drop, but she was alive, and for that I was thankful.

"Ian gave me his dealer's contact information, so that's a start."

"Have you given any thought to calling Chance?"

Chance was retired Drug Enforcement Administration supervisor Chance Goodeve. I'd made his acquaintance when he helped me get out of Mexico and escape from my ex, Roberto Salazar, and I trusted him implicitly. He had extensive contacts that could prove useful in our search for the source of the drugs.

I nodded. "Chance is the one person I trust, but I don't think Mac would like having the DEA in his face."

"Then again, he might welcome the help." Sam studied me for a moment, his dark eyes boring into my soul. Uncomfortable under his scrutiny, I shifted in my chair.

I hadn't told him that I'd been thinking about what I could do to find the source myself. By necessity, the wheels of a police investigation turned slowly. If the DEA got involved it would take even longer. Not only were the police answerable to the state of Washington, the DEA was beholden to government oversight, and going off the reservation opened the agency up to public scrutiny and harsh penalties. Additionally, either agency had to build a watertight case that would hold up in court. I, on the other hand, had no such restrictions.

"What's going on in that beautiful, devious brain of yours?"

Like I said, Sam was spooky.

Shrugging, I looked him in the eyes. "I'm trying to figure out a way to help them in their investigation. You know, speed things up a bit." Which wasn't really a lie. I just didn't elaborate.

Sam leaned across the conference table and took my hand, his expression grave.

"Go through the proper channels, Kate. If you don't, you know where this will lead. You've dealt with these types before."

"It's my sister. I have to do something." I stifled the emotions threatening to overwhelm me. The thought of my baby sister lying in a hospital bed oblivious to the world around her wasn't a memory I wanted to keep having.

He released my hand and leaned back in his chair.

"I know. But think long and hard before you do anything that might compromise their case."

"I promise."

Deciding that it might help bring a faster resolution to the ongoing police investigation, I sent an email with my contact information to Chance's former assistant, requesting that he contact me. Two hours later, my phone rang. It was Chance.

We played catch-up for a few moments—I asked him how retirement suited him (he was bored), and he asked me how life was without Salazar and Anaya. Surprisingly, the first answer that popped into my head was similar to his.

"What can I do for you, Kate? I assume this isn't a social call."

"No, it isn't." I paused, thinking how to frame my request. "I need to talk to someone I trust. Obviously, I'm still leery of going directly to your old organization." When I was on the run from Salazar and Vincent Anaya, the man who took over Chance's supervisory role when he retired turned out to be a mole on Anaya's payroll. He was still out there, somewhere, although both the DEA and the FBI were looking for him.

"Understood. What have you got?"

I told him about the Jason Whitmore case, my interview with Bobby and his subsequent murder, and concluded with my sister's overdose. Then I told him about the Seattle PD's ongoing investigation and my frustration with the lack of results. I left out Ian's role in Lisa's overdose, although told myself I'd give the DEA the information after I found out more about Ian's dealer.

"The attending physician mentioned a spike in fentanyl overdoses over the last couple of weeks. Sam's contact in the SPD confirmed it."

"I'm sorry about your sister, Kate. That's a terrible thing. But I'm not sure how I can be of help." Chance's voice had turned cautious. "I can certainly give your information to my contacts at the DEA, but unless the SPD requests their help with the investigation, there's not much more I can do."

"Thanks, Chance. I appreciate whatever you can manage." The information would be taken more seriously coming from Chance than it would from me. "I can't sit around waiting for the SPD to take action. I need to do something for Lisa."

"I get it. Your little sister's hurting and you feel responsible. But you need to remember, these things take time. Every little bit of information helps these agencies build a case, helps them find the major players. Each operation is different, with myriad details that need to be taken into account and looked at as a whole." Chance paused. "Don't work at cross purposes with them, Kate. Things aren't always as cut and dried as they were with Salazar or Anaya. The SPD could be working on someone higher up in the food chain that you don't know about. Any interference could at the very least cause a distraction, delaying the case. Worst case scenario, an agent winds up dead because you didn't know the whole story."

"Don't worry, I won't. I only want to help."

We ended the conversation with Chance's promise to give the information to the person in charge of investigating the fentanyl overdoses nationally, as well as suggesting the DEA assign a contact I could call in case Sam or I came across anything in our investigation for the Whitmores.

Talking to Chance relieved some of the pressure I put on myself to find answers, giving me the illusion of having done something to find the source of the counterfeit meds. Obviously, someone was going to great lengths to disguise the drug as a legitimate medication, which would put even the most paranoid addicts at ease. People trusted Big Pharma, even though the blessings of the Federal Drug Administration meant less and less these days. The lack of FDA funding and personnel was a recipe for disaster, especially when it involved so much profit for the pharmaceutical companies. Often, important findings fell through the cracks or were cloaked in subterfuge, which made it easier for Big Pharma to market their drugs for far more than the originally intended use.

Which earned them boatloads of diñero.

But I wasn't interested in going up against Big Pharma. I was interested in finding whoever was responsible for Jason's overdose.

And getting payback for Lisa's.

TEN

LISA'S CONDITION DIDN'T change. She was still in a coma and still hooked up to a machine to breathe. Maureen and my father visited Lisa every day, as did I—although I tried to time it so I didn't have to share the space with my stepmother. The occasional dinner with her was enough. As bossy as she was in a normal situation, she was much worse when it came to family. Lisa's doctor visits rarely coincided with my parents', and I suspected the doctor's dislike of Maureen was the reason.

We still hadn't made progress on the Whitmore case, which was now tied to the DEA's investigation of the spike in fentanyl deaths.

"We're hamstrung." I slammed the Whitmore file on the conference table for emphasis. Sam and I had just gotten off the phone with John and Ellen Whitmore. They were disheartened by the snail's pace of our investigation, wondering why we couldn't do more. Sam tried to explain that because Jason's death was now part of a federal investigation we had to move carefully. The Whitmores would have none of it.

I couldn't blame them.

Sam sighed. This wasn't the first time I'd nagged him to let me do more.

"You know as well as I do, these things take time."

"Yes, but why does that mean I can't do *my* job?"

"You can. Look, I'm sorry that Lisa's still unresponsive. That isn't what any of us want. But there are reasons for events beyond our comprehension."

I scoffed. "I thought you said you didn't believe in the crap that shaman told you."

Sam's eyes darkened. "I never said that I didn't believe. I said that I learned more as a truck driver and a cop. And I learned that by observing people and understanding their motives." He walked to the sideboard and poured himself a cup of coffee. "The shaman taught me how to be in the world but not of it. He did it in such a way that he would withhold information from me, which I thought was unnecessary. I realized later he was ensuring that I found the answer for myself."

"Then why should I *not* take things into my own hands? How else will I find the answer?" My frustration got the better of me, and I pushed out of my chair and stood. "Look, I understand that if we go out on our own we might disrupt Mac's and the DEA's investigation, but I think I know enough about what they're doing to be able to stay clear." I crossed my arms and leaned against the conference table. "I'm only going to nibble around the edges. I promise I won't dive into the whole pie."

Sam shook his head. "If this only affected you, then I'd say go ahead. But it doesn't. It involves a lot of other cogs, and anything you do could put the people involved at risk." His expression softened and he came over to stand next to me. He put his arm around my shoulders and drew me closer. "It's going to be fine. There are enough people working on this that there has to be a breakthrough soon. Pull back and look at the big picture."

Sam had a point. I took a deep breath and squared my shoulders.

"Fine. I'll do it your way. For now." I kissed him and headed for the door.

"You want to take the new rig?" Sam had picked up a new Tahoe that morning, identical to the one I'd wrecked, except for being two years newer.

I shook my head. "No. I'm good with the Jeep."

Pausing with my hand on the doorknob, I turned. "If I was in a coma because of some asshole's decision to sell tainted drugs, what would *you* do?"

The look on his face told me he'd feel the same as I did now. Satisfied, I walked out the door and headed for the hospital.

My visit to Lisa left me even more frustrated. Hopelessness washed over me at the sight of her slender frame sprouting lines to monitors, an IV hookup, and God knew what else. I stayed an hour, reading from the book she'd left at the house, alert for a glimmer of awareness: the twitch of an eye, a frown, a slight change in her breathing, the infinitesimal pulse of a finger, anything.

There was nothing.

I rose from the bed and picked up my purse, the bleak feelings even more acute than when I'd arrived. "I'm going to find out who did this to you, Lisa. I promise." I gave her hand a squeeze. Her skin was still cool to the touch, the sound of the respirator even and regular. If I didn't know any better, I'd think she was only asleep.

Seized by an overwhelming need for fresh air, I made it to the visitors' parking lot in record time. I leaned against the front door of the Jeep and inhaled deep, jagged gulps of air, fighting the tears threatening to derail my hard-won composure. An older couple walked by, sympathy plain on their faces. The woman looked like she was about to offer assistance, but her companion gave a terse shake of his head and they continued on. I held back until they were out of sight before giving my emotions their due. All the grief, fear, frustration, and guilt came pouring out. I gripped the door handle to keep from sinking to the concrete and cried until there was nothing left.

Drained, I slid down to sit on the running board and leaned my head against the doorframe.

I should have been there for her. But how? I didn't know she'd been taking so many painkillers. It wasn't like she ever let on. Sam hadn't noticed either, and he was far more observant than I could ever hope to be.

Stop beating yourself up, Kate. She didn't know what she was taking that night.

But Ian should have at least gone with her to the party. A flicker of anger ignited inside of me at the thought of him telling Lisa to hunt down some drug dealer on her own. If she knew there was fentanyl in the painkiller she bought, there was no doubt in my mind that she would have refused to take it. Lisa wasn't a risk taker. Defying our older siblings to come out west to live with me had been a huge leap of faith for her.

With a heavy sigh, I stood and climbed into the Jeep. The long shadows from the late afternoon sun told me it was close to dinnertime and that I should be getting back home. I threw my purse on the passenger seat, and my phone slipped out and onto the floor. The fall must have inadvertently activated my contacts list, because the screen lit up. I glanced at the list. Ian's name was at the top. I scrolled down one and came to Ian's drug dealer contact. Momo. Without thinking, I hit dial.

"Hello?"

"Hi. Is this Momo?"

"Yeah. Who's this?"

"My name is Kate. Our mutual friend Ian gave me your number." My heartbeat spiked.

What was I doing?

"Okay?"

His overly cautious tone told me the idea forming in my head might not be quite as easy as I thought.

"He, um, he said you could hook me up for my neck pain?"

"Ian, huh? Ian…" His voice trailed off as though he was trying to remember who Ian was. "Oh yeah. Ian. Tall hipster dude with a bad back, right?"

"Right."

"Sure, sure. How 'bout we meet under the clock at Pike Place Market. Say, in an hour?"

"I can do that. How will I know you?"

"I'll be the handsome dude in a bright purple ball cap."

"Okay. How much—"

"We'll discuss that in person, a'ight?" he said, cutting me off.

"Oh, sure. Right. See you then?"

Silence.

He'd already hung up. I put my phone away and shrugged off the fear of what I was about to do.

Don't back out now, Kate. You don't have to buy anything. Besides, I'd been intimately involved with people much higher up in the illegal drug world than Momo. Much.

What could happen?

Eleven

AN HOUR LATER, I was standing next to the bronze pig sculpture underneath the huge neon clock at Pike Place Market. The fishmongers had already buttoned up for the day, and the usual crowds had started to thin, with tourists trading the open-air market for a tasty dinner at one of the many restaurants.

I checked my phone for the fifth time. Momo was ten minutes late. What if he didn't come? My idea to make a buy from him wasn't going to work. I'd have to figure out something else in order to make my way up the chain of command in Momo's world. My fingers curled around the fat envelope in my purse. On the way I'd stopped at the bank to pick up the money. I had no idea how much counterfeit meds cost, but I wanted to make a big enough purchase so he wouldn't have it on hand and would need to go to *his* buyer.

I also needed to give him enough that he wouldn't separate the cash. I'd attached a round, flat disk about the size of a quarter to the inside of one of the stacks of bills. It was a small GPS tracker powered by a tiny but powerful battery. I'd be able to keep track of him for a few hours with an app I'd downloaded onto my phone.

After watching the market stalls close down one by one, I slid my phone back into my pocket and turned to leave.

"Kate?"

I glanced at the man in front of me. In his early thirties, he had dark, curly hair and a hard face, with small, deep-set eyes. His bright red coat looked new, and his tennis shoes were expensive. The purple ball cap didn't fit.

"Momo?"

He gave me a quick nod. "Let's take a walk." Momo took my arm and steered me through the thinning crowd of pedestrians and along the street, sidestepping slow-moving cars as we picked our way toward a nearby alley.

Halfway down the length of the alleyway, he stopped and looked both ways. Satisfied that we were alone, he asked, "How much were you looking for?"

"Actually, I was hoping to get a large supply so I wouldn't have to do this again for a while."

"How big are we talking here? Fifty? A hundred?"

"At least a thousand."

His eyes narrowed. "A thousand? You wouldn't be thinkin' of goin' into business for yourself, would you?" He inched closer, sizing me up.

"No, no, no." I put my hands up, palms out. "Believe me, I don't want to do this for a living. I have a good job. Really. It's for the pain." I rubbed the side of my neck for effect. "I take at least three of those pills with the 6767 on the side a day—can't remember what they're called—sometimes four if it's bad. Add it up. A thousand won't even last a year."

His shoulders relaxed a bit, but he still didn't look convinced. "It'll cost you twelve K."

I widened my eyes in surprise. "Twelve dollars each? Are you serious? Last time I made a buy it was only seven." I didn't have a clue if I was supposed to haggle, but it sounded good.

He shrugged. "That's the price. Take it or leave it." He looked me up and down. "I'm gonna need a few thousand up front. That's a big order, yo."

"How do I know I can trust you? I'm not comfortable handing over that much to a complete stranger. What's stopping you from taking off with my money?"

He smiled. "But I ain' no stranger. We have a mutual friend." Momo gave me an annoyed look and added, "And why in hell would I steal your money when you bringin' more bank?"

Good point. "Tell you what. How about I give you five hundred now and the rest on delivery? That way, we both get peace of mind."

He scoffed. "Ain' no such thing as peace of mind." He took out a pack of cigarettes, shook one free and lit it. Studying me, he exhaled a blue cloud. Then he said, "A'ight. For a friend of Ian's I'll see what I can do. Make it two thousand and we're good."

"Cool. Do I pay you here?"

He sighed as though he couldn't believe how naïve I was. "Where else you gonna pay me?" He spread his arms to encompass the empty alley.

With an embarrassed smile, I dug in my purse for the money and slipped the stack of fifties with the GPS inside along with an additional thousand dollars into an envelope. I opened it to show him and then quickly closed it before handing it over. He took it from me and slid it into his coat pocket.

"When will you have it?"

"Should be early tomorrow. I'll give you a call."

I nodded. "Okay. And you're sure you can get the same kind, right? The ones that say 6767? Nothing else seems to work as good."

He took one more drag off his cigarette and flicked it against the brick building. It sputtered out in a shallow puddle. "I'll see what I can do."

"Great." I hesitated. "Are we done?"

One side of his mouth quirked up, and he shook his head again. "Yeah, we good." He pushed off the wall of the building and sauntered back the way we came. I stayed behind and waited for him to turn the corner.

As soon as he was gone, I took out my phone, found the app I was looking for, and logged in. A little red dot blinked steadily.

Now I just had to follow the money.

Rush hour was long since over and traffic was light. The streetlights glowed blue-white in the crisp evening air. I followed Momo south onto I-5, where he exited the freeway a few miles outside of Tacoma. The red light on my phone continued to blink, tracing Momo's route. A few minutes later the red light stopped. I squinted at the screen. The map indicated a park.

Following the outskirts of the deserted park, I spotted Momo's newer-model Acura parked next to an open-air pavilion. Stationary barbecues dotted the green space, with dozens of trees breaking up the expanse. Glowing light circles from the occasional street lamp peppered the area.

I pulled to the curb and turned off the lights. Reaching into the console, I took out my camera with the night vision zoom lens attached. After the last stakeout, I'd made sure to stash it and a pair of night vision binoculars in the Jeep. The directional mic was in the shop. The delicate hardware had been damaged from the collision with the van the night of Bobby's murder, so I wouldn't be able to listen to their conversation.

A dark-colored van sat several yards from Momo's Acura, on the same side of the street. He climbed out of his car and headed toward it. I shot a number of photographs of both Momo and the other vehicle. The side door to the van slid open, and a man in a hooded sweatshirt got out. Momo said something to him and handed him an envelope, larger than the one I'd given him. The man in the hoodie disappeared inside the van, reappearing a moment later with a square bundle wrapped in plastic. He handed it to Momo, got back inside the van and rolled the door closed. Momo returned to his car while the other vehicle drove off. I glanced at my phone—the red dot was moving. My bundle of money was now inside the van.

I waited until Momo left before I shifted into gear and followed.

The van drove out of the park and back onto I-5, headed south toward Olympia. I wasn't too worried about the men in the van catching sight of me following them. They had no reason to believe Momo had a tail. He was a small-time dealer. Within the larger distribution scheme he wasn't important.

The van continued past the city of Olympia and exited the freeway. I recognized the neighborhood. A knot formed in my stomach as the van turned left onto a familiar street and pulled into a familiar driveway.

Where did you think you'd end up?

I turned around at the next intersection, drove past the house where Bobby had been killed, cut the lights, and pulled to the curb. The van was idling in the driveway. The windows were dark, and there were no other vehicles. Keeping my eyes on the van, I groped in the passenger seat for the camera.

According to my contact at the DEA, they were still at the gathering evidence stage and did not have plans to move on whoever owned the home. I would have thought that the man who ordered Bobby's murder would have vacated the premises. He'd certainly heard about the car accident that killed the van's driver that night. Whether he thought the timing coincidental or not, he had to have weighed the pros and cons of staying. But if there were no repercussions from the murder, why leave?

At that moment, the garage door scrolled open and the van moved forward into the darkened space. The night vision lens gave the scene an eerie green hue. Two men jumped out of the van—the guy wearing the hooded sweatshirt who had done the deal with Momo, and another, thinner man. They walked around to the side and opened the door to reveal multiple plastic containers stacked three and four high. I started taking pictures.

The men transferred the containers to one side of the garage, stacking them three high before starting another row. Fifteen minutes later, the two men had emptied the van, closed the cargo door, and went into the house. The man in the hooded sweatshirt hit the button to shut the garage door as he walked inside.

Without the directional mic, I wouldn't be able to hear their conversation. I wasn't in the mood to stay put and pull an all-nighter. Other than my 9mm, the night vision camera and binoculars were the only equipment I'd brought with me.

Conducting physical surveillance usually required more preparation, not the least of which was staking the place out beforehand to get an idea of the subject's activity. I glanced down at my black shirt, black pants, black sneakers, and black jacket. It was a start.

I needed to find out what was inside those containers. Securing the camera around my neck, I slid my gun into a bellyband under my shirt and exited the Jeep.

The hydrangea bushes gave me the cover I needed as I skirted the house past the window where I'd heard Bobby murdered. There were no lights on that I could see, so I continued to the back. Normally, I would have done more reconnaissance, but I hadn't tripped any alarms the last time, so I figured it was safe enough. A few feet from the hydrangeas, I came to a tall wooden privacy fence with a gate. I tried the latch but it was locked. I checked the immediate area for something to stand on to help me climb over the top. There was nothing. Rather than waste time looking, I pulled out my set of lock picking tools.

It was a simple mechanism, and two minutes later, the lock tumbled and I opened the gate. I stepped through and eased the gate closed.

Rounding the back corner, I came upon an expansive patio with a lap pool and an outdoor barbeque. The blue light from the pool cast amoeba-like shapes on the trunks of the trees surrounding the perimeter. I skirted the patio and caught a glimpse of a lamp through a pair of French doors to the left of a huge window. I hugged the wall and crept closer.

It was a cavernous room with an entertainment center lining the back wall and a U-shaped leather sectional oriented toward a big-screen television, but there was no one visible. Somewhere inside, a dog barked, quickly joined by another.

That wasn't good. I eased away from the doors in case someone came downstairs to investigate. Remembering what Quinn had taught me in the Yucatán about reconnaissance, I kept to the shadows, moving from cover to cover, always keeping something between me and the place I was surveilling.

I cleared the backyard and made my way along the far side of the house. This time, there were no hydrangea bushes to hide behind, only a massive HVAC system and a pump house for the pool and hot tub. The distance between the fence and the house was much narrower than the other side. A sturdy six foot-high privacy fence stood between me and the neighbor's side yard.

The windows on that side of the house were above my head, so I climbed on top of the pump house roof and eased to a standing position to peek in the nearest window.

Inside was a mudroom-slash-laundry room, with two doors. The door to my left sported a deadbolt and more than likely led to the garage. Another door, which was open, led to a hallway. Hanging cabinets filled one wall, with a front-loading washer and dryer underneath. Open shelving with a bunch of cleaning products stood near the back, and a deep utility sink took up space nearby. Two of the plastic tubs I'd seen in the van were stacked in the corner.

Shadows fell across the open doorway. I stepped back as two men entered the laundry from the hallway. Neither of them looked up. One was the guy in the hooded sweatshirt from the van. Of medium height, he had a buzz cut and a bolt through his earlobe. The other one was tall and thin and had spiky blond hair. He wore ripped black jeans and a black T-shirt underneath an old army jacket. His bone structure was pronounced—sharp cheekbones and bony shoulders gave the impression of a man on the verge of starvation. An indeterminate amount of piercings and tattoos covered what I could see of his body.

They went out to the garage, returning a few minutes later carrying two more tubs from the van, one stacked on top of the other. They set them down next to the others and went back through the door, returning with two more. This continued until the containers took up most of the space in the room. The guy with the hoodie left through the door to the hallway. The one with the spiky blond hair stayed with the tubs.

Spike crossed his arms as he waited, then crossed and uncrossed his legs. He cracked his neck first one way, and then the other, and scratched the side of his face, his fingernails leaving a trail of red welts. Unable to keep still, he shuffled from foot to foot, and yawned dramatically. He raised both hands in the air in a stretch that ended with one hand casually draped across a stack of tubs. A few seconds later, Spike craned his neck to look out the door into the hallway. Then he sauntered into the hall and checked both directions.

He walked back into the room and headed for one of the stacks of tubs, where he eased the top off a container, checking behind him like he was afraid of getting caught.

A slow grin spread across his face as he removed the lid. The tub was filled to the top with plastic baggies that contained what looked like hundreds of white pills. My heart beat faster as my camera quietly whirred, recording the contents.

That was a lot of meds.

Were the pills the same kind that killed Jason and put Lisa into a coma? I could only guess. Either way, I was now one step closer to keeping them from ending up on the street. I'd contact the DEA as soon as I got back to my Jeep.

Spike checked behind him once more before grabbing one of the baggies and stuffing it into his jacket pocket. He replaced the lid and turned as his friend in the hoodie walked into the room, leading another man behind him.

The new guy was older than the other two by at least a decade—his salt-and-pepper hair gave him a more distinguished appearance, as did his long-sleeved shirt, pressed slacks, and shiny leather shoes. But the heavy gold chain around his neck didn't do anything for his ensemble. Neither did the gaudy gold pinkie ring.

But that could just be me.

They exchanged words, and then the three of them walked out of the laundry room and into the house.

The show was over. Slinging the strap across my body, I slid the camera around my back to keep it safe and then eased away from the window and climbed down from the pump house. Somewhere in the backyard a door slammed followed by a chorus of barks and the scrabble of claws on patio bricks.

I'd forgotten about the dogs.

Panicking, I scrambled back onto the roof of the shed, frantically searching for a way to escape. Except for the laundry room window, this side of the two-story house was all smooth siding with no handholds anywhere.

With the barks getting louder, I eyed the distance to the fence.

And jumped.

TWELVE

I LANDED HALF on, half off the top of the
wooden privacy fence as the first snarling dog
rounded the corner. The barks grew louder as the
rest joined in the hunt. I lunged upward, hooked my right
leg over the top, and launched myself into the neighbor's
backyard, landing on my side with a thud. The wind
knocked out of me, I rose to all fours and tried to suck in
a breath, fervently hoping the neighbors didn't have guard
dogs, too.

The snarling and growling intensified as the dogs
began to paw wildly at the ground under the fence. I
climbed to my feet and stopped. My gun was no longer in
my bellyband. I pivoted, searching the ground, but the
semiauto was nowhere to be seen. Retracing my steps
wasn't an option. I took the loss and sprinted for the
Jeep.

Chacon's outdoor lights popped on, illuminating the
front yard, and the barks turned to howls. Realizing that
I'd be easy to spot on the street, I adjusted my trajectory

and headed for the stand of cedars I'd parked by the first time I was there.

My lungs close to exploding, I raced into the small copse of trees and ducked behind one of the largest ones. I was dead meat if they let the dogs loose in the street. They'd pick up my scent and find me in no time. I stared at the Jeep, mind feverishly searching for some way to get to it.

The sound of the dogs barking their heads off upped my anxiety level. Being attacked by snarling canines wasn't an option. I had to move, now. Slinging my camera back over my shoulder, I eased out from behind the grove of cedars and calmly walked to the Jeep. I had to slow myself down so I wouldn't look like I was running away.

Even though I was.

Blood pounding in my ears, my hand closed around the driver's side door handle.

Almost there, Kate.

I yanked the door open and stowed the camera safely in the console. I was about to climb behind the wheel when the unmistakable sound of footsteps signaled there was someone behind me. Heart in my throat, I slid into the driver's seat and was about to close the door when someone gripped my arm and jerked me out of the Jeep. Whoever it was wrenched my arm up between my shoulder blades and pinned me face first against the Jeep. I let out a yelp. Something hard pressed into my spine. The strong scent of onions and cigarettes nearly made me gag.

"Where do you think you're going?" The man's voice dripped with malice, matching his iron grip.

"What the hell are you doing? Let me *go*." Every time I tried to move he wrenched my arm higher. Pain rocketed into my shoulder. There was no way to escape, especially with a gun in my side.

"What were you doing in the backyard?" The man's voice was more like a growl.

"I wasn't *in* a backyard."

He tightened his grip and shoved my arm higher. I bit my lip to keep from crying out. A dislocated shoulder appeared imminent.

The dogs sounded like they'd been contained—the barking had subsided, dwindling to the occasional whine. I assumed the owner had ordered them quieted before someone called the police to complain. I craned my neck to see if any of the neighbors were coming outside. It looked like there was someone standing in the street, although it could have been one of the other men I'd seen at the house.

Maybe I could force the guy's hand by screaming. If a neighbor heard me they might call the cops. I'd rather take my chances in police custody.

I took a deep breath, but my handler wrenched my arm further up my back, turning my scream into a pathetic whimper.

The man grunted and yanked me away from the Jeep. Still behind me, he whispered in my ear, "If you scream, I will shoot you. No one will hear."

I assumed that meant he had a suppressor on his gun.

"You're hurting me." The fear in my voice was annoying.

"You don't know the definition of hurt. Now move." He frog-marched me back toward the house, my stomach sinking like a stone with every step.

The man who brought me back to the house turned out to be the guy in the hoodie. He shoved me down a long hallway, past several closed doors, and into a back bedroom.

"On the bed."

His words chilled my blood. When Hoodie saw my expression, he grunted and motioned for me to hold out my hand. When I hesitated, he grabbed my wrist, yanked it toward him, wrapped a cord around it numerous times, and then tied me to the headboard. He did the same with my other wrist and left.

Relief tunneled through me at the reprieve. Hopefully none of the occupants were interested in adding rape to their rap sheet. I scanned the room for something I could use to get free. There wasn't anything in the room other than the bed, two nightstands with a pair of matching lamps, a chair, and a dresser against a far wall. An *en suite* bathroom was to my left.

Why hadn't I let Sam know what I was doing? At least then he'd be able to retrieve my dead body.

The door opened and the man with the salt-and-pepper hair walked in. He moved to the foot of the bed and stopped. His expression was a cross between stone-cold killer and annoyed businessman. I opted to focus on the businessman.

"You need to let me go. I was expected home an hour ago. My husband is probably looking for me right now."

He smiled, obviously amused. "And he will know where you are, how?" He had a slightly nasal accent, like the guy I'd overheard the night of Bobby's murder.

I gave him what I hoped was a confident stare, although I was feeling anything but. "He knows where I was going."

"Ah." He nodded as if that answered everything. "And why were you sneaking around outside my home?"

"Your bodyguard, or whoever he is, is mistaken. I was nowhere near your place. I was visiting a client." I kept my voice even and enunciated slowly, as though speaking to a child.

Ignoring my condescending tone he asked, "Who was your client?"

"I don't think that's any of your business."

With a shrug, he walked to the dresser and opened the top drawer. He pulled something out and turned to face me. In his hand was a .45. The long black suppressor extended the barrel's length by several inches. His expression didn't change as he moved closer to the bed.

I cleared my throat. My desiccated tongue stuck to the roof of my mouth.

"Just what do you think you're going to do with that?" My heart beat an annoying staccato in my ears.

He considered the weapon in his hand. "What do you think I should do with it? Or with this?" He reached behind him with his free hand and pulled another gun from his waistband. It was the semiauto I'd dropped in my mad dash to get away from the dogs.

I acted like I didn't recognize it. "Nothing. Cut me loose and let me go and we'll forget this ever happened."

"Or else what?"

And that was the problem. What could I say that would make him think twice before he pumped a round into my head? I doubted any threats on my part would interest, much less scare him into letting me go. No, he was convinced I was the intruder. There wasn't much I could say in my defense.

I opted for the truth. Sort of.

"All right." I sighed, like I was giving in. "You win. That's my gun. I'm a private investigator looking for someone's kid. I received word that he'd been seen in the vicinity, and I was checking out the neighborhood to see if I could find him. Yours was the only house on the block with any activity, so I decided to take a closer look."

Salt-and-Pepper shook his head in amazement. "Still you lie to me. Do you know what will happen to you if you don't answer me truthfully?"

"Torture?" I shrugged. "Statistically, it's been shown to be ineffective." I neglected to tell him I knew from experience. "Besides, I told you the truth."

"You are not afraid to die?"

I'd have to appeal to his common sense. As long as he had some. With criminals, that could be a crap shoot.

"If you kill me, then you'll have a dead body to get rid of. Think of all the DNA I'll leave behind. Add to that the hassle of disposing of the body. It's not like you can just bury me in the backyard, right?" I could tell by the look in his eyes that he was listening. "If I turn up missing, I guarantee that somebody will come snooping around. I wasn't lying when I said my husband knows where I am, and he's got a lot of friends you don't want to meet."

"Why should I believe you?" He brought up the silenced gun and aimed it at my chest. I winced, preparing for the worst. Just then, there was a knock at the door.

"Yes?" Obviously frustrated, Salt-and-Pepper scowled at the interruption.

The door cracked open, and the guy with the spiky hair poked his head into the room.

"The cops are here, Mr. Chacon. Said a neighbor complained about the dogs." His gaze darted between me and his boss and the two guns.

Chacon let out an irritated sigh. "Watch her." He handed him the .45 and glared at me as he slid mine into the drawer and pushed it closed. "If you even think about screaming, know this: as you can see, my associate is now holding the gun with a silencer attached. He has been instructed to shoot if you utter a word." He opened the door and walked out. Spike closed it behind him and turned to face me. He weighed the gun in his hand while a grin spread across his face. Then he raised the barrel with both hands and aimed it at my head.

"You mind pointing that thing somewhere else?" If the gun went off accidentally they wouldn't be able to hear it at the front door, not with a suppressor. I didn't want to have to cope with a bullet wound.

Or dying.

Keeping one hand on the grip, Spike lowered the barrel and absentmindedly scratched at his neck with his free hand. Like before, his nails left long red marks on his sallow white skin. Eyes twitching, he moved his hand to his shoulder and then his arm, scratching like a dog with a bad case of fleas. He was still wearing the army jacket, even though it was warm inside the house. Either the coat was infested or he was a quart low on his drug of choice. He walked over to the chair and sat. His leg bounced wildly as his gaze roamed the room. I cocked my head. I had one play. It could go well or very, very badly.

"You still have that plastic baggie full of pills?" I nodded toward his jacket. He stilled and narrowed his eyes.

"What pills?"

"The ones I saw you take out of the plastic tub and hide in your jacket pocket."

"Fuck you." Scowling, he stood and paced the floor. Midstride he stopped and pointed the barrel of the gun at me. "And how the fuck do you know anything about any pills? Unless," he moved closer, a cruel smile on his face, "you really were watching us."

I held my breath, wondering if he'd be willing to kill me to hide the theft.

"And if I was? What do you think your boss would say if I told him you were skimming off the top?" I neglected to tell him how deadly the fentanyl-laced ones were. He wouldn't have thought that was a bad thing, probably. Addicts tended to think in terms of how high they could get, not how dead.

A troubled look skated across his features but then cleared. "He won't believe you. He'll think you're lying to save your ass." He sneered. "Besides, all's I have to do is put the stuff back and he'll never know."

"Unless he already suspects you." I shrugged. "No skin off my ass, but he looks like the kind of boss who wouldn't be very happy to catch an employee in a lie, much less outright theft."

Spike scowled, but I could tell he was worried. The scratching began in earnest. I wondered if someone could scratch themselves to death. Soon, he was on his feet, scratching and pacing, pacing and scratching.

"Look. I don't want to tell him, but if it will delay the inevitable, then, yeah, I'm going to say something." I fell silent, letting him think.

He stopped midpace and took a step closer. His eyes gleamed in the lamplight. He brought the barrel of the .45 up and forced the end of the suppressor against my temple. I tried to swallow, but failed.

"He'll be pissed off if you kill me. He wants to interrogate me, not dispose of a body." I was amazed that I got the words out.

"I'll just tell him you tried to escape." The stench emanating from his open mouth was enough to make death preferable.

Taking shallow breaths, I replied, "True, but"—I peered at the rope around my wrist— "he'll have a hard time believing you if I'm still tied up and leaking brains all over the bed."

Spike appeared to consider the implications. He lowered the gun and took a step back.

I let go of the breath I'd been holding and added, "But he doesn't *have* to know."

Like a moth to a flame, he drew closer.

"What do you mean?" he asked.

"Let me go." At the look of disbelief on his face, I hurriedly added, "We'll make it look like there was a struggle. Tell him you untied me so I could use the bathroom. I promise he won't have a clue about the pills."

Spike appeared to be weighing the offer in his sketchy, flea-infested brain. I was betting on his need for the pills over his need to be a good soldier.

The pills won.

With a quick glance at the door, he untied the wrist closest to him and stepped back. I didn't wait for an invitation. I untied my other wrist, leaped to my feet, and started for the window.

"Wait." Spike grabbed my arm. "We have to make it look like something happened."

"Oh. Right." I glanced at the lamp on the dresser and then at him. He followed my gaze and gave me a little nod.

"Yeah. Hit me just enough to give me a bruise. That'll work."

I grabbed the lamp and smashed it against the side of his head with as much force as I could muster. The heavy base made a cracking sound but it held together. He dropped like a stone. I grabbed my gun from the dresser and slid it into the band around my waist. Then I raced to the window, eased the screen off, and let it slide to the ground before I climbed through. The window opened onto the side of the house near the gate with the lock I'd picked earlier. The dogs must have been corralled inside—they were nowhere to be heard.

I lowered myself to the ground and sprinted around the side of the house, headed for the street, praying that Chacon's men weren't looking in my direction.

"Moving targets are hard to hit." I repeated the mantra and broke into a flat-out run for the Jeep.

The red taillights of the police cruiser were disappearing down the street. I made it to the Jeep before the dogs started yowling. A door slammed, followed by a man yelling as I jumped in and turned the engine over. I rammed the accelerator to the floor, and the tires chirped as the Jeep rocketed away from the curb in the same direction as the cruiser.

Half a block away, I glanced in the rearview mirror at the three dogs hurtling after the Jeep, growing smaller and smaller.

THIRTEEN

M Y HEART RATE didn't return to normal until
I'd made it onto the highway and was sure no
one was following me. I pulled my phone from
my purse and dialed the number for my contact in the
DEA, and left a message letting him know I'd discovered
a large shipment of counterfeit pills, but that I didn't
think it would be there long. I gave him the address again
to make sure there was no confusion, and ended the call.
He'd get an immediate alert that he had a new message.

It was then I remembered that Chacon was the name
of the guy Mac's informant, Charlie Krueger, had
mentioned before he was shot to death. I figured I should
let Mac know what was going on, although the city of
Olympia wasn't his jurisdiction.

Chacon wouldn't keep the shipment of pills around,
not after having been compromised. He didn't know if
I'd been telling the truth, and would probably err on the
side of caution. The DEA would have to move quickly if
they wanted to stop the counterfeit drugs from ending up
on the street.

I checked the time. 10:40 p.m. The little icon on the bottom of my phone told me I'd missed two calls. Sam would wonder where I was. He answered on the first ring.

"Where are you?" His nonchalant tone didn't fool me. He was concerned.

"I'm headed home right now."

"That doesn't answer my question."

"I was out doing a little investigating, that's all. No harm done." I hoped, anyway.

"Uh huh." He paused before continuing. "Are you all right?" His voice was quiet.

"Totally fine," I lied. "You know how I get after visiting Lisa."

"Yeah. Have you eaten yet?"

My stomach growled, letting me know that I'd completely forgotten about dinner. Being afraid for your life could do that.

"No, but I'll scrounge something up when I get there."

"I saved you a plate. Your parents were over. They brought dinner from The Brooklyn."

The Brooklyn was a Seattle institution and had fabulous food—they grilled a mean steak and their salmon was to die for. "Let me guess—Maureen didn't like whatever the last meal was that I made and thought she'd bring over something she could actually stomach?"

"You know, I think she actually means well."

"She has an odd way of showing it."

"Let it go, Kate. She's stressed about Lisa. We all are."

"I know, I know." My eyes rolled so far up all I could see was black. "It's just hard when she keeps blaming me for all the world's ills."

"That's dramatic."

"Maybe, but it sure feels that way." I glanced at the next overpass. "I should be home in twenty." I ended the call feeling surly. I wouldn't be able to tell Sam what had happened with Chacon. He'd be upset, tell me that I could have compromised the DEA's investigation. Hopefully the message I left my contact would have the opposite effect.

I couldn't just sit around, twiddling my thumbs. Not only were the Whitmores unhappy with our progress on their deceased son's case, but my sister was lying comatose in a hospital bed because of assholes like Chacon and Momo and Spike and Hoodie—people who couldn't care less about what happened to their customers once they'd gotten their money.

My anger spiked at the injustice of it all. I'd never been good at feeling helpless and I didn't want to start now. No, if anyone found out what had happened tonight, I'd be damned if I'd apologize. Even to Sam.

Sam picked up on my mood when I got home but didn't press for details. We talked about our days and then turned in. I slept like the dead.

The next morning I received a call from my contact in the DEA. Agents had moved on the house outside of Olympia, but they were too late. Chacon had already transported the drugs. No evidence of wrongdoing was found. No guns, no drugs. No evidence that a homicide had occurred. I wondered how they had managed to wipe the place of Bobby's DNA. My contact then told me that he was being assigned to another case. When I asked if I would get another contact, his answer was vague.

Momo called and left a message telling me he had the drugs. I slid on a pair of big sunglasses and a ball cap to hide my hair in case anyone from the night before was hanging around, and met him at the same park where he'd scored the drugs. Twelve thousand dollars seemed a bargain to keep that many pills off the street, but after what happened the previous night, the extent of the problem loomed large. I hid the pills in the garage back at the house underneath a blue tarp. I'd hand them over to Mac with an explanation later.

Depressed by my failure to achieve something worthwhile from my near-death experience with Chacon, I nosedived into a funk. I woke late and stayed in bed, staring at the ceiling. Food lost its allure. I avoided my father and Maureen, and soon even my dad stopped calling. Sam left me alone for the most part, understanding that I needed to deal with the grief from my sister's overdose, unaware of my part in the failed bust.

Chance called several times, wanting to know what happened that night. I finally called him back and gave him my side of the story, which didn't go over well. Apparently, I was persona non grata with the DEA, and for good cause.

Burning bridges seemed to be my strong suit.

I'd never kept anything from Sam. Our relationship became strained, mainly because of the guilt I was feeling, but also because of the distance I created from everyday life. If he suspected what happened, he never said. Sam kept on being Sam, and I tried to keep on being me.

The cases that we were able to make progress on failed to motivate me, and Sam finally called me on my lack of enthusiasm.

"Look, I'm trying." I slammed the kitchen cupboard closed and put my hands on the counter for support.

"Maybe you should take a break." Sam's soft tone stood in stark contrast to the anger simmering inside me. I closed my eyes and took a deep breath.

"I can handle it—I just need a little time, that's all."

Sam skirted the counter and came up behind me. Gently, he wrapped his arms around my waist and pulled me to him. I went rigid at his touch but then melted as his warmth seeped into my skin. He kissed my neck and we stood still for a moment, listening to each other's breathing, savoring the quiet eddy in our lives.

I broke away first and turned to face him. Searching his eyes, I said, "Maybe you're right. Maybe I do need to get away." The thought of leaving my sister tugged at my emotions, and I almost took back what I'd said. But something stopped me. If I didn't get my head straight and work through my anger, I'd be of no use to anyone, especially Lisa.

"But what about Dad? I can't just leave him here to deal with both Maureen and Lisa."

"He'll be fine. I'll invite them over for dinner and make sure he's holding up." He caressed my cheek. "He'll understand. And, I hate to say it, but Maureen will probably be less combative with you out of the picture for a while."

"What if Lisa comes out of the coma? Or worse, what if she dies? I won't be here. I'd never forgive myself if that happened."

"You have a phone. I'll call if there's any change in her condition. Just make sure you're within range of a cell tower or have an internet connection. Besides." Sam's gaze locked into mine. "You aren't going to be MIA that long, are you?"

I smiled, letting him know he didn't need to worry. "No, you're right. A few days alone somewhere is all I need." I leaned over and gave him a kiss. "I love you, Sam Akiaq. I don't know what I'd do without you."

He kissed me back, and for the first time in weeks I felt my passion ignite. It was obvious that he felt it too, and soon our clothes were on the floor. He lifted me onto the counter and I wrapped my legs around him. We moved in concert, both of us wanting, needing, reveling in the release, our pent-up emotions and physical needs urging us forward into oblivion.

FOURTEEN

I TOOK MY time driving to the coast. The sunny, unseasonably warm weather had broken, and a fine rain accompanied me to the cabin I'd rented for a few days. The rustic one bedroom was one of only three on an isolated bluff and had everything I needed: a stove, a refrigerator, dishes and pots and pans, a queen-size bed, and a river rock fireplace. There was no cell service, but the rental agency assured me that the high speed internet was reliable. All I had to do was bring food, wine, and my computer tablet, and I was set. I relished the idea of spending a few days alone on the wild and windswept Washington coast, walking the beaches with only my thoughts for company.

I unloaded the Jeep, and placed a loaded Beretta in the top drawer of the nightstand next to the bed. After putting away a few clothes I grabbed a bottle of red wine from the back seat of the Jeep and went into the cabin to pour myself a glass. The cabernet went down easily, and was a great complement to the sharp tang of the aged cheddar I'd picked up along the way. Kicking off my shoes, I settled onto the comfortable sofa and soaked in the vista before me. The huge picture window perfectly framed the deserted sandy beach below, punctuated by a number of stunted, windblown pines. As I contemplated the trees' sheer tenacity, I realized their contorted trunks matched my mood—exhibiting strength against the elements but twisted and misshapen from the changeable winds.

There's beauty in surviving.

And I was a survivor. Lisa's condition wasn't my fault, and my thinking it was wouldn't help her. I had to come back to myself, get grounded again. Otherwise I'd continue to make bad decisions, allowing emotion to dictate my life. Like I'd always done.

And here I thought I'd left that tendency behind me.

Memories came flooding back of the years spent running from my past, all the pain and the loss I'd experienced and caused, and how much I'd grown. Back when I'd first been caught in Roberto Salazar's web, I'd been fresh and new and expected the best from life, never having faced significant hardship or disappointment. Then it all changed, and in a *big* way. All from one, unimportant decision.

Or so it seemed at the time.

My ill-fated choice to stay with Roberto in Mexico had been an impulsive act, a personal rebellion against the safe life trajectory of working for a financial firm in downtown Minneapolis and living the dream of my older sisters and high school friends. I'd been confident of being on the fast track, had dedicated my life to climbing the corporate ladder, when my best friend suggested a vacation in Mexico to have one last hurrah as single college grads. It sounded like the perfect antidote to all the late-night studying and the stress of keeping my grade point average up, not to mention the job waiting for me. Little did I know that trip would change my life, and not for the better.

The reverberations of my past were still evident—my inability to trust, my edginess every time I entered a building or a new street or someone's home. Strangers walking by were assassins sent to kill me or innocent bystanders who might be in danger should my old lover's reach extend to wherever I'd run. Constantly on edge, I still made sure to choose the chair that would allow me to sit with my back to a solid wall, and I'd catch myself automatically searching for the exit, no matter where I was.

And I never left home without a gun.

Even now, on this remote stretch of the Pacific Coast with no people in sight, I'd locked the door behind me and knew exactly which windows I could use for an emergency exit. The back door was the weak link in the sturdily built cabin. Although equipped with a deadbolt, a sheer curtain covering the upper half of the wooden door was the only thing that stood between the six-paned window and the lock. If someone wanted to break in, all they'd have to do was knock out the pane closest to the deadbolt, slide the lock free, and open the door.

Relax, Kate. You're safe here.

Restless, I set my wine glass on the coffee table and stood. The wind had kicked up, lashing the window with rain, but I needed to move, to burn off the nervous energy coursing through me. I grabbed my rain gear and the keys to the cabin and stepped outside.

Securing my hood against the weather, I set off along the bluff, hands shoved deep in my pockets. The landscaping, if you could call it that, consisted of a split-rail fence running the length of the bluff. A few rustic planters filled with primroses dotted the way.

Several yards from the cabin I came to a gravel path carved into the bluff. I followed the narrow trail down to the beach, enjoying the feel of the rain on my face. When I reached the bottom I kicked off my shoes and socks and struck off along the beach at a fast clip. The gray waves crashed against the sandy beach, the foamy water stretching toward the tree line.

Forty-five minutes later, I decided I'd gone far enough and turned around, intending to head back. In the distance, a lone figure walked toward me, head bowed to the rain and wind. By the person's gait, I guessed it was a man. My instincts immediately went on high alert. Where did he come from? I hadn't noticed cars at either of the other two cabins, and there weren't any nearby parks.

Wishing now that I'd brought my gun, I veered left, moving closer to the bluff side of the beach. I needed a good look at the stranger, whoever it was, before I'd take any chances and get too close. The thought that Sam had followed me there crossed my mind, but I discarded the idea. He knew I needed time alone and wouldn't impose. If anyone understood the need for solitude, it was Sam. Besides, I didn't recognize the coat.

My next thoughts gave me pause. *No one but Sam knows you're here. You're being paranoid.*

Feeling foolish, I forced myself to relax. If this guy was a fellow cabin dweller, there'd be no sense putting him off by being overtly rude. I knew how to guard my privacy. It didn't take much to let someone know I wanted to be left alone.

As we drew closer to each other, I glanced at his face. Clean-cut and in his early to mid thirties, he was average in height and weight. His nondescript features didn't ring any bells. He noticed me looking at him, and he smiled and waved. Forcing a smile, I waved back, but kept moving.

"Nice weather we're having," he called out, trying to be heard over the wind.

I nodded and shrugged. *We're in Washington, dude.* Rain was on the menu nine months out of the year. We passed each other, and I continued for a few yards before turning to see if he was still walking in the opposite direction. He was.

Relieved I wouldn't have to make small talk or worry about his presence, I continued back to the cabin for another glass of wine and dinner for one.

A four-door sedan was parked next to one of the other cabins. Apparently I was no longer alone.

After dinner, I washed and put away the dishes and then dug out my tablet from the suitcase. The rental agency had been right. The internet was good, almost as fast as the office. I sent an email to the rental agency to ask if any of the other cabins had been rented for the same dates, and spent time on a couple of social sites but quickly grew bored. For over an hour, I mindlessly clicked on whatever took my fancy. I tried watching a movie, but my restlessness kept me from getting interested. Frustrated that I had nothing to show for the time I'd just wasted, I surfed to an online bookstore and downloaded the latest thriller by one of my favorite authors.

By now, the rain and wind had turned into a full-fledged storm, raging against the tiny cabin. The lights flickered, so I put down my tablet and went to build a fire in the fireplace in case the power went out. A few minutes later, the flames leaped to life, crackling and snapping and sizzling from the moisture in the wood. I breathed in the smoky scent of burning cedar and fir, and settled back on the couch.

About an hour later, there was a sharp knock at the door. Engrossed in my new book, I jumped at the intrusion. Frowning, I set my tablet down and went into the bedroom to grab the Beretta. Checking to make sure there was a bullet in the chamber, I slid it into the waistband of my jeans.

The door had no peephole, so I angled myself near the window to get a look at who was standing outside. It was the guy I'd passed on the beach.

I went to the door and cracked it open, keeping my foot jammed against the bottom. A gust of wind raced through, and I moved behind the door.

"Sorry to bother you, but I'm afraid my power's going to go out, and I can't find any matches to light a fire." Two pools of water had formed near his feet from rain dripping off his Columbia raincoat.

"Oh. Sure. Hold on a minute." I closed the door to give him the idea I wasn't open to visitors, then grabbed a handful of matchbooks from the kitchen drawer. I walked back to the door and cracked it open again. "Here you go," I said, handing him the matches.

"Thanks." He leaned forward and glanced at the bottle of wine on the table, his expression telling me he'd be open to an invitation to share.

I pushed on the door, narrowing the gap.

"Anything else?" My body language and actions screamed *leave me alone*. Was he that dense? Finally, he got the drift.

"Uh, no. These should do just fine. Have a good night—"

I shut the door.

After checking through the window to make sure he was gone, I walked back to the table and poured myself another glass of wine. I placed the Beretta on the couch, within easy reach. Earlier, when I'd gotten back from my walk, I looked through the windows of his locked car but didn't find anything noteworthy. The curtains on his windows were drawn, so I wasn't able to peek inside his cabin.

Oh, stop it, Kate, I chided myself. *He's probably a really nice guy who's getting over a divorce or a layoff or something like that. He's probably just lonely.*

I wasn't here for lonely. I was glad that the third cabin appeared to be empty.

I read for a couple more hours before deciding to call it a night. The storm still raged, but I'd gotten used to the sounds and found them oddly comforting.

As I was getting ready for bed, I glanced out the bedroom window. A light shone from a small window in the other cabin. Assuming the structures all had similar floor plans, it would have been the bathroom. The idea of someone staying in one of the other cabins didn't sit well with me, even though he seemed harmless.

I slid the Beretta under my pillow.

FIFTEEN

I'M IN *A hallway in a hospital, peering into each room as I pass by, looking for Lisa. All the beds are full except the last one I come to. It's a private room, with people crowded around an empty hospital bed. Relieved to see my father and Sam, I enter the room. Two doctors, two nurses, and my two older sisters are there. I walk over to ask them where Lisa is but they morph into Maureen, who is wearing the most hideous makeup I've ever seen—dark green eye shadow, exceptionally pink cheeks, yellow lipstick. Instead of her hair, a nest of vipers sway hypnotically around her head, their forked tongues flicking in and out. Their slit-pupiled gazes latch onto me as though honing in on their next meal.*

Shuddering, I turn to Sam, who is now sitting at a card table, immersed in a game of poker with my dad and the two nurses. The doctors look on, making side bets on who has the best hand. I try to get Sam's attention, but he doesn't hear me. I yell and scream, but no one pays me any mind.

A loud banging, like the sound of a pile driver, can be heard down the hall. I turn to see what's causing the noise, but Chance blocks the doorway. He grabs me by the arms and shouts "Wake up, Kate. You need to wake up."

Swimming back to consciousness, I opened my eyes to inky black. The banging hadn't been a dream. Every few seconds a loud slam from outside the cabin punctuated the stillness.

The glowing red numbers on the bedside clock read 3:34.

I threw back the covers, grabbed my raincoat and the Beretta, and slid on a pair of jeans and my shoes. Peering out the window was no use—I couldn't see anything. There were no perimeter lights, which had been part of the appeal of coming to this secluded section of the coast. At least it appeared that the worst of the storm had passed.

Rummaging through the kitchen drawers, I found a small blue Maglite. I slid the gun in the front of my jeans and partially zipped my coat, allowing me access if I needed it but also to keep the material from flapping in the wind. I opened the door and stepped onto the dark front patio. The rain had stopped, leaving a brisk wind in its place. The air had a fresh, briny scent. Waves crashed below me, near the base of the cliff. The banging sound was coming from my right, near the other cabin. I peered around the corner but couldn't see anything.

Sweeping the beam of the flashlight on the ground in front of me, I followed the noise to the back of the other occupied cabin. A loose shutter slammed against the outside wall. Hoping for an easy fix, I walked over to inspect the problem when a rock skittered behind me. I turned, shining the flashlight toward the sound.

The guy from the beach held his hand up, squinting in the beam. I lowered the light so it wasn't directly in his eyes.

"Is it the shutter?" he asked.

"Yeah." I turned back around and shined the Maglite at the loose mounting bracket. "Have you got a screwdriver?"

"Something better." There was a click and a bright light washed over the side of the cabin.

"Thanks." I turned off the Maglite and stowed it in my pocket as I inspected the shutter. "But I still need a screwdriver." When he didn't answer, I turned around and squinted at the bright light.

"Put your hands behind your head." The friendly voice was gone. "There's a .45 pointed directly at your chest. If you do as I say, I won't have to use it."

Fear rocketed up my spine. It wouldn't matter if I screamed. No one would hear me. He hadn't killed me yet—something he could have done easily. The Beretta felt solid against my stomach underneath my coat, but I didn't dare draw attention to it. Not until I knew what he had in mind.

"Put your hands behind your head," he repeated.

I did as instructed, averting my eyes from the larger flashlight's beam.

"Who are you?" My voice wavered from the combination of adrenaline and fear marching through my veins.

Ignoring my question he said, "Start walking toward the beach." The light spilled past me into the darkness beyond. I took a tentative step.

Play for time, Kate.

"Listen. I'm sure we can figure something out. I have money. Who do you work for?" My first thought was he could be a remnant from my past with Salazar and Anaya. Maybe this guy had been contracted to kill me and didn't get the memo that they were dead. Kind of like the Japanese soldier who'd been living in a cave on an island in the South Pacific that wasn't aware World War II had ended.

No answer. I continued walking.

"Who sent you?" I had to yell over my shoulder—we were nearing the bluff. The waves pounded angrily against the beach. Slowing my pace I added, "If someone wants me dead, then why don't you just shoot me?"

"My employer prefers to make it look like an accident."

That wasn't good. *Think, Kate. He doesn't know you've got a gun.* The waves grew louder. Time was running out. Either he'd break my neck and then roll my body over the cliff, or he'd simply push me onto the rocks below and hope the fall did the job. I didn't think a professional would take the chance, though.

He'd go with the first scenario.

The flashlight beam bounced in time to his gait, making it difficult to navigate the uneven terrain. Walking with my hands behind my head didn't help. I tripped over a rock and barely caught myself in time.

Okay. That could work.

Maybe.

I didn't have long. The split-rail fence materialized in the beam of his flashlight. It was only a couple of yards ahead. Beyond was the cliff.

It's now or never, Kate.

I took a step and pretended to twist my ankle. With a yelp I brought my arms down like I was trying to regain my balance. Crouching, I reached under my jacket, my fingers closing around the Beretta's grip. I slid it free as I stumbled the rest of the way to the ground. Dropping my shoulder, I rolled onto my side and then up to a sitting position, keeping the gun hidden behind the folds of my jacket. I squinted into the beam of the flashlight, aimed the barrel of the gun where I thought he stood, and squeezed the trigger.

The Beretta bucked as the brass ejected and I fired twice more. There was a groan and the flashlight toppled to the ground. Shaking, I scuttled backward, away from the cliff and the gunman, and climbed to my feet. I waited for the hot, searing pain of a round from his gun.

None came.

Blood rushed through my ears and I grew lightheaded, a physiological reaction to the adrenaline racing through my veins. The crash of the waves below sounded like the cymbal section of an orchestra. Salt water stung my eyelids and nose, and the cold, damp air sank into my skin. Violent shudders I couldn't control coursed through my body. My synapses, overloaded from the adrenaline dump into my bloodstream, felt like firecrackers going off in my head. I took a deep breath to calm myself.

That worked well.

Still holding the pistol and shaking even harder now, I stumbled over to his flashlight. I tried to swallow, but my mouth had gone dry. I picked up the light and did a sweep. A few yards away, the gunman lay on his back, his arms splayed out like a snow angel.

He wasn't moving.

Not sure if he was dead, I edged closer to the body. His .45 lay a few inches from his outstretched hand. I kicked it out of the way before I nudged him in the ribs with my foot. Hard.

No reaction. I aimed the light at his chest and waited. No telltale rise or fall of a living, breathing man. The left front of his shirt to his shoulder was a mass of blood.

A lot of blood.

Hot bile climbed my throat. Turning away from the body, I bent over and put my hands on my knees, sucking in large gulps of air.

Eventually the feeling passed. I straightened and turned back to the dead gunman.

Just to be sure, I leaned over and felt the carotid artery in his neck. There was no pulse. Gingerly, I checked his pockets for ID. Nothing.

Was he from Salazar's or Anaya's organization? It didn't make any sense. Both of them were dead. Their people had more than likely scattered to the remaining cartels. It's not like they could run things from hell.

Right?

Shaking off the visual of Roberto Salazar and Vincent Anaya ordering demons to do their bidding from a fiery cell in Hades, I picked up the .45, slid it and the Beretta into my coat pocket, and walked back into the cabin.

I went straight to the open bottle of wine. My arm shook as I poured myself a glass, and red wine splashed onto the table. Ignoring it, I sat on the couch and stared at my reflection in the window. My hair was mussed from having woken in the middle of the night, and my jacket was askew. Other than that, I was looking at a normal, thirty-something woman.

Who'd just shot someone dead.

Again.

I drained my glass and set it on the table. That made at least three people where I'd personally pulled the trigger: the commando in the Yucatán, Roberto Salazar, and now the nameless hit man. Murder was beginning to feel a little too much like a habit.

I pushed aside concerns regarding my homicidal tendencies and ran through the options for contacting the outside world. It was no use trying to call out on my cell phone since there was no service, so I turned on my tablet, connected to the internet, and called Sam via VOIP.

He answered on the third ring.

"I was just thinking about you."

My heart rate slowed just hearing his voice.

"Me, too."

"What's up?"

I cleared my throat. "Would you call the sheriff or the police or whichever agency has jurisdiction out here and have them come to the cabin?" I surprised myself with how calm I sounded.

"Wait—what? What happened?"

I paused. "I just shot a man."

Silence. "You what? Jesus."

I imagined Sam was having a hard time wrapping his mind around what I'd said. I told him about meeting the guy on the beach and then waking up from a sound sleep to the banging outside the cabin. Then I told him what the guy had said about making it look like an accident.

"Are you all right?"

"Yeah. A little shaken up."

Another pause. "Who was it? And why the hell was he after you? There's no reason for Salazar's or Anaya's guys to come after you anymore."

"You know, I didn't check for ID and he didn't tell me before I shot him, so I have no idea."

Sam ignored the sarcasm. "I think the sheriff has jurisdiction over there. I'll contact them and then jump in the car. I should be there in"—there was a brief pause—"a little under three hours. Lock the door and close the blinds, if there are any. You have a gun, right?"

"The Beretta." I forgot to mention the .45.

"Good. Get some rest if you can. I'm not sure how long it will take before the sheriff shows up." There was another pause. "And Kate?"

"Yes?"

"Don't worry. We'll figure this out."

After the call ended, I felt marginally better. Although, a dead body outside on the ground wasn't exactly conducive to getting any rest. Making sure to have the gun handy, I went outside to check the guy's car. It was locked. Not wanting to disturb evidence in the cabin, I resisted the urge to go inside and look around. I doubted I'd find anything except maybe more weapons. Although still open to question, if this guy was actually a professional hit man, he wouldn't have ID. At least not anything with his real identity.

I spent the next half hour wondering two things. First, who had the resources to hire someone to kill me? And second, who wanted me dead? Aside from the fantasy of Salazar and Anaya reaching out from the grave, I couldn't think of anyone other than Luis. Even he was a stretch, since I'd already handed over the incriminating information to the FBI linking him to Vincent Anaya's operation. Yes, he was on the run, and yes, he might be angry enough to kill me, but he wouldn't waste time or precious resources on revenge. Not when both the DEA and the FBI were looking for him. And he certainly wouldn't care if it looked like an accident.

Then the penny dropped.

Chacon.

Of course. The night I'd been at the house and saw the drug shipment in the laundry room, the guy in the hoodie had grabbed me right as I was about to get into the Jeep. Anyone could have written down the license plate number. It wouldn't have taken much digging to figure out who owned the vehicle. I had no doubt that Chacon had the resources as well as the inclination to hire a hit on the woman who sent the DEA to his door.

My face warmed, and the self-recrimination started. How could I have been so stupid? The sad excuse of being messed up because of Lisa's condition rang hollow in my mind.

Once again I'd put someone I loved in danger. What if I hadn't taken the trip out to the ocean? Would Chacon have sent someone after me in my own home? *Sam's* home?

Of course he would. Criminals didn't play nice.

I got back on my tablet and fired off a message to Chance Goodeve, telling him my suspicions. He'd hear about it eventually. I looked at my watch. There was no sense trying to contact Sam again; he was already on his way. I'd bring him up to speed when he got to the cabin.

Sixteen

THE SHERIFF ARRIVED within the hour. The two detectives assigned to the case weren't far behind. I gave my report and answered questions while law enforcement taped off the crime scene and gathered evidence. One of the detectives confiscated the Beretta, since that was the only gun that had been discharged. I handed over the .45 giving them the excuse that I felt safer not having a firearm lying on the ground where anyone could grab it. It was my word against a dead man's regarding who pulled a gun first, although the autopsy report would show that I'd been near the ground when I shot him, which would help substantiate my story.

Sam showed up a little while later. He had a word with the lead investigator, who came over to tell me they'd gotten what they needed and that I was free to go. Sam and I walked back inside the cabin to gather my things. I'd already packed, so it was more a matter of making sure everything inside the cabin was as I'd found it. The owner had been notified, but she lived in California and wouldn't arrive until the next day.

Thinking about what to say to Sam, I straightened up the living area, making sure nothing was out of place. Sam carried my suitcase out to the car and came back inside.

"I need to tell you something."

He looked at me expectantly.

"I need you to hear me out before you get pissed off. Do you remember the night I came home late?"

He crossed his arms and leaned against the door. "Sure."

"Well, I didn't exactly tell you everything."

The corner of his mouth twitched. "Really." The sarcasm wasn't lost on me.

I took a deep breath and let it go. It was unnerving that he knew me so well.

"Yes, really. Smart aleck." I lifted the bag out of the kitchen garbage can and tied it closed. "That night, the two men I followed in the van had just done a drug deal. They ended up at the same house where Bobby the Barracuda was murdered."

"Chacon's place?"

I nodded.

"And?"

"And they offloaded a shipment of pharmaceuticals—I assumed they were counterfeit. I think that Chacon's place was a distribution hub for the bad fentanyl. Anyway, I watched them through a window."

Sam didn't move, his expression unreadable.

"They didn't see me at first, until someone let out the dogs. I tried to run, but they caught me."

"Jesus, Kate." Sam put his hands on his hips and looked at the floor. When he finally raised his head, his eyes were the darkest I'd ever seen them. "You could have been killed."

"I realize that."

"How did you get away?"

"A neighbor complained about the dogs and the police showed up. As Chacon was dealing with them, I made a deal with one of his guys. He looked the other way while I climbed out a window." I figured Sam didn't need every little detail.

"I think Chacon sent that guy." I nodded toward the door, indicating the hit man lying dead outside. "He knew what I was driving."

"And you're telling me this because you think the house is compromised?"

"I'm pretty sure that's the case. How else did the guy know that I was headed to the coast?"

"Did he ever have possession of your cell phone?"

"Not that I'm aware of. I put it inside the Jeep before Chacon's goon grabbed me."

"You might want to check the battery, just to be sure."

I rummaged inside my purse and pulled out my phone. A quick check showed nothing unusual.

"How about the Jeep?" He crossed his arms again. "They could have attached a tracker."

"I didn't think of that. Wouldn't the batteries have run out? I mean, we're a week out from the night in question."

Sam nodded. "They could have switched it out, or put a tail on you. Or he tapped into the battery. Takes longer, so I'm leaning toward either a tail or a slap and go."

"I wonder why he waited so long?"

"I imagine Chacon had other concerns occupying his time, like moving his operation. Add to that the fact that we both keep strange hours. There's no discernible pattern, which makes it difficult to stage a clean hit. He probably figured he'd be able to isolate you eventually." He opened the door. "We'll have to wait for daylight to run a thorough check on the Jeep, but I can give it a quick once-over before we leave here."

"So."

"So."

"I suppose this means you won't trust me again, right?"

Sam closed his eyes and shook his head. "No. I trust you, Kate." He glanced out at the team of law enforcement working the area under bright spotlights. "God knows why, but I do."

Why did I always screw things up? I was a walking disaster. People needed to stay far, far away from me. The bad spirits that guy told me about in Mexico a lifetime ago still hadn't left me alone.

Um, you can't blame bad spirits, Kate. That was too long ago.

I never said I wasn't good at denial.

Grabbing a flashlight from his rig, Sam did a quick check underneath the Jeep for a tracking device but didn't find anything suspicious. As soon as all my stuff was secured in the back, we headed for home. The drive gave me time to consider what happened and to try to formulate a plan to keep Chacon from coming after me again.

I'd have to do something, and do it quickly. But what? If he hadn't already, Chacon would be moving into a new place to conduct business. Sure, I could use Momo again to find the guys in the van and track them to Chacon's new location. That was if Chacon was the only supplier they used, and if Momo would sell me another big order.

Big ifs.

And then what? The DEA was no longer interested in dealing with me. Chance's anger at what I'd done, coupled with not having a contact familiar with the case, spoke volumes. I couldn't blame them. They acted on information I gave them and ended up with a big fat nothing. And, Chacon made them look foolish. I'd be pissed off, too. I was lucky they didn't bring me up on charges for interfering with a federal investigation.

There was still time.

Three hours later, we were home. Exhausted, I dumped everything in the closet, intending to sort it out later. Sam cooked some eggs while I glanced through the news on my tablet.

While Sam plated the eggs, I laid the tablet on the counter in front of me and cleared my throat. "I was thinking."

"That's dangerous," Sam said without turning around.

"Funny man. But seriously, when that guy pointed a gun at me, I didn't know how to respond, and I had a gun. What should I have done in that situation?"

Sam turned away from the stove, a plate in each hand, and set them on the island. He'd added some strawberries and a couple of slices of melon on the side. I stabbed a strawberry with my fork and ate it. He picked up the salt and pepper before coming around the island to sit beside me.

"That depends." He ground a liberal dose of pepper on his eggs and offered me the grinder. I shook my head and he set it down. I reached for the hot sauce and poured it on my eggs until the Scoville heat unit would kill a rhino.

"On what?"

"Size and position of your assailant, for starters." He shoveled a forkful of eggs into his mouth, chewing as he thought. "Your ability to handle a gun, which, in your case is pretty good, especially since you've been practicing at the range."

"But what *should* I have done? I couldn't have just pulled out the Beretta and shot him. Even though he didn't know I had a gun and I had the element of surprise, I don't have the confidence or speed to try something like that." I nibbled on a piece of melon. "What would you have done?"

Sam shrugged. "From the scenario you described, I would have most likely feigned surprise, spun around, and blinded him with the Maglite while drawing the Beretta." He speared his fork into one of the strawberries. "Of course, I've had a lot more training than you and I'm pretty fast. But for your skill level, you did just fine." He smiled as he popped the berry into his mouth. "You survived. That was the main objective, right?"

"I guess." I played with my eggs. "Can you teach me? I learned a lot training with Quinn's guys, but it's been awhile since I've used any of the moves. I'm rusty."

Sam nodded. "Good idea. I can show you what they taught me in the Academy, and add some specialized martial arts into the mix. That way"—he brought his hand up and stroked my cheek—"I won't have to worry so much."

Later on, after I'd gotten a few hours of sleep, I called Chance.

"If you don't already have one, I would suggest that you and Sam install a security system at the house," he said. "Make it the best you can afford. A man like

Chacon—if indeed it was Chacon—will have access to thugs who know how to avoid detection." He sighed. "Until this is over you're in danger, and by proxy, so is Sam."

"Have you heard whether the DEA is going to bring me up on charges?"

"I haven't heard, but I'll let you know."

"Thanks, Chance. I owe you."

"Don't be too hard on yourself, Kate. If anybody owes anyone, it's the DEA. Because of you, two of the most elusive drug traffickers in recent memory are dead, and the Feds are well on their way to finding the power behind the drug cartel throne. I'd say that's damned fine work. You just need to tone things down, stay the hell out of their way for a while."

We ended the call with Chance promising to have someone at the DEA contact me for my version of events at the cabin. He also promised to put in a good word toward getting someone assigned as a new contact.

The next day, Sam purchased an alarm system for the house, complete with audio and video feeds and a computer backup. When I offered to pay for it, he brushed me off, telling me he'd been thinking about installing one for years but hadn't gotten around to it yet.

I just hoped it was enough.

SEVENTEEN

Sam and I started training that weekend. Sessions were broken up into morning and evening, and divided between weapons handling and hand-to-hand combat. He taught me foundational skills like assessing an opponent's strengths and weaknesses and how to play to my own strengths while being aware of weaknesses in my defenses.

One of my *aha* moments came when Sam taught me to work *with* my opponent's moves rather than try to block them with force. There was energy in an attack that I could use to my advantage. Learning how to guide the force of the attacker so that his body ended up in a position where I could better immobilize him was key to giving me more confidence in my abilities. Even at a rudimentary level, the art of reading the other person's subconscious physical cues took work, but Sam was a firm taskmaster and didn't give me any slack. I practiced over and over until identifying common initiating moves started to become second nature.

During our weapons sessions, Sam glossed over semiautomatics, AK-47s, MP5s, and Uzis, since I'd already been trained on those kinds of guns. First by my bodyguard, Eduardo, when I lived in Sonora with Salazar, and then by Quinn and his group when I joined forces with the commandoes deep in the Yucatán. Instead, we concentrated on non-traditional methods of self-defense: using a pen, a set of keys, or a telephone cord to shut down an opponent. He tested me on a person's most vulnerable points—the groin, throat, and eyes were the best choices, followed by the wrists, instep, kidneys, and if you had enough room to make it count, the back of the knee. After training with Sam and going over what others had taught me, I felt better able to handle whatever Chacon or someone like him would try to throw my way.

When I asked him to teach me the best way to kill someone, Sam gave me a strange look and said, "We're not doing offense. Only defense. Offense is a whole other mindset."

"Okay, then let's play what-if."

Sam crossed his arms and leaned against the garage wall, where we'd been practicing throws and kicks.

"What if someone kidnaps you and leaves a note saying that the only way I'll see you again is to come to such and such an address? What should I do then?"

Without missing a beat he said, "Call the FBI."

I rolled my eyes. "Yes, of course, but what would you do in that situation?"

"Call the FBI."

Shaking my head, I blew out a frustrated sigh. "You're not going to work with me on this, are you?"

"Nope."

Leaving it for the time being, I talked him into doing some worst-case scenarios. We continued sparring and role-playing well into the night. The more I learned, the more I wanted to try. Training made me feel powerful, like I could handle anything that came my way. Sam must have sensed it, because the holds grew more difficult to outmaneuver. More than once I ended up on my back on the mat, staring up at him, trying to catch my breath.

I got the feeling he enjoyed the training a little too much.

Sunday evening, my parents came to dinner. Maureen was subdued, and I found it easier to talk to her. Dad even noticed. He came into the kitchen to help with the dishes and joked that he didn't know what we put in the water, but he wanted to bottle it.

"Maureen seems distracted. Is there news about Lisa?" I'd been to see my sister the day before, but it was possible something had happened since then.

Dad shook his head. "No, I think she's just homesick. You know, all of her lady friends are back at the country club having their lunches and whatnot, and she's been out here, tending to her daughter." He shrugged as he dried a wine glass and put it in the cupboard. "You know how they talk, and Maureen's not there to run interference. I'm sure the rumor mill is running amok in our absence."

Maureen cared a lot about what everyone else thought, trying to control what was being said about the family and keeping up appearances. Not only was Lisa's condition emotionally devastating, but the fact that her biological daughter was in intensive care because of a drug overdose had to be terribly embarrassing.

At least when I messed up, she could blame someone else's DNA.

"It's got to be exhausting trying to control what people know about you and your whole family. Maybe this will help her not to care so much about what people think."

A smile tugged at his lips as he stifled a laugh. Pretty soon we were both guffawing at the thought of Maureen learning that particular lesson. When the laughter subsided, I gave my dad a big hug and a kiss on the cheek. Releasing some of the pent-up emotions I had surrounding my stepmother's disapproval went a long way toward lowering my anxiety levels. I hadn't felt this light since Lisa had asked if she could move in with me.

"Thank you, Dad."

"Anytime, sugar pie." He paused. The towel in his hands grew still.

"Looks like something's weighing on your mind. Can I help?"

Dad frowned before he resumed drying the pan he was holding and put it on the counter. "Maureen and I are leaving the day after tomorrow." He stared into the distance for a moment and then shook his head. "The doctor says it could be months, hell, years before Lisa comes out of the coma, if she ever does. We've got a life back in Minnesota, and Maureen's not happy here."

I knew what he was going to say next, and it twisted my insides. I didn't want to lose the tenuous attachment I'd regained with my younger sister.

"Maureen—I mean, we, think that Lisa would do best if she was moved to a care unit in Minneapolis, close by where we can check in on her."

Even though every cell in me wanted to protest, I realized he was right. Lisa needed to be home. Maureen and my sisters would visit her every day and give her the care she needed if she ever came back to us. It wasn't my decision. It was never my decision.

There was no guarantee that Lisa would ever come out of the coma. Yes, if she stayed I would visit her as often as I could, and I assumed that Ian would do the same, but that wasn't going to be enough. The finality of my father's words hit me hard. My dream of having a normal relationship with my family evaporated.

"I understand." I placed the last bowl into the rack and pulled the plug in the sink. The water receded, giving a final gurgle as the last of it drained out. I looked at my father. He gave me a sad smile and wrapped his arms around me in an all-encompassing hug.

"I know how much you two were looking forward to getting to know each other again."

Hot tears brimmed in my eyes. I took a step back and wiped at them with the back of my hand.

"Aw, sweetie, you know I love you. Lisa's going to be fine. She'll come out of this even better than before. I promise."

I smiled through the tears at his valiant attempt to try to make me feel better. It looked like I wasn't the only one in denial.

Eighteen

MAUREEN AND MY father made arrangements with the hospital to transport Lisa back to Minnesota right away. When the time came, the doctors and nurses let me have a few moments alone with her to say my goodbyes. I wondered if I was ever going to see her alive again.

She looked so peaceful lying in the hospital bed. It was almost like she'd wake up and ask me how the PI business was doing.

My conversation with my father the day before may have brought me back to reality, but saying goodbye to her made it all seem final.

I sat on the edge of the hospital bed and took Lisa's delicate hand in mine, thinking about what I should say to her. Would she hear me? Would the news that Maureen and my father were taking her back to Minnesota have a detrimental effect? It sure as hell depressed me. I opted to keep that part to myself.

"Hey, Lisa. It's me, Kate." I stroked her hand with my thumb, unsure if she could even feel it. "I just wanted to say goodbye for now. Looks like Maureen and Dad are moving you back to Minnesota where they can take care of you better." I took a deep breath, fighting back the tears. "I'll come and see you, I promise. It just might not be as often as I'd like." The thought of going back to Minneapolis and dealing with my two older siblings and Maureen on their home turf made me shudder.

As though she was listening, I continued until my list of current events was exhausted. A nurse appeared at the door and gave me a kind look that said I should wrap things up. I nodded and turned back to Lisa.

"Be well. I love you." I leaned over and kissed her cheek. Then I stood and shrugged my purse over my shoulder. With one last, final look, I walked out of the room.

I drove the streets of Seattle aimlessly, not wanting to go home but not wanting to stop anywhere, either. When I found myself near the house in Green Lake where Ian was supposed to meet her that fateful night, I pulled to the curb and shut off the engine.

Why did I even bother? Every time I tried to start a new life, something I could be proud of, things went sideways. And it usually involved the ones I loved the most getting hurt. Yes, I'd made a big mistake when I hooked up with Roberto Salazar, but even after I extricated myself from that hellacious nightmare he'd come after me, upsetting all the careful plans I'd made. I'd run to Alaska to get away from him, but he found me there. Or, more accurately, Angie McKenna tracked me down with the help of a private eye who lost his life for the trouble.

Sam helped me get away, but in doing that I lost everything. I ran to Hawaii, where I trusted an old friend who turned out to be just as dirty as Roberto, and had to leave again. Finally, I changed my name, my hair, and my address once more, hid out in the little town of Durm, Arizona, and I was safe. At least for a while.

Five years later, John Sterling, an associate of Salazar's, tracked me down and tried to kill me. But he died in a mine collapse, or so I thought, and I rebuilt my life yet again. Soon, he and Roberto Salazar caught up with me, and the nightmare began again. Angie made another appearance and shot the man I was involved with to try to get to me. He survived, but later events ultimately led to my losing him. Fortunately, I found Quinn and together we put my trouble with Salazar to rest.

That was, until Vincent Anaya got wind that I still had his money. Again, I'd asked Quinn for help and he'd obliged.

The two years that had passed since then had been relatively quiet. I was beginning to relax, to not jump quite so high when a car revved its engine, or hit the decks whenever someone lit a firecracker. Sam said I had PTSD, or Post Traumatic Stress Disorder, and he was probably right. Fighting for my life for so long left me with nightmares and a deep anxiety that I just assumed would be my new normal.

Years ago, an old man in Mexico had told me bad spirits surrounded me, that I wouldn't be rid of them until I had lost everything.

He'd been wrong.

I'd lost everything many times over. No matter where I went or what I did, bad luck followed me. And God help anyone who was a friend of mine.

A soggy blanket of depression enveloped me, dampening my already low spirits. I turned away from what was once going to be a bright, shiny future and started the Jeep.

What the hell was I doing? My life stood for nothing. *I* stood for nothing. I was a waste of space. A living, breathing bag of flesh and bones. That was it.

Screw that.

Pushing away feelings of self-pity and hopelessness, I pulled away from the curb and into traffic. My confidence grew as I planned my next steps. I was going to make a difference.

And I was going to start with Chacon.

NINETEEN

M Y CALLS TO Ernesto, the owner of a hotel in the Yucatán who could usually find Quinn, went nowhere. The woman who answered the phone at the Hotel Maya didn't sound familiar. Like the manager before her, she displayed the same fierce protectiveness of Ernesto.

Time was running out. I didn't have the luxury of traipsing down to Mexico to try to find Quinn and his group of commandoes. That could take days, possibly weeks. Quinn wasn't one to stay in the same place for long. Depending on which cartel he was targeting, he'd break camp every few weeks or so. His life's work of eradicating the ranking members of powerful Mexican drug cartels took him and his recruits into some seriously gnarly situations, which I knew from first-hand experience. If it hadn't been for Quinn, I never would have broken free of Salazar's or Anaya's murderous grip.

I poured myself a third glass of wine and checked my watch. It was past midnight. Sam was pulling all-night surveillance for a new client who wanted proof his wife was having an affair with his business partner. Neither Sam nor I enjoyed taking those types of cases, but they were the bread and butter of a private investigation agency and every once in a while it had to be done. I was glad it was Sam's turn.

The wine was doing a fine job of helping me forget how my little sister's life had shifted forever and how frustrated I was waiting for the DEA to bring the perpetrators to justice. Again, I'd asked Sam to teach me lethal combat, knowing that he wouldn't. Which led to my attempt to contact Quinn. I knew if I asked, he'd agree to teach me what I needed and not only because I'd pay. When I left Mexico two years before, he'd offered to help anytime, anywhere.

Since that hadn't worked, I had to think of a plan B.

Who did I know that would train me to kill? The idea sounded ludicrous. Even though I'd shot three men, in my heart I wasn't a murderer. Far from it. But if I wanted to go after criminals like Chacon, I needed them to be afraid of me.

And I needed to be able to kill them if I had to.

I got onto my laptop and surfed the dark web using encrypted technology to hide my identity. Soon, I veered down the rabbit hole that led me to a place where a girl could get herself into some pretty serious trouble if she didn't know what she was doing.

Good thing I knew what I was doing.

With a few clicks I accessed a message board that Sam and I had stumbled across in a previous case. We'd been trying to prove a client's change of heart in contracting a hit on her husband, and had left a message hoping to get in touch with the alleged contract killer. She'd filed for divorce, but the husband had balked at signing the papers. It turned out that the wife had, in fact, contacted a hit man through the message board but changed her mind before any money exchanged hands. The assassin corroborated her story, and we were able to convince the husband not to press charges. Immediately afterward, the husband signed the divorce papers.

The hit man had been congenial and quite helpful, and claimed that he was available for a consult, should we ever need his expertise in solving a case in the future. He'd served in the military, claiming to have been a member of an elite black ops force, and had decided to continue to work as the killer he'd been trained to be.

The wine was doing its thing by erasing any semblance of caution a normal person might have. So, using the fake name I'd given when we interviewed him, I posted a request for the hit man to contact me regarding a case ASAP.

I was having a hard time staying awake, so I turned off the laptop and went upstairs to bed, not giving another thought to my late-night request.

The next morning I eased out of bed, trying not to wake Sam. He'd come home a few hours earlier, obviously exhausted, stripped off his clothes, and fell into a deep sleep as soon as his head hit the pillow. I padded along the hallway and down the stairs to the kitchen to get a cup of coffee. As I passed the office, I paused, remembering the message I'd posted the night before.

My brain still fuzzy from the wine and barely awake, a jolt of fear kicked me into overdrive.

I had to delete the message before anyone took it seriously.

Why on earth did I think getting in contact with a hit man was a good idea? I hurried to my laptop, brought up the encryption app, and clicked over to the message board to find my request. There were four replies.

I took a deep breath and opened the first one.

My name Bob. I help. Where we to meet?

Obviously it wasn't the man I was looking for. He'd used the name Ron and could write in complete sentences. I opened the second and third replies. One was an advertisement for a male enhancement remedy, and the other was a rant from some sociopath incensed about the United States government who was trying to drum up subscribers for his hate-filled vlog.

Relieved that no one seriously considered my impulsive request, I clicked on the last reply.

Ron is currently indisposed, but I may be able to help you with your case. Depending on your requirements, my fees are considered reasonable. Results oriented, with nearly 20 years in the business and a close rate of 99%, I am one of the best in the field.

The respondent listed a contact email, and signed off with the name Lucy.

I sat back in the chair, pondering her reply. A female assassin? The way her message read, she was a businesswoman with a penchant for killing.

Stop it, Kate. Are you seriously considering working with a complete stranger? Even I thought I was nuts. With a shake of my head, I deleted both my request and Lucy's message and shut down the laptop.

That was the stupidest idea you've ever had.

I hated when I was right.

That still left me with the problem of what I could do to stop Chacon from releasing his little pills of death onto the street. What I really wanted to do was find out who his supplier was. That way, I might be able to figure out how to stop the drugs at their source. A normal criminal would worry that he was killing his customers, but if Chacon was linked to a Mexican drug cartel, normal didn't enter into it. The way they figured, their customers wouldn't dry up anytime soon—there were always more where they came from. Especially in the US.

No, it was mainly the little guy who wanted to hook his or her customer and keep them coming back for more. There was so much money changing hands in the illegal drug trade, the big players never concerned themselves with small-time hustler priorities. And it was the big distributor's call which drug the street hustlers got to sell.

Chance had gotten the DEA to assign another case manager to me, but it was obvious that the contact was only there to keep an eye on me when I became impatient at how long things were taking. The Whitmores had all but given up on Akiaq Investigations, and it bothered me that we couldn't do more for them. I couldn't imagine how hard it must have been for them to know that their son was just another number in the DEA's investigation. Sam took it all in stride. Having been in law enforcement, acceptance of the time it took to close a case as well as dealing with the inevitable restraints of a federal investigation was easier for him. He knew what it took to build a case that would hold up in court.

I'd never been accused of being patient.

There had to be some way I could help bring closure to the Whitmores in the death of their son and do something to avenge Lisa's overdose by finding out where the deadly painkillers were coming from.

Restless, I poured myself a cup of coffee and went into the den. I grabbed the remote, turned the television on, and clicked through to one of the 24-hour news sites.

CNN was running a story about a recent murder in downtown Portland, Oregon. The reporter used the word "peaceful" when referring to the state of the victim, and "clean" when describing the method of murder. Indeed, when the camera panned over the crime scene, all that was visible was the deceased sitting on a bench with his eyes closed and his hands folded neatly in his lap. There was no blood, no signs of struggle. In effect, "clean."

Cycling through a few more stations, I was about halfway finished with my coffee when a red banner with the words "Breaking News" scrolled across the bottom of the screen. I turned up the sound as the news anchor reported fourteen confirmed overdoses in Seattle in the previous twelve hours. Most, if not all, were thought to be the result of painkillers laced with contaminated fentanyl. Three of the victims had died, with two others in critical condition. Heart skipping, I leaned forward in my chair.

Three more people died because I haven't done anything.

Anger burned in my chest at the thought of Chacon enriching himself by selling deadly drugs to unsuspecting addicts—many of whom became dependent because their doctors overprescribed opioids when something far less addictive would have done the job.

I couldn't blame the DEA for not arresting Chacon. There was no proof that he'd been involved. My testimony wasn't enough to put him behind bars. Although Chacon was laying low as a result of the botched raid on his home, my DEA contact assured me that they were watching his network, waiting for him to make a mistake.

Maybe I could help them out.

TWENTY

I HAD IAN make plans to meet Momo the next afternoon for a buy similar to the one I'd done before. It was possible Chacon's boys put the word out that they'd had a problem with a woman fitting my description, so I thought it best to use a go-between. Ian was to wait for Momo at a park a few blocks from the wine bar where he worked. Guilt about Lisa's condition weighed heavily on his conscience, and he appeared eager to make amends.

Half an hour before the scheduled time, I parked Sam's new Tahoe at a strategic location, giving me a good view of the surrounding area. The Jeep would stick out among the other vehicles parked along the street, and even more so if Chacon's thugs had circulated a description. To counteract any unwanted attention, I wore a big pair of sunglasses, a Mariners ball cap, and had tied my hair back, altering my appearance just enough to throw off suspicion.

The day was warm and sunny—one of those glorious, blue-sky days prized by those who live in the

Pacific Northwest. Happy children dressed in bright-colored clothing played on the jungle gym while their minders looked on. Ian had taken a spot on a park bench and was checking his phone. A gentle breeze floated through my open window, bringing with it the faint scent of garlic and onions from a nearby Italian restaurant. An idyllic afternoon, soon to be marred by a drug deal. Sure, it was possible the people taking advantage of the park and the lovely day wouldn't notice the illicit activity. All the same, acid churned my stomach at the dirt bag conducting business so close to so many kids. The idea of getting enough information on Chacon so that he'd spend his days behind bars helped assuage the anger.

The hairs along the back of my neck prickled, and I scanned the vehicles parked nearby. No one was visible, but that didn't mean a lot. I slumped in my seat and pulled the ball cap lower on my forehead, and at the same time brought up my phone to make it look like I was checking the screen.

Right on time, Momo pulled next to the curb, his window rolled down. Ian grabbed his messenger bag and got to his feet, then strolled over to the dark gray Acura. He reached the car and rested his forearm on the roof as he leaned down to speak to Momo.

The buy happened in a matter of seconds. If I hadn't been watching the transaction take place, I doubt I would have even noticed. Ian straightened and slipped something into his bag before zipping it closed. Then he backed away from the car and gave Momo a quick nod as the dealer pulled away from the curb. I waited until a couple of cars were behind the Acura and followed.

This time, instead of the park where he had met the van before, Momo drove to an industrial area along Highway 99 and turned into a dirt lot. An old brick warehouse stood near the back. A cream-colored van and an older model Buick were parked near the entrance. Concertina wire had been installed along the top of the chain-link fence, giving the place an unfriendly vibe.

I continued past the property for a short distance, pulled to the side of the road, and shut off the engine. Checking to make sure no one was nearby I waited for a line of cars to pass. Not seeing anyone, I took my gun out of the console, shoved it into my shoulder holster, and exited the Tahoe, making sure that the gun was somewhat concealed by the light jacket I wore.

I walked toward the fence, searching for a weak area that I could breach without too much trouble. I'd just located a good-sized hole in the fence when the deep rumble of a car engine echoed through the air. Seconds later, a blood-red Aston Martin slid in behind the Tahoe and parked.

The side windows were dark, and I couldn't see who was driving. My breath shallow, and acutely aware of the press of my gun, I paused, hoping like hell that whoever got out of that sports car didn't have anything to do with Chacon or Momo.

My heart beat staccato in my ears as the door opened and the driver climbed out. At first I didn't recognize her because of the oversized tortoiseshell sunglasses. When her identity finally dawned on me my breath caught, mind feverishly tumbling toward an explanation.

That smile. Like a Cheshire Cat with a cadre of mice at her disposal. She'd changed her hair. Again. The last time I'd seen her in Mexico, it had been short and iceberg white. This time, Angie McKenna had toned things down a bit, opting for a warmer, caramel-and-tan inverted bob.

How the hell did she find me?

The assassin's ensemble of black cigarette pants, cream-colored blouse, and fitted black jacket screamed East Coast chic except for her flats, which had serviceable written all over them. The gold glinting at her ears, neck, and wrists made a tasteful if overly upmarket statement. Even when she was closing in for the kill, I couldn't help but admire her fashion sense.

"Angie." I stayed where I was, preferring not to get too close in case there was still a contract out on me.

"Kate, darlin'. How *are* you? It's been an *age*." Angie's southern drawl flowed over me like raw honey.

Thick, viscous, sticky honey.

"I've been all right. Thanks for asking," I added. It seemed the thing to do. Acutely aware all that separated me from death by assassin was the streaming traffic and probable witnesses, my brain searched anxiously for reasons why she was there, but came up empty.

Except for the unfinished business of my death.

How did she even *find* me? I doubted she knew where Sam lived.

Or did she?

With a smirk, Angie crossed the street during a lull in the traffic and stepped onto the curb. "Oh, jus' fine, honey. Jus' fine." Crossing her arms, she turned her head and studied the razor wire on top of the fence. "That looks serious. Just what the hell are you doing here?"

"I was going to ask you the same thing." I shifted my stance so my body was at an angle to her, making me less of a target. "How did you find me? Or, more to the point, why? Vincent Anaya's dead, or hadn't you heard?"

Angie waved the comment away and leaned against the car. "I'm not here because of Vincent, Kate. Don't you think I would've killed you already?" She shrugged, looking at our surroundings. "I'd have opted for your house, though. Fewer witnesses."

"My house? So you followed me from the house?"

She rolled her eyes. "Well, of *course*, darlin'. How else?"

"How long have you known where I was living?"

She glanced at her watch. "About two hours, give or take."

"Maybe I should ask *how* did you know?"

"Oh, please. I'm not going to give away *all* my secrets."

"Why are you here, Angie?"

"You tell me. You're the one who left the message."

No. It couldn't be. "You—you're Lucy?"

A slow grin spread across Angie's face, and she stretched her arms wide. "At your service."

"But—" The whole encounter was beginning to take on a surreal quality. Having a conversation with someone who'd been hired to kill you can do that.

"You're wondering where Ron is?" She studied her fingernails, which had been painted a particularly obnoxious shade of green. "Let's just say I'm not a fan of competition."

Well. One less hit man in the world wasn't necessarily a bad thing.

A semi roared by, the screech of its Jake brakes making conversation difficult. Angie grimaced and waited for it to pass.

"Listen. I know a great little restaurant nearby where we can get a proper drink and something to eat. I'm *famished.*" She checked the elegant timepiece on her wrist, and then her eyes met mine. A faint glint of amusement sparkled in them. "It's a tad quieter there, and public." She emphasized the word public and smiled. "I can tell you need some convincing that I'm not here to kill you. Honestly, I'm not. No one wants you dead, hon." She shrugged again, giving me a look that said *sorry*.

Well, part of her statement was true. Roberto and Vincent were both taking the big dirt nap which precluded them from contracting a hit on me, but Chacon was a new threat altogether. One that I needed to put an end to, and soon.

"Yeah, I don't think so, Angie. Thanks for the invite, though." Did she seriously think I was interested in breaking bread with the woman who was hired to kill me on at least two different occasions? Who had, in fact, shot two of my lovers? Thank goodness she'd been distracted, or both Sam's and Cole's deaths would have been on my conscience, too.

A look of supreme annoyance crossed her features. "Oh, for Christ's sake. You're the one who put out the call for help. I came all this way for nothing? I don't think so. It's the least you could do." She pulled a pack of cigarettes from her jacket pocket and lit one.

"What do you mean, the 'least I could do'?"

Angie snorted. White smoke streamed out of her nostrils. "Remember the ninety-nine percent success rate I quoted in the message?" She wrinkled her nose in distaste. "You're the one percent."

"Really. I find that hard to believe." I couldn't have been the only target she didn't kill. I wasn't that good at escape.

She dropped her partially smoked cigarette and mashed it into the ground with the toe of her sensible shoe. "Shit. I'd kill you now if it would make a difference." She sighed dramatically. "But it wouldn't."

"What, assassins have a code or something?"

She gave me a sharp glance. "Of course, darlin'. We have our pride."

"So, correct me if I'm wrong. You're pissed off because I'm the one hit you were unable to complete, but you can't kill me now because of professional pride?" This conversation was getting bizarro.

"Exactly."

Really? Huh.

"Okay. Let me put this another way. Unless someone contracts with you to kill me, either now or in the future, I don't have to worry that you're going to tie up loose ends?" I used finger quotes around the words *loose ends*.

"Correct. Why on God's green earth would I do a job with no remuneration at the end of it? That would be like asking a lawyer to represent you in court for free. It's not like I *enjoy* killing people. I'm just good at it."

I shook my head to clear it, but the gesture didn't help.

"Darlin', I can see that the concept is evadin' you. How about you let me buy you a drink and we can talk about it?" She smiled brightly. "I assume you were going to pay ol' Ron for whatever expertise you needed, right?"

"Maybe." I hated to commit to anything. Not with Angie, anyway.

"Well, then. Let's be civilized and discuss business over drinks." She put her hands in the air, palms out. "No expectations. No obligation. What d'y'all say?"

My good girl was in full attendance at this point, asking what the hell I was doing, and prodding me to turn back at every corner as I followed Angie to a small bistro nearby that she assured me had a rockin' wine list. I could just hear Sam telling me that consorting with known assassins was a boneheaded move.

Okay, he would probably use a stronger word, but it still didn't stop me.

She doesn't have a contract to kill me, and could have done so many times over. Why not hear her out? I decided to blame Sam for not giving me the training I needed. I wouldn't have gone looking.

But that dog didn't hunt, and I knew it.

We settled into a booth at the back of the restaurant, far from the other customers. Dim lighting combined with the subtle wall color and antiqued wood floors elicited a sense of calm and suggested low conversations. At this time of day only a few of the tables were occupied, and no one paid any attention to two women enjoying a late lunch. A waiter came by to take our orders and then disappeared into the kitchen. Taking advantage of Sam's non-presence I ordered a hamburger. He would have frowned on my adding cheddar cheese, fried onions, and French fries.

"I'd have pegged you as a lettuce-wrap kind of girl." Angie took a sip of her Campari and soda and set it back on the table. She'd ordered the tri-tip, rare, and a green salad.

I shrugged. "Sometimes you just gotta have a burger."

She gave me a smile. "I suppose living with a health-nut will do that to you."

"Sam's not—wait a minute. How do you know who I live with?"

She gave me a look. "Give me a little credit, darlin'. Just because you were difficult to find once doesn't mean I'm not good at my job."

"That brings up a great point." I leaned forward, my elbows on the table. "How did you find me this time?"

"I have my ways, darlin'. It helped that I was in the area. Portland, to be exact." She studied her nails. "And next time? You might want to access the deep web from software on a thumb drive and make sure to close your browsers."

Apparently Angie had been able to track my IP address. Had I left a different browser open when I was accessing the deep web that night? If so, there might have been some bleed-through of information. Obviously, I needed to do more research on anonymous web browsing.

"I'll be sure to take your advice."

"So. Why were you trying to contact Ron?" Her sharp gaze caught and held mine.

"It's nothing. Just something having to do with a case I'm working on."

"Anything to do with that warehouse?"

"Maybe." I took a sip of my iced tea and watched her for a moment. She returned the stare.

The first to break eye contact, she shifted in her chair and said, "You know, Kate. No hard feelings. Being the one I missed gives you some distinction in my circle." She smiled and shook her head. "I should have dropped you back at your house, just to keep up my stats."

"Wait a minute. What was all that back there about professional pride?" I reached for my purse, feeling distinctly like a mouse having lunch with a cat.

She burst out laughing. "Oh, shoot. Don't worry. The look on your face—" She wiped tears from the corners of her eyes. "I was just havin' a little fun."

"Can you blame me? You tracked me for years."

Angie took another sip of her drink, waving my concerns away. "And you gave me a bum foot for my trouble. Remember that day up there in that godforsaken, frigid Alaskan forest? You damn near shot my foot right off. Thing still throbs when it rains." She winced at the memory. "I want to tell you, I was never so glad as when you popped up on my radar in Arizona, of all places. Much better than freezin' my ass on the tundra, believe me."

"Well, as long as there are no hard feelings."

The waiter arrived with our orders. After making sure everything was all right, he left.

"So? Aren't you going to tell me what you wanted ol' Ron for?" she asked, reaching for the pepper. "I promise, I won't *kill* you."

"How can I be sure?"

"Kate, darlin', there is something you need to know about me and about assassins in general." She leaned in close, dropping her voice to a whisper. "We really are in it for the money." She leaned back and commenced to grinding pepper onto her perfectly grilled steak.

Huh. Learning how to kill from someone who tried to kill me. Oh, the irony.

You're out of your mind, Kate. Back away from the assassin.

"Hypothetically speaking, how much would you charge to teach someone…offensive maneuvers?" Taking my hamburger in both hands, I sank my teeth into the juicy hunk of meat and waited for her reply.

She put down her knife. "You want me to teach you how to kill someone?"

My face heating, I scanned the room to make sure no one was near enough to have heard her.

"Keep your voice down," I hissed. I envisioned some employee overhearing our conversation. Did I bring enough cash to pay for my meal? I didn't want to use a credit card with my name on it, in case someone had.

Angie's eyes widened. "You're serious, aren't you? Well, well." She frowned as she carved off another bite of steak and popped it into her mouth. "I'd have to think about that." She cocked her head to the side as though she was sizing me up. "You know your way around a gun, at least."

"And I've killed people before."

"Did you like it?" she asked with a conspiratorial wink.

"Not particularly. My life was in danger."

"Killing a person has to be learned. It's not a natural act for most human beings." She tapped the side of her head. "A lot of it is mental." Then she placed a hand on her chest. "And emotional. You have to wall off those pesky feelings. Can you do that?"

"I have in the past."

"But you had to in order to survive, right?" She flapped her hand at me. "That's easy. I take it you're asking me to show you how to do things real quiet-like. Cloak and dagger stuff, am I right?"

Now it was my turn to wince. "Not exactly, but yes, that's the gist." Maybe working with Angie wasn't such a great idea. This lunch had already headed into surreal territory. But the pragmatic part of me thought, *Why not? She hasn't killed you and has said that she won't. She's in it for the money, which you have. She has the skills that you don't. Why not give it a try?*

"Let's go at this another way." Angie leaned forward. "How much are you prepared to pay me for my services? Give me a number and I'll work up a plan to fit your budget." She took the last bite of her salad and waited for me to answer.

"I hadn't gotten that far yet. I assumed Ron would quote me a price."

Angie rolled her eyes. "Okay. How about we start at twenty-five thousand? I know you got away with Salazar's money, I just don't know how much. I assume you have some of it left?"

I ignored her question. "What will that get me?"

"Let me work up a proposal and I'll send it to you by tomorrow morning."

"Sure. You can use this email address." I pulled out a notepad and pen and scribbled a throwaway email address on it before sliding the piece of paper across the table. She picked it up and glanced at it before putting it into her purse.

"Perfect," Angie said. "Now, if we're done, would you mind picking up the check? I seem to have left my pocketbook in the car."

TWENTY-ONE

Y TRAINING WITH Angie McKenna, assassin, began the next afternoon in an abandoned warehouse south of the town of Lakewood. Her proposal gave me everything I was looking for and more. I couldn't deny it, working with my former enemy was hard to wrap my mind around, but after a while it was almost normal.

Almost.

She was a good teacher, albeit a tad impatient. When I didn't get something right away, she'd rant about how I could never learn to be a top-flight assassin. This would be followed with a string of expletive-laced insults the likes of which would have made a sailor blush. I reminded her that I wasn't looking to become the next Jason Bourne, just that I'd like to know what I was doing in case things went south, but she ignored me, apparently wanting to believe that I was her protégé.

I didn't bring it up again. Arguing with an assassin skirted bat-shit crazy territory. I didn't want to remind myself training with an assassin was, in fact, bat-shit crazy.

The idea of taking on Chacon was, too, but I couldn't come up with a better way to deal with my anger other than to exact revenge. Lisa's coma had unearthed a part of me that I had no idea existed.

Except when I shot Salazar.

After Salazar's death, I'd convinced myself that the incident was a one-off. I had to kill him or he would have killed me. A case of self-defense that could have happened to anyone.

What I hadn't counted on was the power I'd experienced in the aftermath. The long-denied ability to direct my own life on my own terms had come roaring to the surface. The power to make my enemy pay. A thick, black vengeance coursing through my veins. Now I understood why the cartels struck back, hard, any time their right to exist was threatened. The fury with which rival cartels went after each other made a little more sense now. Not that it was right, or that I empathized. Just that I understood.

Well, I could play that game, too.

Angie's training consisted of rigorous drills using knives, guns, and household items to dispatch a life-size dummy, along with a mind-blowing amount of online research-slash-homework—the use of poisons and their effects, the vulnerable points on the human body, especially those that were lethal, weapons characteristics, ammunition. The studying and skill-building kept my mind off of Lisa and how I'd failed the Whitmores, a miracle in itself. During the first week, I dutifully called my DEA contact and asked him how things were progressing but I could tell that he was only there to make me feel better about staying out of the way and letting the agents do their jobs.

I couldn't blame them. They didn't want some civilian with a personal stake in the case trying to help them out. They had a job to do.

So did I.

After the first week, I quit calling.

Underlying all of this were the lies I told Sam about where I was going when I left for "class." I told myself they were only little white lies that wouldn't hurt our relationship in the long run. That he'd ultimately understand. I hated deceiving him, knew he'd be hurt and angry if he found out what I'd been up to, but I couldn't stop. The idea of meting out justice to whomever was responsible for distributing the deadly painkillers had begun to consume me. Let Sam and the Feds do their investigating by the book.

I was taking things in another direction.

When I stopped long enough to think about it, the idea was liberating. I convinced myself that I was only doing what law enforcement wanted done but was hamstrung from carrying out. They had to follow the law. I didn't.

I just had to make sure I didn't get caught.

One morning, Sam and I were having our usual breakfast of fruit, yogurt, and coffee. I could tell something was bothering him. He'd hardly said a word throughout the meal. Even though Sam's a man of few words, this was unusual. He took our dishes and silverware to the sink and ran water into the basin. Shutting the water off, he turned to look at me.

"What?" I put down my coffee cup and tilted my head, giving him a little smile. He didn't return the sentiment.

Clearing his throat, he glanced at the floor as if trying to formulate his thoughts. I waited for him to speak.

"Are you seeing someone else?" His voice was tight, as though taking a deep breath wasn't possible. He raised his eyes to mine.

My heart melted at the raw emotion I saw in their depths. I reached across the counter for his hand. He didn't move.

"No. A thousand times no. I would never do that to you. You know that."

"Then what's going on?"

"There isn't anything going on. What do you mean?" The lie slipped out before I had a chance to think. His question caught me off guard and I needed time to formulate a response.

He frowned and shook his head. "I know when you're lying, Kate." He crossed his arms. "And you're lying now."

My mind raced for something to say to ease the worry on his face. I yearned to tell him everything but didn't know if he'd understand. How could he? He was Sam Akiaq, ex-cop turned private eye. Righter of wrongs, seeker of justice, man of integrity. He'd never understand my need for revenge, for some sort of closure. I couldn't let him know what I'd been doing. If I did, it might be the end of us.

I blew out a long sigh. Something. I had to tell him something.

"Okay. You're right. But it's intensely personal." I ran my thumb along the back of his hand and looked him in the eyes. "I'm working through my feelings about Lisa the only way I know how, and I'm not ready to let you in yet." I let go of his hand and walked around the counter to wrap him in a hug. His shoulders inched lower as he relaxed into the embrace and leaned his head against mine. "I love you, Sam. I would never hurt you like that."

Sam sighed and pulled me closer.

"I don't know what I'd do if you found someone else."

"I won't. We're meant to be together. Just give me some time." I pulled back to look into his eyes. "I'll work through things and then we can talk, okay?"

Sam nodded and kissed me. The sweetness of the kiss nearly stole my breath, and I melted into his arms.

Maybe Angie can wait. I glanced at the clock on the stove. I was already fifteen minutes late. Knowing Sam, it would be another hour, which would probably piss off Angie so much she might not stick around. Already regretting my decision, I took a step backward, breaking off the embrace.

"Hold that thought until tonight, okay?" I gave him a lascivious grin and wiggled my eyebrows. His smile didn't quite reach his eyes as he dropped his hands to his sides.

"Sure. I'll see you tonight."

Angie's Aston Martin was still parked at the warehouse. I skidded into the parking lot and slammed on the brakes. A cloud of dust enveloped the Jeep as I shifted into park and jumped out.

Entering the cool, dark building, I waited until my eyes adjusted before spotting Angie. She sat on a folding chair, arms crossed, looking like she wanted to put me out of my misery. Her phone was in a docking station on an old card table, attached to two small speakers.

"What's up?" I asked, peeling off my sweater to reveal a T-shirt. She glanced at the image of Kurt Cobain on the front and rolled her eyes.

"You're half an hour late."

"I got held up. Sam had something he wanted to talk to me about."

Angie's eyes glittered in the low light. "How is ol' Sam, anyway? You never talk about him."

"Fine." I didn't like where the conversation was headed and changed the subject. "So what are we working on today?" The drills had been relentless. To help me concentrate she'd added a noise component by streaming heavy metal through her phone combined with smashing garbage can lids together, and occasionally firing a gun. All while screaming at me.

Needless to say, I learned to tune out distractions.

"Well, darlin', I think it's time to try out your newfound talents."

"You what?"

"Don't you want to try out what you've learned?"

My stomach did a little flip at her smile.

"Why, I would think you'd be rarin' to go, what with all the practicin' you've been doing."

"I am, I mean, of course I want to, but are you sure I'm ready?" My mind scrambled for what Angie would deem "trying out my newfound talents."

She chuckled and rose from her chair. "The only way you're going to learn is to actually use what I've taught you. Now." She moved closer to where I stood. "Who's the first target?"

This was moving too fast. I needed to back her up. "I wouldn't necessarily call him a target. More a person of interest. I need more information from him before I pick my target."

"Ah. So that's why you were so interested in the enhanced interrogation techniques we covered on Wednesday." She nodded, tapping her chin. "Well, then, let's run over a few more things before we plan the operation. Have you been surveilling the subject?"

"I know where he's conducting business, if that's what you mean."

"Let me guess. The warehouse where I followed you that first day?"

I nodded. "That's the one."

Angie paced in front of the small table, head down, thinking. "I don't like the location. Too many variables. You need to follow him home, find out his vulnerabilities."

"What if he doesn't have any?"

She smiled. "Oh, believe me, he has them. Everyone does." Walking over to a satchel resting near her chair, she pulled out a sheath containing two fixed-blade knives. "Let's do a little more practicin', shall we?"

TWENTY-TWO

URVEILLING CHACON TURNED out to be simple. He was staying at a Craftsman-style home in a busy Seattle neighborhood, which made it easy to watch his comings and goings. Most of the older homes only had room for one or two cars. Everyone else had to find parking on the street. My Jeep was one of dozens of vehicles lining the curb. I just had to make sure I got there before five o'clock in the afternoon or I'd be out of luck.

The owner of the home was listed as John Hastings, the same guy who had owned the Honda driven by Bobby the Barracuda's homeboys, the Exterminator and Bruce Wayne.

Visitors to the house were few. It looked like Chacon was using the warehouse solely for distribution. I'm sure my actions had a hand in that decision. Especially after the DEA descended on his home in Olympia. There was another plus to his new situation: no dogs at the house. They were back at the warehouse, guarding the goods.

A few days into my surveillance, Angie insisted I'd done enough. It was time to try out my new skills. I argued that I hadn't had enough time to really get his routine down, but she pooh-poohed my objections.

Fine. It was time to put up or shut up.

I chose to break in on Friday evening. My presence would be less likely to raise questions since more people would be out and about at the start of a weekend. I went in the back way, in case the DEA had the place under surveillance. Angie had insisted I put up a motion sensor camera with a wide view of the backyard when I first started my surveillance. The photographs were rife with raccoons and neighborhood cats, but no agents appeared in the frame, leading me to believe that either the DEA didn't know where he'd moved to yet, or they were only watching the front of the house.

Apparently Chacon hadn't yet bothered to add security to the home, and getting in the back door proved easy. I used a glass cutter to scribe a hole large enough for my hand to fit through, making it easy to unlock the deadbolt. Carefully picking my way through the darkened first floor, I took long, deep breaths to quiet my hammering heart. When I reached a stairway, I slowly made my way to the second floor, making sure to use the outer portion of each step.

From Angie McKenna's School for Would-be Assassins, Module 2: Breaking & Entering Without Discovery. Stair treads tended to be weaker near the center.

I reached the second floor and stood in the darkened hall, listening for movement, and went over what Angie had taught me. The semiauto had heft, a last-minute gift from my mentor. I knew all the moves, had practiced them with relentless determination, unwilling to make a mistake when I did the deed.

Committed the act.

Went off the rails.

What are you doing, Kate? Whispers from my good-girl self, long buried all these years, echoed through my head.

Shut up and let me do what needs to be done. I'll deal with the fallout later.

But isn't that how you've always done things? Act first, ask questions later?

This is different.

How?

Be quiet. I'm in no mood to argue.

Angie had delivered her last lesson that morning. The memory came galloping back with a force that was difficult to comprehend.

I'd been lucky to survive.

My gaze cut to my right arm, as though I could see through the darkness and under the bandage, at the angry red wound it covered.

Angie didn't dick around. I'd been shocked when she took a slice at me during our sparring session. I shouldn't have been. She'd waved away my angry retort with "I wanted to see how you'd react to bein' wounded."

I shouldn't have been surprised that she'd wanted to help instead of kill me. Money dictated her loyalties. With no current, remunerable contract connected to my death, she couldn't have cared less if I was standing in front of her at point-blank range, handing her a gun.

In her world, Kate Jones had ceased to exist.

But wave a bundle of crisp, hundred-dollar bills at her? *Why, yes ma'am, what can I do for you this fine evening?* Her southern head turned so fast, I was afraid she'd get whiplash.

A relief, really. After all those years of running, of looking over my shoulder, waiting for Angie or one of the others to strike.

Gone. Poof.

One minute I'm scanning restaurants and street corners for suspicious activity, and the next, nothing. Nada.

Zilch.

From what I understand, it's a lot like giving up smoking. All of a sudden, you have too much extra time on your hands. You're at a loss, really.

And so it is with normal life. No more running. No more death threats.

No more fear.

But then again, there's all that muscle memory. The fight-or-flight response that's hardwired into our brains.

That's no way to live when no one's trying to kill you.

The bedroom door opened, and I moved deeper into the shadows. Soft footsteps padded along the corridor to the bathroom. The silhouette confirmed my suspicions.

It was time.

My inner good girl had evidently left the building, her recriminating voice finally silenced.

I crept toward the bathroom, my feet whispering silently along the polished wood floor. I was glad I'd used the disposable booties like Angie suggested. Not only did they reduce evidence left behind by my sneakers, but they silenced my footsteps as well as if I'd been wearing socks.

What if Sam finds out?

There she was again.

I thought you left. Good girls need their sleep, right?

Not gonna happen, Kate. You know me. I'm tenacious.

The idea of Sam finding out that this was my doing gave me pause. My sister Lisa's face sprang unbidden into my mind. My cheeks flushed warm and my respiration increased, tightening my chest and giving rise to a mini panic attack. I took a deep breath and slowly released it, just like Angie taught me to do, and the bands around my chest loosened. The assassin's ability to remain calm under pressure still amazed me, although I don't know why. She was a stone-cold killer with the personality to match.

At the sound of the toilet flushing I snapped back to the present and sprinted along the hallway to the open bedroom door.

You shouldn't be here. Go home to Sam, now.

Ignoring the good girl and wondering where the hell my bad girl had gone—because I really could have used her at the moment—I crossed the room, skirted the bed, and slipped inside the closet, leaving the door cracked open while I waited. The smell of cedar laced the air as I kicked a pair of shoes out of the way.

The bathroom door creaked open, followed by the sound of feet scuffling into the bedroom. I gripped the gun and waited as the occupant kicked off his slippers and sat down heavily on the bed. The sound of covers being thrown back and a faint sigh as he settled in told me it was time.

I waited until Chacon's breathing deepened and grew more even before I stepped from the closet into the room. Gripping the silenced gun with two damp palms, I advanced toward the bed and stopped a few feet away. I adjusted the mask I wore to be sure he wouldn't recognize me.

Moonlight sliced through the window, giving his skin a blue cast. Gathering my courage, I listened to his breathing for a moment and then cleared my throat. His eyes popped open, the whites glistening in the dim light. His Adam's apple bobbed, once, as he swallowed. A hoarse protest bubbled from his lips.

"Quiet. I'll do the talking." Surprisingly, my voice sounded strong and steady. Keeping the gun trained on him, I walked to the nightstand and turned on the light. The blanched white skin of Chacon's face contrasted markedly with the midnight blue sheets.

Chacon clamped his mouth closed and frowned. He didn't recognize me. Good. His chest rose and fell with shallow breaths, emphasizing a capital C stitched in cursive on the breast pocket of his pajama top. A bead of sweat rolled down the side of his face.

Good. He's afraid. Unbidden, a picture of Sam floated through my mind. I mentally shook it off and returned my focus to Chacon.

"Where did you get these?" I reached into my pocket, pulled out one of the painkillers from Lisa's stash, and held it up. He started to shake his head, but I lowered the gun barrel until it was in line with his crotch and he stopped.

"Who are you?" His voice wavered slightly.

"Answer my question." I took a step forward, bringing the suppressed pistol closer. Angie's interrogation techniques were based on three essential requirements when prying information from a recalcitrant subject: be relentless, unemotional, and stay on task. That way, there would be no misunderstandings.

Chacon eyed the gun. A sheen of sweat on his forehead gleamed in the lamplight. "Who are you and why are you here?" This time the question lacked force. The confident, dangerous man I'd encountered at the house in Olympia had disappeared, leaving a deflated and frightened low-level drug dealer.

Having a gun pointed at you in the middle of the night while wearing your jams can do that to a person.

The tension in my neck and shoulders drained away. I'd threatened way more dangerous characters than Chacon. I flashed on a similar confrontation from years earlier when I'd pointed a gun at Vincent Anaya's right-hand man, Frank Lanzarotti. It seemed so long ago. I'd been a different person then. Cocky. Self-assured.

Maybe it was time to resurrect my old self. I was getting tired of scaredy-Kate.

"Wait. Who's holding the gun?" I asked, dripping sarcasm. I'd always had good luck with sarcasm.

Chacon remained silent. Even though he gave the impression of being afraid, he wasn't going to make this easy. Looked like I'd have to resort to what Angie called "Fun and Games," also known as torture. My stomach squeezed tight at the thought. Would I be able to go through with it?

You have to, Kate. You've gone too far to turn back now. Remember Lisa.

I reached into my back pocket and slid out a six-inch fixed-blade knife, another gift from Angie. Staring at the wicked-looking weapon, Chacon scooted backward so that he was flush against the headboard.

"What are you going to do with that?" His eyes were fixed on the blade.

I inspected the knife as though it was something new. Then I cocked my head and gave him a look. "Well, I don't know. What do *you* think I should do?" With the gun still aimed at him, I used the tip of the knife to flip the bedspread off of his right leg. He winced as though anticipating the pain.

The thought of actually cutting Chacon stopped me. What if I nicked an artery? He'd bleed out before I could get the information. I took a deep breath, trying to control my thudding heart. Why couldn't he just give me what I wanted?

Or try to fight back. At least then I could justify my actions with self-defense.

Well, except for the whole breaking and entering in the middle of the night thing.

Damn it, Kate. You're losing your advantage. Just do it! Angie's recriminations cascaded through my head. *Remember why you're here. What he's responsible for.*

He must have picked up on my hesitation, because he shifted his leg and his foot disappeared beneath the covers. Taking a page from my encounter with Frank Lanzarotti, I stepped forward, shoved the gun between his legs, and fired into the mattress.

Even though the pistol had a suppressor, the result was impressive. Chacon yelped and tried to disappear into the headboard. When that didn't work, he covered his face with his hands and choked back a sob.

That was more like it. I stepped back, once more aiming at his crotch. I doubted I could actually shoot him.

But he didn't know that.

"Who's your supplier?" I asked again, this time with more force.

Chacon's sobs had degraded into hiccoughs, and his shoulders heaved with each breath. Lowering his hands, he shook his head. "He'd do worse to me than you ever could."

"Yes, but if you're dead, that won't really matter, will it?" That was a good line. And, I sounded confident.

I was getting the hang of this.

He spread his arms, providing a larger target. "Then you're going to have to kill me. I can't do what you ask."

Crap. I'd practically shot the guy. Even Lanzarotti had capitulated when he'd been faced with the choice of losing his bits. The supplier must be a heavy hitter. I'd have to actually cut him or shoot something. My stomach lurched at the thought of him bleeding all over the mattress.

At that moment, the door slammed open and bounced against the wall as a dark figure burst into the room. Angie McKenna's expression could only be described as massively annoyed. She marched to where I stood, grabbed the knife from my hand, and turned on Chacon.

"Who the *fuck* is your supplier?" she growled, brandishing the knife.

What the—why was she *here?* My mind raced for an explanation. The only thing I could think of was that she was checking to see how I did on my first foray into the world of intimidation and torture.

Not well, apparently.

Chacon's wide-eyed gaze flickered from Angie to me and then back to Angie, alarm obvious on his face.

"Who are you?" he asked, his voice hoarse.

"Your worst nightmare."

Twenty-Three

I HAD TO admit—Angie looked impressive wielding the knife. I would have told her whatever she wanted to know.

She advanced on Chacon, her body coiled tight like a well-dressed leopard ready to pounce on her unsuspecting prey. All she needed was a long tail to swish behind her.

Except that would have ruined the look.

"I—I—" Chacon worked his mouth like a fish out of water, eyeing the blade in her hand.

"You're going to tell me now, or you lose the top joint of your right pinkie finger. First."

Attention riveted on Angie, Chacon tried to swallow but could only make a dry smacking sound.

She shrugged. "All right. Your choice." She seized his right hand, pinned it to the nightstand, and brought the knife down, hard, chopping off the tip of his little finger. Chacon screamed and yanked his arm away, clutching what was left of his pinkie.

Damn. That blade was sharp. My stomach churned at the blood flowing from his hand, and I gawked at Angie, who acted as though she'd just diced a carrot. I was relieved that he'd only lost the top of his pinkie. Knowing Angie, he could've been missing a whole lot more than that.

Still think you're cut out for this? Good Kate asked. If she'd been real, she'd have smacked me upside the head.

"One more time. Who is your supplier?" Angie loomed over him. "This time I think I'll take a bigger chunk. What do you think?"

Chacon shook as he stared at her through pain-filled eyes.

"His name is Mick Dobson," he said, stifling another sob.

I guess you just never knew who was going to fold and who was going to play the tough guy.

"And where can we find him?" Angie held the knife aloft, its razor-sharp tip shining in the lamplight.

"He's the CEO of Pro-Pharma."

My mouth dropped open in surprise. Pro-Pharma was one of the largest pharmaceutical companies in the state of Washington. My little operation to try to find the main distributor for the tainted pills had just blown up. If Chacon was telling the truth and the executive officer of a legitimate pharmaceutical company was involved, then this was way bigger than I'd anticipated.

"You mean that Pro-Pharma knowingly released contaminated drugs onto the street?" I asked. Pro-Pharma's reputation as a progressive, green drug company was well known. Their tagline was "Give. Growth. Goodwill." They prided themselves on being a different kind of corporation. As in, putting people before profits.

Chacon looked at the floor. "Not exactly."

"Then how did they get there?"

"Wait a minute. Let me get this on video." Angie pulled out her phone and aimed it at Chacon's face. He winced.

"If this gets out, I'm dead."

"Honey, if you *don't* tell us, you're dead. And I promise it won't be as pleasant."

Chacon closed his eyes for a moment and then continued. "The full batch was slated for the DRC. None of them were supposed to have been distributed here."

"The DRC?"

"Democratic Republic of the Congo. In Africa," he added helpfully.

"And that makes it all right? Sending deadly drugs overseas to unsuspecting patients?" My anger spiked at the thought that some executive somewhere thought it would be okay to ship their mistakes to another country. "What happened? Why did some of the drugs make it to Seattle?"

"If I tell you, you have to promise that you won't cut off anything else, and that you'll let me go."

"Deal." Angie nodded at him to continue. Apparently, Chacon believed in honor among thieves.

Me, not so much.

"It was Dobson's idea to have the drugs manufactured overseas. To save money. When the batch came back and was tested, Pro-Pharma discovered the contamination. It was bad. The whole lot would have to be destroyed. It was a huge shipment representing a massive loss for the company."

"That doesn't tell us why the pills ended up on the streets." Was he stalling for time?

"I'm getting to that. According to Dobson, rumors were going around that his future was on the agenda of the next board meeting, and it wasn't looking good. So,

Dobson contacted me to divert the tainted goods and ship them overseas for pennies on the dollar. That way, Pro-Pharma still made some coin, the pills were gone, and no one was the wiser."

"Except," Angie added. Chacon nodded. The skin around his eyes sagged in the lamplight.

"Except. Dobson never told me the drugs were contaminated. The way he made it sound, the only problem with the pills was that there was too high a dose of fentanyl in them." He shrugged. "Shit, junkies live for fentanyl. Figured I'd rake it in, maybe take a little vacation, you know. I skimmed some off the top before shipping the rest to the Congo, and then gave 'em to my guys to sell." He shook his head. "I had no idea they were that bad. I lost one of my own."

I thought back to the night I'd been tied up in the bedroom in Chacon's house in Olympia, back to the kid I'd talked into letting me go and the pills he'd stolen. Then I thought of Lisa. And the Whitmores. These guys didn't care what happened to the people who bought their drugs. All that mattered to them was the bottom line. My face warmed as I fought to control my anger.

"I'll need his contact information, if you don't mind," Angie drawled.

Chacon nodded at the desk on the other side of the room.

"In my laptop. Bottom drawer."

Angie walked over to the desk and sat in the chair. She opened the bottom drawer and brought out his laptop, which she placed on the desk.

After booting it up she asked, "What's your password, darlin'?"

Chacon leaned his head back, still clutching his pinkie. His hand was covered in blood, as was the bedspread. "Bring it here."

"I asked you a question." Bristling, she glared at him from across the room. "Now give me your goddamn password."

The color drained from his face. His voice cracking, he recited a string of letters and numbers. Angie typed in the information and smiled.

"Bingo. Now where would I find Mr. Dobson's information?"

"In my contacts."

Angie cocked her head. "Kind of an obvious place for such important information, don't you think?"

Chacon didn't reply. Angie shrugged and pulled a flash drive from her pocket, which she inserted into a USB port.

"What are you doing?" Chacon started to get up, but I waved him back with the pistol. He sank onto his pillow.

"Just a little insurance in case you're not telling the truth."

Chacon closed his eyes in defeat and slumped further onto the bed.

"Hold on a second." If what Chacon said was true, then I needed clarification.

He gave me a wary look.

"This doesn't make sense. Why would Dobson risk selling tainted drugs to the Congo? Pro-Pharma's number is stamped on the pill. They could be traced back to them. Isn't that illegal?"

Again, Chacon didn't reply.

"Good question," Angie said. "Well?" She looked pointedly at Chacon. His gaze darted from the knife on the desk next to Angie back to me holding the gun, and he licked his lips.

"All I know is occasionally pharmaceutical companies will sell subgrade drugs to other countries at a big discount."

"You'd call the poisons found in these pills subgrade?" I stared at him in disbelief. "People are *dying*."

Chacon raised his hand, wincing with the effort, I assumed to slow the bleeding from his mangled pinkie.

"People die every day from legitimate meds. If the pharmaceutical companies can defray the cost of manufacturing by selling at a discount then they do it. It's business 101."

It looked like the cartels had nothing on Big Pharma. Both were ruthless in their assessment of the bottom line. At least the cartels were up front about their methods.

"Excuse me, but last time I checked, other countries were comprised of actual human beings, just like the US." My anger was exceeding my ability to hold my finger off the gun's trigger.

Calm down, Kate. Angie got the information you need. Don't do anything rash. There's no going back if you do.

"Did y'all tell him who you were, Miss Kate?" Angie asked from across the room.

"I didn't feel the need," I replied, a warning in my voice. She'd already gone too far by using my first name.

Angie removed the flash drive and tossed it to me before she sidled over, her full attention on Chacon.

"Remember when you sent that man to kill a woman out on the wild Washington coast?" she asked, directing the question at Chacon. Before I could stop her, Angie grabbed the mask I was wearing and slid it off. My breath caught and I glanced at Chacon.

Recognition lit his eyes.

"You," he sputtered, his eyes narrowing.

"Was that really necessary? He knows where I *live*." My anger mounted at her cavalier attitude toward Sam's and my safety.

Angie clucked like a mama hen to her chicks. "Then I guess you'll just have to *kill* him, won't you?" She grinned and batted her eyelashes at me. "For Sam's sake, of course."

It was my turn to glare at her. "Are you fucking *kidding* me?"

Angie's soft chuckle filled the room. Clearly alarmed, Chacon glanced from me to Angie, his eyes wide.

I turned toward her and spoke in a low voice so Chacon couldn't hear me. "I had this under control, Angie," I said through gritted teeth.

"Really?" Angie glanced around me at Chacon. "It doesn't look that way to me."

Exasperated, I folded my arms across my chest. "I wasn't going to kill him," I continued in a low voice. "He might have more valuable information. Now you've totally screwed things up."

Frowning in annoyance, she pursed her lips and stepped to the side. In one rapid movement, she hurled the knife at Chacon. The tip of the blade speared his throat with a sickening thud, impaling him against the headboard. Chacon's lips moved but no words came out, a wet gurgle the last sound he would ever make. Blood spilled from the wound, pooling on his monogrammed pajamas.

I stared at the rapidly dying drug dealer, words of protest sticking in my throat. Angie walked over to Chacon and, carefully avoiding the puddle of blood forming on the floor, pulled the knife free and wiped it clean on a sheet.

"Time to go, sugar," she said over her shoulder. "I think we need a debrief."

For once, I was speechless.

It wasn't that I was going to miss Chacon. He was a scum-sucking, criminal middleman, a distributor of deadly drugs, a man who tried to have me killed and was responsible for my sister's coma and dozens of deaths. I believed he deserved to pay for his crimes. But in that singular moment I realized I didn't believe he should die.

For one thing, death was an easy out. He wouldn't have to suffer for what he did, and oh, how I wanted him to suffer for what happened to Lisa. Another realization struck me hard. Did I have the right to take someone's life just because he was scum? If that were the case, then what was stopping me from killing anyone I thought deserved to die? The fact was that I didn't, not unless my life or that of someone I loved was in jeopardy and my actions would prevent that from happening.

What right did I have to act as judge and jury?

There was one other small problem. If I was caught, I could now be charged with murder. Or, at the very least, as an accessory to murder.

Angie walked out of the bedroom, and after a moment I followed her. Without saying a word, we left the same way I'd entered the house—through the back door and into the alley. We both removed the paper booties from our shoes and stuffed them in a plastic grocery sack I brought along for the purpose. The nitrile gloves followed, along with the knife and pistol, both of which were wiped clean, just in case. Inside I was fuming, but I didn't say anything, didn't trust myself to be civil. I'd let her have it as soon as we were clear.

I'd parked two blocks away and headed in that direction, keeping to the shadows. I shoved the panic down as far as it would go. Freaking out wouldn't do any good and might bring unwanted attention. Angie accompanied me, still silent.

Angie had swapped her Aston Martin for a nondescript sedan, which she'd parked behind my Jeep. She pressed the key fob and the running lights blinked. Body thrumming with tension and a dozen chaotic thoughts, I climbed into the Jeep and fumbled with the key, which I dropped. Like a ghost, Angie appeared at my window. Startled, I did my best to ignore her and finally inserted the key into the ignition. The engine sprang to life.

"We need to talk." My words came out clipped.

"Yes, we do. Why don't y'all follow me?" Without waiting for a reply, she walked back to her car, got in, and pulled away from the curb.

I followed her to a deserted parking lot next to the water a few miles from Chacon's. Even though I was still seething, my rapidly beating heart had calmed enough so I couldn't hear it in my ears anymore, and the urge to scream at Angie had passed.

Sort of.

She got out of her car and leaned against the hood, the cold white glow from a nearby street lamp surrounding her like a halo. I waited a moment, working to calm myself before I climbed from the Jeep with the bag of weapons and joined her.

"Dump them in the sound," she said, nodding at the bag in my hand. Without saying a word, I walked to the edge of the parking lot and onto the grass median where I had a clear shot. With as much strength as I could muster, I threw the bag containing the booties, gloves, gun, and knife as far as I could, listening for the splash. Then I returned to the parking lot.

"So what did we learn?" Angie's professorial tone grated on me and I narrowed my eyes.

"That you don't listen and would just as soon kill someone as look at them."

The ghost of a smile arced across her face. "Well now, darlin', that's a mighty interestin' viewpoint comin' from a gal who can't conduct a proper interrogation." She shook her head and gave me a reproving look. "We covered all of this in module eight. If the subject won't talk, you're supposed to do one of three things." She counted on her fingers, "Cut, maim, or mutilate—"

"I shot the man between the legs."

"But you didn't do any *damage*. You have to mean business. Especially with these low-level types. They feel like they *must* resist. You see," Angie leaned forward, as though letting me in on a secret. "Those types have to prove their *manhood*. They've got no control over anything except their little fiefdoms, if that. Then some upstart woman comes along, steals their balls, and poof! What've they got to lose?" She waved her hand and leaned back. "That kind of person is harder to break without deliverin' some kind of pain. Preferably excruciatin'."

"But you killed him."

Angie frowned and cocked her head to the side. "What's your point?"

I closed my eyes and dropped my chin to my chest as a long sigh escaped me. Finally, I raised my head and looked her squarely in the eyes.

"I can't do this. I'm not cut out for it."

Angie opened her mouth as if she was going to say something, but I shot her down with a look.

"Our relationship ends, now."

"But darlin'—"

"No buts. I'm done. I no longer need your services."

"Aw, sugar, you're just cross because I muscled in on your little operation. I get that. I really do. It's just that you were doin' so *badly*."

Okay. That stung. Although I had no idea why I cared. I turned and started to walk back to the Jeep. Angie sprang to her feet.

"You can't just end this, Kate." The threat in her tone sent a chill skittering along my spine.

I turned to look at her. The flashing anger in her eyes and set of her chin should have tipped me off that she was in no mood to argue, but I'd had enough.

"We're paid up. I don't owe you anything. Let's quit while we're ahead, okay?"

She crossed her arms over her chest. "But there are two more modules."

I raised my hands, palms forward. "You've done enough. Really. I can take things from here."

Angie slowly shook her head, her gaze never leaving my face. A lump formed in my throat and I tried to swallow.

"*I* say when we're finished."

Don't push her, Kate. She's not exactly stable. Remember, she kills people for a living.

"Look. I appreciate your help. The training has been far superior to anything I could have ever imagined." Maybe a little flattery would work. Angie tended to be on the vain side. "But, with a heavy heart, I realized tonight that I'm not cut out for this vigilante stuff."

Please, let her understand and leave quietly.

"But what will Sam think? I mean, you haven't told him about our little arrangement, right?"

"Look, Angie. I can't do this. I'm never going to be the student you're looking for. I don't have it in me." I figured the whole "It's not you, it's me" argument might work, since the current scenario felt like a breakup with a psycho ex-boyfriend. I didn't know what I'd do if she told Sam.

"Oh, hon, c'mere." Angie's expression softened. She skirted the car and wrapped me in a fierce hug, putting a nice little cap on the bizarre evening.

I endured the hug, even patted her back, kind of. Finally, she stepped away and wiped at her eyes. Then she took a deep, cleansing breath and gave me a watery smile.

"I've never had a protégé."

My expression must have betrayed my incomprehension because she nodded a few times, a wistful look on her face. If you could call any look from Angie wistful.

"You're my first." She placed a hand over her heart and looked like she was tearing up again. I started to slowly back away. Making a run for it flitted through my mind.

Wrapped in her own little fantasy, at first she didn't notice my attempt at an exit. I'd almost made it to the Jeep when she called out, "Same time tomorrow? We'll get those two li'l modules over and done with, and then we'll have us some *real* fun."

TWENTY-FOUR

THE NEXT DAY was intense. I couldn't figure out a way to quit the training without raising Angie's ire and was seriously afraid of what she might do. So I did the next best thing: I humored her.

Angie insisted on my going over the enhanced interrogation module until I got a perfect score on the pop quiz. Once I met that objective we went on to the next module, which dealt with clean-up and destroying evidence. Humoring her came with a price. The friendly camaraderie was exhausting, especially since I had to work at it. Her unnerving unpredictability aside, stalling her seemed the best course of action as I worked out the best way to extricate myself from her tutelage.

Interestingly enough, I did learn some useful information. Things like chlorine bleach might destroy DNA but could also leave traces of hemoglobin which could be detected with luminol. Or that when clearing a crime scene to remember the drains. And that latex gloves don't prevent the transfer of fingerprints. When I challenged her on the point, she proved it by showing me how my own prints bled through the glove onto a glass. Good thing I used nitrile at Chacon's house.

Angie was in all-out mentor mode, which was much worse than her raving bitch act. I found myself wishing she'd go back to screaming. Overly solicitous, her attempt at kindness and compassion struck me as forced and unnatural, kind of like Ted Bundy trying to care.

At the end of our session I gathered her "teaching materials" and put them into the plastic bin she'd brought with her. The guns, knives, bleach, luminol, and ammunition were all par for the course. On the other hand, I think she'd taken things a little too far with the supply of bloodstained clothing.

I didn't want to know where it came from.

"Join me for a drink?" She worked at giving me a friendly smile and stiffly wrapped her arm around my shoulders.

"Gosh, you know, I'd love to, but I haven't been home much lately. Sam's mentioned it a time or two."

"Oh, c'mon. It's only a *drink*, for Christ's sake."

"Really, Angie, I—"

But she'd already picked up the keys to my Jeep and dropped them into her bag.

I groaned inwardly. There had to be something I could do to get her off the mentor kick.

"Fine. One drink. That's all." Maybe it would come to me at the bar.

Angie chose Elliott's Oyster House on the Seattle waterfront. The restaurant was popular with locals and tourists alike and served great food. Oversized windows brought in ambient light even on the inevitable gray days, and the place was usually packed.

Angie ordered a gin and tonic and I decided on a margarita. Once the waiter brought us our drinks, Angie moved so that we were sitting side by side. It was all I could do to keep from shifting my chair around to the opposite end of the table.

"I have a confession to make." She brought her glass to her lips and leaned her head back. The entire drink disappeared in two swallows. Wiping the back of her hand across her mouth, she signaled a passing waiter for another.

I sipped at my margarita, wondering how many drinks she'd be able to put into her slender, five-foot-six-inch frame before getting seriously trashed. By the looks of it, she was no lightweight.

The waiter brought her another gin and tonic. She drained the dregs of the first one and set it on his tray. When he asked if we wanted to order anything to eat, she waved him off with a fifty-dollar bill.

"Keep 'em comin' though, okay, sweetheart?"

The waiter nodded and disappeared into the crowd gathered near the bar.

"You were saying?" Against my better judgment, my curiosity was piqued. What kind of confession would a cold-blooded assassin like Angie make?

And could I use it against her?

She glanced to each side, making sure no one was within earshot before sucking down her second drink. She set the glass on the table, squared her shoulders, and shook her hair back. As if on cue, the waiter appeared with another gin and tonic.

"I don't have many friends." Her gaze flickered out the huge window before settling on me.

"No. Seriously?" I doubted she caught the sarcasm.

She shook her head. "Hard to believe, isn't it?"

Nope. Hadn't caught it. I remained silent and let her continue. Clearly, she wasn't looking for a response.

"I used to. Back when I was a deb—that's debutante for you Yankees—I was one of the most popular girls in my class. Got invited to *all* the parties." She smiled at the memory but then appeared to snap back to the present. "You'd think my fashion sense and ability to put together a sit-down dinner for eleven hundred at a moment's notice would have stood me in good stead, but nooo." An annoyed expression flitted across her face. "When I won the Miss Confederate Angel pageant you'd have thought Hitler himself had been nominated, judging by the town's response." She turned to me with a puzzled expression. "Just because I used a little creative genius to take care of the competition."

"Are you telling me that you killed a contestant?"

She waved her hand as if swatting a fly and polished off her third gin and tonic. The waiter was right there with another as soon as her glass touched the table.

"Heavens, no." She took a dainty sip of the fourth. "I went straight for the judges. Let me tell you, the whole town was in an uproar." She sucked on her straw and then stabbed the ice with it. "Especially since one of 'em was actually a sitting federal judge."

I had to ask. The idea of her confessing pulled at me, sucking me into her recollection. It was a lot like not being able to pass by a car wreck without looking. "You killed a federal judge to win a beauty pageant?"

Angie giggled, the booze finally beginning to show an effect. She leaned in close and stage-whispered, "I didn't kill 'em, silly. I sent 'em a note *promisin'* to kill 'em. Said that if they didn't select li'l ol' Angie McKenna as the winner, that they were all gonna die. And not in a good way." A loud belch erupted from deep inside her. I turned my head to avoid the stench.

"I take it you did time for threatening a federal judge?"

She emphatically shook her head. "No. I was careful. I used gloves and cut the words out of a magazine and pasted 'em into the note. They never did figure out it was me." She smirked and took another drink. Then her face turned dark. "I did time for something else." She shrugged. "It was worth every year I spent behind bars. I learned a lot. When I got out I was ready for a lifestyle change."

I tried to stop myself from asking the next logical question, but failed. It wasn't every day that I was privy to the inner thoughts of an assassin.

"Can I ask why you *did* do time?"

She gazed across the room, a moody expression on her face. "My asshat of a husband, that's why."

Assassins got married? The idea of Angie hooking up with anyone other than Charles Manson or Hannibal Lecter was a hard sell. That particular train of thought must have shown on my face because Angie's expression morphed from glowering anger to hurt in a nanosecond. The rest of her drink disappeared, and the waiter materialized with another. I signaled that I was ready for one more, as well. He nodded and hurried off.

"You think I can't love anybody because of what I do for a livin'?"

"It's not that, I just—"

"Believe you me, I most certainly can feel love. Probably a lot deeper than your skinny ass." I expected her to add, "So there."

"I stand corrected." A small, persistent voice in my head told me I needed to finish my drink, thank her for the nice chat, and vacate the premises while I still could. Maybe it was the tequila, but my fascination had grown and I wanted to find out the rest of the story. I decided my best course of action was to stay quiet and let her talk if she wanted to.

The waiter brought my second drink and Angie's sixth, and we sat in silence. I was about to suggest that we order an appetizer when she sighed and shifted in her seat, almost losing her balance. Her purse slipped off the back of the chair and fell to the floor with a clank. Part of a gun barrel peeked out from the opening. With a confused expression, Angie looked around her for the source of the noise. I bent down and grabbed her bag, shoving the nine millimeter back inside before anyone noticed. Then I pulled my car keys out and slid them into my pocket. Zipping her purse closed, I hung it on the back of my chair with my own bag.

"Where was I?" Angie muttered.

"Something about your asshat of a husband."

"Oh, yeah. Tha's right." She sipped at her G&T, her gaze unfocused. Whether from the gin or reminiscing, I wasn't sure.

"He was *gorgeous*. Really, *really* handsome." A dreamy sigh escaped her. "Definitely my weakness."

"Why was he an asshat?" I prompted.

"His gorgeousness worked against us. Women from ten counties came cattin' around, wantin' a piece of him." She let out a low whistle. "My, my. He was *somethin'.*"

Okay. I got it. The guy was good in the sack. Moving on.

"So he cheated on you?" I said, hoping to yank her out of her reverie.

"He didn't just cheat, darlin'. Oh, no." She shook her head, getting into the telling of it. "He was an artiste, a *maestro*. Played every last one of us like a damned orchestra."

I figured I knew where the story was headed.

I was wrong.

"One day I came home from work and there he was, face down on the bed, a kitchen knife stickin' out between his shoulder blades." She gave a little shudder before continuing. "I must have been in shock, because I went right over and pulled the damned thing out. Now, I *knew* I shouldn't have touched anything, and I knew in my brain that he was dead, but for some stupid reason I couldn't stand to see him that way. I even explained it to the detective who showed up after I called the police, but do you think he believed me? Or even gave me half a chance?" Angie shook her head, resentment plain on her face. "Of course not. The actual killer used gloves and didn't leave any prints, and the detective in charge was gunnin' for mayor, so makin' sure I was sent away for a long time became his priority.

"All I can say is, those five years in prison surely made me what I am today. I learned more about killin' in there than anyone had a right to."

"Five years? For murder?" That didn't sound right. My bullshit detector went on alert.

Angie gave me a wry smile. "The actual perpetrator confessed five years later. It was like magic. One day I'm doin' hard time for a murder I didn't commit, and the next day I'm a free woman with no home, no friends, no money, but a whole lotta newly acquired knowledge." She finished her drink, waving the waiter away when he reappeared with another. "Turned out to be one of his little girlfriends from the roadhouse. Couldn't take sharin' him, I guess. Ironically, she got assigned to my cell block just before I was released, and I slit the little bitch's throat. No witnesses came forward and I went my merry way. The rest is history."

My phone pinged in my purse, and I took it out to see who it was. It was a text from Sam that dinner was almost ready. I gave Angie a look and she rolled her eyes.

"Fine. We'll go. Jus' one more toast." She raised her glass and I picked up mine. "I'm pleased to say that you are the *first* graduate of Angie McKenna's School for Assassins." We touched glasses and both drained our drinks.

"Really? You mean we're done?" I tried to keep the excitement out of my voice. I didn't want to press my luck.

"Yep. Fini. I have one last parting gift to give you."

I waited in anticipation, relieved that our association was finally over. When she didn't specify what she meant, I asked, "And that is?"

Angie gave me an enigmatic look. "You'll see."

TWENTY-FIVE

I REPLIED TO Sam's text, letting him know I'd be home soon and to hold dinner. After much arguing, I drove Angie's car back to the Jeep, and then called her a cab. Giddy with relief at finally ending things with her, I found myself humming a happy tune in anticipation of spending some quality time with Sam. Twenty minutes later, I parked the Jeep in the garage next to Sam's new rig and climbed the stairs to the kitchen.

The mouthwatering scent of Sam's signature vegetable lasagna greeted me as I walked in the door, the air redolent with fresh garlic, basil, and marinara. I tossed my purse on the counter and glanced inside the oven. Ricotta and mozzarella cheese bubbled in the deep pan, promising a tasty dinner. The counter had been set for two, including a lit taper, a bottle of red and two wine glasses, and a basket of crusty French bread. Sam wasn't in the kitchen, so after washing my hands at the sink, I moseyed into the living room. He sat on the sofa with his back to me. The muted television was broadcasting a local news station.

"Hey there," I said, skirting the end of the couch. His stony facial expression was the first clue that he wasn't happy. He held his phone loosely in his right hand, as though forgotten.

"What's wrong?" I sat down beside him and put my hand on his arm. He turned his head and gave me a look I'd never seen him use before. I tried to guess at his mood—anger? Sadness? Shock? "Talk to me."

Sam returned his attention to the television and unmuted the channel. The news anchor was in the middle of reporting a breaking story. A still shot of a familiar Craftsman home could be seen behind her. The scrolling marquee on the bottom of the screen read *Rival Gang Brings Down Crime Boss.*

"Edward Chacon had moved to the quiet Seattle neighborhood just one week before his brutal murder…"

My heart skipped a beat. They'd found the body. Even though I knew it would happen, it was still shocking to see it play out on TV. I glanced at Sam. This time his expression was easy to read.

Sadness.

"What are you looking at me like that for? You think I had anything to do with this?" My mind scrambled for the right thing to say to ease the pain I saw in his eyes.

"I know you did."

"No, I didn't. What are you even talking about?"

"Don't lie to me, Kate." He muted the TV and set the remote on the side table. "I just got off the phone with a mutual acquaintance."

Something shifted inside of me and my heart sank. *She couldn't have.*

"Who?"

"Angie." He watched me closely. When I didn't respond, he continued. "She told me everything, right down to the knife in his throat. And she emailed me this." He turned his phone toward me and pressed play.

It was the video Angie had taken of Chacon's confession. At first the framing was tight to Chacon, but a few seconds into the replay the scene widened to include the back of me holding the gun. My voice was unmistakable.

A wave of weariness swept through me. It was too much effort to hold myself upright, and I slumped back against the sofa.

"I didn't kill him, Sam."

"But you hired her to teach you how." He shook his head. "What were you thinking?"

I didn't know what to say. I'd never be able to make him understand how powerless I felt when I first saw Lisa in that hospital bed. Or when the Whitmores demanded more information about the people responsible for their son's death and I couldn't give it to them. The pain in their eyes would stay with me for a lifetime. Sam never let things affect him that way.

"I wanted to know how to do things that would get results. Chacon's the kind of criminal who only understands violence, Sam. You know that. I thought if I could learn what to do and expect, then I'd have better luck finding the person responsible for so many lives cut short and make them pay."

"And have you?"

Remembering the thumb drive with the information from Chacon's laptop, I nodded. "Another clue, at least."

"The man died, Kate. And Angie has evidence that you were there." He leaned forward, his body taut with tension.

"I never intended for it to happen, at least not that way. Angie just showed up." I spread my hands wide, as though that should have been enough of an explanation.

Sam watched me for a moment before responding. "You do get that you're responsible for his death, right? You hired an assassin. If you hadn't done that, he'd probably still be alive today."

A tiny spark of rebellion ignited in my chest. "I didn't 'hire an assassin' to kill the guy. Besides, he was a dirt bag with no regard for human life. The world won't miss him one bit. Will you?" Just where did Sam get off judging me for trying to do what was right?

"Kate—" Sam's surprised expression added fuel to my fire.

"What did you expect? I've lived for years looking over my shoulder, being afraid for my life and the lives of those I loved. That's no way to live, Sam. You should try it some time." I was on a roll, now. "Chacon was responsible for my sister's coma, not to mention all those other deaths linked to those painkillers. How could I do nothing?"

Sam closed his eyes and shook his head. "Who have you become?"

"What's that supposed to mean?" The anger inside of me was burning out of control. A part of me watched the scene play out, knowing where this was headed but unable or unwilling to stop the emotional runaway train.

"I think we need a break. I've been operating under the assumption that you and I were of like minds." He stared into space. "What happened with Angie and Chacon tells me a different story."

"So we're breaking up?" The words came out defiant but my heart was in shreds. *I don't want to lose you, Sam,* I thought. But I didn't say it. I couldn't form the words.

Wouldn't.

"I hear a lot of I's in your explanation. No we's. I've been thinking of us as 'we.' Obviously you haven't."

I opened my mouth to speak, but Sam shut me down with a look.

"You can tell yourself that Chacon deserved to die, deserved to be tortured. That you haven't really done anything wrong. You can see it any way you want. Let me tell you how the criminal justice system will see it if they figure out you were a part of this. They could charge you with Murder One, or barring that, accessory to murder, which means a prison term. I guarantee you won't like prison, Kate. People tell you what to do there. All. The. Time.

"If prison doesn't bother you, how about the position you've put me in? Thanks to your new BFF sending the video to me, now there's a record that I know who committed the murder. What do you think the police will do if they catch up with Angie or find her phone? My number's on her call list." Sam leaned back and crossed his arms. "How the hell did she even get my number?"

"I—I don't know. She must have gotten a hold of my phone." She'd had plenty of opportunity. My heart stuttered in my chest. I waited for him to continue, but he didn't.

We sat in frozen silence, both of us unsure what to say, knowing the next words would make or break us. My phone pinged in the kitchen, telling me I had a text. Grateful for the distraction, I rose from the couch and blindly made my way to see who had sent it. I wiped at the tears forming in my eyes before fishing my cell out of my purse and glancing at the screen. It was a message from my father.

Lisa's had a turn for the worse.
Call me asap.

Palms sweating, I punched in his number, willing the call to connect faster. Finally, on the fifth ring, he answered.

"Maureen and I are at the hospital." He sounded like he hadn't slept. "Lisa went downhill overnight. They've been working to revive her." He drew a ragged breath. "They don't know how long she's got."

My stomach twisted and I closed my eyes. *Please don't leave, Lisa. You have to hang on.* The words formed in my mind like a mantra. "I'll be on the next plane to Minneapolis."

"No, Kate." He paused. "It would be better if you didn't come, love bug."

"Why not?" Shock replaced worry and my hands clenched. "I can take the redeye and be there by morning."

There was a hesitation before he said, "Maureen and your sisters don't want you here. They don't even know I'm calling you." His voice softened. "I'm sorry, honey."

Shock gave way to hurt, which quickly turned to anger. I tried to slow my breathing as my face heated.

"Lisa's my sister, too." I bit through the words.

"I know, love bug, I know. It's just that right now it would be best if you weren't around. They're angrier than a nest of hornets and blame you for everything."

"But you don't, do you?"

"Of course not. I know you mean well. It's just that—" Another sigh. "It would just make life a whole lot easier if you stayed in Seattle. I promise to keep you posted, okay?" Muted voices floated through the other end of the line. "I've got to go, love bug. Take care, okay?"

"Okay," I replied, but he'd already ended the call.

Numb, I set the phone down on the counter and stared into space. Lisa was fighting for her life and I wasn't there to help. My own stepmother and sisters didn't want me around, thinking that everything was my fault. I could have gone to Minneapolis, could have made a reservation to fly out of SeaTac that evening, but what was the point? I'd be lucky if Maureen would even let me see Lisa. She'd probably already given my name to the head nurse to bar me from visiting her.

"Is everything all right?" Sam's voice echoed in the empty kitchen. I looked up, and my gaze met his. He stood in the doorway leading into the living room.

"Lisa's worse."

"What time are you flying out?"

I shook my head. "Maureen and my sisters don't want me there." Tears pricked at my eyes, and I wiped at them with the back of my hand. The loss of both Sam and my family in the space of a few minutes was too much to bear. The kitchen walls closed in on me, claustrophobia clawing its way to the fore.

I had to get away, had to leave, now.

Fuck them. An ember of long-buried anger ignited at the outright loss of Sam and my family, such as it was. Not that I cared what Maureen thought, but my two older sisters feeling the same way stung. Somehow Maureen had turned them against me. They'd at least been willing to talk on the phone at Christmas and birthdays. And why didn't my father just leave Maureen? My mother and she were polar opposites. We'd all been surprised when Dad had popped the question.

Too bad my real mother was gone. I could've used her wisdom about now.

Sam walked over and wrapped his arms around me. At first I stiffened, but then leaned into the embrace, thankful for that small measure of comfort as my world crashed down around me in bright, fiery flames.

Twenty-Six

S AM AND I decided to take an extended break, and I moved to a hotel downtown. My life was a mess. In addition to giving Sam space, I needed new scenery, something to take my mind off things. Traffic and people and Seattle's hectic, hive-like activity seemed like just the ticket.

All the fury I had toward Angie's betrayal had nowhere to go—she'd disappeared and wasn't answering her phone. Implosion was imminent unless I could find a distraction. Rather than mope around my room, I spent the next three days at the Seattle Public Library—that pantheon of progressive Dutch architecture and some engineer's primal, unleashed imagination—using their Wi-Fi to search for more information on Pro-Pharma and Mick Dobson.

Pro-Pharma's corporate headquarters boasted a platinum LEED certification for responsible and sustainable building practices—the highest level granted by the US Green Building Council. The completed structure had been used as an example for projects around the world and was a great source of Seattle pride. According to an article in the *Seattle Times*, not only was Pro-Pharma's corporate headquarters one of the greenest buildings in the Pacific Northwest, but it had a security setup that would have made the Pentagon weep.

Aside from the usual Wikipedia entry and a few articles written for online business magazines like *Forbes* and *Fortune*, information on Dobson, the CEO of one of the largest pharmaceutical companies in the Pacific Northwest, was surprisingly sparse. Nowhere did it say where he lived, other than the greater Seattle area, or what charities he supported, or supply any identifying information. To add to the problem of locating the guy, he also wasn't on Facebook, Twitter, or any of the other social media sites I checked. After deploying all the ideas in my arsenal to track the guy down, I still came up empty. And I couldn't go to Sam with this, not now. I decided to call Jax, our IT guy, to see if Jason Whitmore's computer had anything on it that I could use. But Jax was uncomfortable with what I asked him to do as it involved a local company with a good reputation, so he declined my request to hack into Pro-Pharma's website.

In my quest for avoidance, I'd made it a habit to stop off at the hotel bar for a drink before calling it a night. Although considered an upscale lounge according to Seattle standards, Rudyard's generous happy hour attracted people from all walks of life. Stopping by for a drink helped me pretend that all the laughing, animated people in the bar were prospective friends, and that I had a home to go to and a family that loved me.

After a particularly unproductive day hunting for information, I almost bypassed the bar, intending to go to my room and hang out under the covers for the rest of the evening. My self-pity meter was in the red zone and I didn't feel up to giving myself a pep talk. When I reached the elevator and the doors pinged open, I hesitated. The thought of spending the evening alone in my empty, sterile room sounded worse than making the effort to visit the bar. With a deep sigh, I turned around and made my way to Rudyard's.

I sidled up to the sleek mahogany bar and ordered a margarita on the rocks. The bartender fixed my drink and had it on a cardboard coaster in front of me in seconds. I paid, tipping her accordingly, and took a sip before checking out the early evening partiers.

The lounge's low lights and subtle earth tones flattered everyone, which probably made it great for getting lucky, especially if a liberal dose of alcohol was involved. Most of the patrons were in groups of three or four, with a couple of larger tables of six and nine. Many were animated in that uninhibited way a person gets after a long day at the office and a couple of stiff drinks. A dark-haired woman in her mid to late twenties wearing heavy makeup and black fingernail polish sat in a dimly lit corner of the room, engrossed in a sticker-covered laptop on a low table in front of her. Out of everyone in the bar, she looked the most interesting. I probably would have approached her for a chat if she hadn't been sequestered in a far corner. Her position in the bar and closed-off body language screamed *leave me alone*.

Resigning myself to people watching, I struck up a conversation with the bartender, whose name was Greta. Greta's story was typical of bartenders throughout the country; she was working her way through college, getting her master's degree in environmental science, and bartending was the best paying job with the quirky hours she needed to finish her studies. When I jokingly asked her if she knew anyone who could hack into a national pharmaceutical company's website, she shook her head.

"Sorry. Now if you wanted to know how to rig a compostable toilet, then I'm your girl."

"That's all right, darlin'. I do."

My stomach twisted and I squeezed my eyes shut at the sound of that evil southern drawl. I sighed as I opened my eyes and stared at my drink.

I'd never be rid of her.

Serves you right. You were the one who put out the call for an assassin. I resisted the urge to tell my good girl to shut the hell up.

Wariness evident on her face, the bartender glanced nervously from Angie to me, and after collecting money for Angie's drink, made herself scarce.

Without looking at Angie I asked, "What are you doing here?" With calm deliberation I took a sip, control in every movement.

"Well, darlin', you've been spendin' a little too much time by yourself lately. It's unhealthy, if you ask me."

I set my drink on the bar and turned to glare at her. "You've been surveilling me?"

Angie's smile grated on my nerves. "Well, of course, sugar. After everything that's happened, I thought it best." She returned the glare. "Can't have my best pupil checking out, now, can we?"

Hot, bitter anger toward her climbed like lava in my chest. Not wanting to make a scene, I picked up my purse and slid off the barstool, intending to go up to my room.

"Leaving so soon?" Angie clucked at me, disdain obvious in her voice. "I'd think you'd want to hear what I have to say." She put her hand on my arm. "It concerns a certain CEO we both know."

I froze at her touch. My face grew hot with unexpressed rage. "Take your hand off me. Right. Now."

She complied. "Well," she huffed. "That's no way to treat someone who has gone through great lengths to find what you're looking for."

I took a deep breath and let it out, slowly. "And just what am I looking for? An address?"

"No, silly. Even better." She nodded at the dark-haired woman I'd seen earlier near the back of the room. "I have *her*."

I looked across the room at the woman with the black fingernails. Her gaze was riveted to her laptop, oblivious to the world around her.

"And who is that?"

"Her name is Eve and she's very good at obtaining information. Especially information that can't be found."

"And I should be ecstatic that you're trying to help because you're an upstanding citizen who cares deeply for humanity?"

Angie narrowed her eyes. Her heart-shaped face and long, narrow nose combined with the sharp green eyes made me think of a fox. The rabid kind. She was just missing the foam.

"No. You should be ecstatic I haven't uploaded the video I took of you yet. You should also be ecstatic because I'm going to help you get revenge on Dobson."

"I don't need or want your help." I threw back the rest of my margarita and started for the door.

"Not one more step, sugar." The warning in her voice had me rooted to the spot. Would she actually use the video?

Of course she would. Like it or not, I was Angie's bitch. I had to play her game. For now.

At least until I could get the video and destroy it.

"Or what? You've already taken the one thing from me that was worth a damn."

Angie slid off her stool and came to join me. "Oh. You must mean Sam." She waved at the air. "Don't you worry about him, hon. He's better off, don't you think? He doesn't need a shit magnet like you around, does he?"

Humiliation mixed with a spark of anger flamed my cheeks. I wanted to argue with her, but I had to admit she was right. Sam *was* better off. Chacon was dead, so no one was going to try to sneak into the house to kill Sam in his sleep. Angie would presumably leave him alone as long as I played her game.

Face it, Kate. You're both where you need to be. On your own.

"I'm sure you feel as though you have nothing to lose, and that's just how I want you in order to pull this little operation off."

"What little operation?"

Angie grinned, the Cheshire Cat making another appearance. "You'll see, sugar. You'll see."

Angie grabbed her drink from the bar, and we made our way across the busy room to talk to Eve.

"This is Kate." Angie set her drink down on the table in front of her. "She has a business proposition. Mind if we sit down?"

Eve gave me a look that said I had better make the interruption worth her while or I'd be talking to security. I wondered if she knew what Angie did for a living.

"Knock yourself out." The room's temperature dropped a couple of degrees.

Angie sat on her right. I took the club chair to her left and made myself comfortable.

"So you're looking for someone with computer experience." Eve's brown eyes had a fathomless quality that made her hard to read.

"Actually, I'm looking for someone with a talent for hacking websites. Angie here suggested I talk to you."

Eve kept her eyes trained on mine. "I don't think I'm your girl. I don't know how to hack anything except maybe that blockbuster movie you don't want to pay to see."

I glanced at Angie, who dipped her head, encouraging me to keep going.

"Useful, I'm sure," I continued. "But what I'm really looking for is someone who could hack a major pharmaceutical company's site."

"Which one?" There was a glimmer of interest in Eve's eyes.

"Pro-Pharma."

Eve arched an eyebrow. "Not that I'd be able to help, but you're going to need a good reason to go after those guys. They're local. Most folks think they're a different kind of pharmaceutical company." She used air quotes around the words "different kind."

"Oh? Why is that?" Angie asked.

Obviously, Angie hadn't done her research.

"Just look at the hype. They've built their reputation on being progressive and responsible. They recycle. They participate in the community. They donate drugs to those in need. Pretty much the perfect business model for emerald-green Seattle, right?" She shrugged. "You know what they say around these parts—think globally, shop locally."

"Hate to burst any preconceived bubbles, but I have reason to believe that the CEO, Mick Dobson, is responsible for dozens of fentanyl overdoses in Seattle."

Laptop forgotten, Eve's gaze riveted to mine. Obviously, I had her attention. "I'm listening."

Angie leaned back as I told Eve about Lisa and Jason, and a partial explanation of what we'd uncovered through Chacon about Pro-Pharma's link to the tainted painkillers. Eve leaned forward, a determined look on her face.

"Obviously you aren't Homeland Security or FBI." She glanced at Angie. "This lady here wouldn't dream of betraying me or my people. Would you, Miss Angie?"

Angie smiled and sipped her drink, answering my unasked question of whether they knew each other.

Eve sat back in her chair. "Why not take this information to the DEA?"

"Because they move too slowly," I said. Maybe this woman really could help me get to Dobson. "They have to build an airtight case that will stand up in court. I don't. I want to stop this asshole from putting more drugs on the street before someone else is killed."

"What's your plan?"

Angie replied, "We've got a couple of ideas, but the first thing we need to do is track the man down and see what kind of information is available on him. If we can't manage that, then there isn't any way to continue."

Eve nodded, apparently satisfied with her answer.

"Listen," I added. "I can pay you. I'm not asking you to do this out of the goodness of your heart."

Eve smirked.

"Think about it? You'd be doing a lot of people a huge favor. Maybe save some lives in the process."

Minutes ticked by while she gave the offer some thought. I sipped my drink, giving her as much space as she needed to reach a decision. Angie remained quiet, watching both of us closely, like she was perusing a couple of bugs pinned to a bug board.

The noise in the bar crescendoed as the place began filling up. Greta disappeared behind a wall of customers, now three deep at the bar.

Finally, Eve gave a small nod like she'd made up her mind. She held out her hand.

"Looks like I am your girl, after all."

I left Eve and Angie in the bar and took the elevator to my room. Eve said she'd get in touch the next day after she did some preliminary investigating. I assumed that meant checking my background as well as Mick Dobson's. It would be interesting to find out what kind of information she'd be able to uncover about me. There was no need to hide anymore, but I still used the name Kate Jones, the alias I'd had the longest, which was a far cry from my original last name of Schroeder. In the beginning, I chose Jones in order to throw Salazar and Anaya off my trail and keep my family safe. It was either that or Smith, and I didn't relish calling myself Kate Smith. Now that Maureen and my sisters had made it abundantly clear they preferred I kept my distance, there was no compelling reason to go back to using my real name.

Besides, my current passport, driver's license, and credit cards were all under Kate Jones, which worked fine. The thought of buying another fake passport didn't appeal to me. I wanted out of that life, had spent too many years trying to remember my name. I was good with Kate. Kind of liked her, in fact. A persona I could call my own.

Events leading up to my split from Sam along with the meeting with Angie and Eve in the bar raced through my mind, the thoughts searching for a place to call home. I didn't like where they landed.

I was heading back into the mistake of a life I'd created before, and this time there was no choice but to do what Angie wanted. Once again, my impulsive and impetuous nature had driven me away from Sam and into a life marred by vengeance, criminals, and death. I should have known once Angie had her hooks in me that I wouldn't be able to make a clean exit. Why hadn't I realized she'd find a way to blackmail me?

What I needed to figure out was why Angie was so interested in helping me find Dobson. Obviously she had ulterior motives. I assumed it had everything to do with money.

Not yet tired, I turned on the TV and flipped through the channels. So many channels, so little interesting content. I sighed and shut it off. Restless, I got up and walked to the window.

A light rain pattered against the windowpane. Traffic was scarce at that hour, although the occasional honk and screech of brakes floated up to keep me company. The lights of Seattle flickered below as a melancholy mood wrapped itself around me, threatening to swamp my determination to avoid thinking about Sam.

What have I done?

Bleak thoughts crowded my mind, shoving each other out of the way in an attempt to gain first position. Sam was the one person I could trust. The one person who had loved me in spite of my past. I'd ruined the tenuous connection we'd built.

What was wrong with me?

No matter what I did or how well-meaning I tried to be, I always found a way to screw things up. Especially when it came to love. Maybe I didn't believe I was worthy. I gave that some thought but quickly abandoned the idea. My inner critic would have none of it.

Stop trying to psychoanalyze things. And for God's sake, quit feeling sorry for yourself.

I'd never been too interested in self-analysis. It seemed indulgent, ego-driven. Leave the questions of motivation to philosophers and shrinks. Well, that, and the margarita didn't help. With another sigh, I turned from the window.

Maybe after all was said and done, I'd find another place to live, some little house in a vineyard in Eastern Washington. Get a bunch of cats. Better yet, maybe I'd go back to Arizona. It was the last place I remembered being really happy. I could reapply for my old job driving Jeep tours. I drifted back to a happier time. Fresh air, new people, beautiful scenery, a great boss.

The idea of running into my ex, Sheriff Cole Anderson, stopped me from going any further.

Yet another relationship I'd managed to screw up.

I just had to own it—I was no good at love. Or dealing with family.

Or living my life.

No, I needed to finish this business with Angie and Dobson and then leave for parts unknown with no forwarding address. Make a clean break. Moving to a location where no one knew me had a strong appeal. I could be someone with a normal past. I'd make new friends, get a job somewhere. Yeah.

The one thing I was good at.

Leaving.

TWENTY-SEVEN

THE NEXT DAY Angie texted me a location in a nearby neighborhood and asked me to meet Eve there at noon. At twelve o'clock sharp, I pulled up to the nondescript, five-story brick building and parked next to the curb. I made a mental note of the two-hour parking limit and walked up to the entrance where I hit the button for apartment 16-A. A moment later, someone on the other end buzzed me through.

The apartment was at the end of a long hall, last door on the left. The corridor was painted beige and smelled of pine cleaner. Cheap dome lights dotted the ceiling. Two of them had burned out, leaving a portion of the hallway in shadow. Somewhere behind a closed door a baby cried.

Before I could knock, the door to apartment 16-A opened and a pale, delicate oval face I didn't recognize peered out at me. The sleek, close-cropped black hair, dark eyeliner, and nose ring didn't give any cues as to gender, but my instincts told me the person was more than likely a she. Not that it mattered.

"I'm here to see Eve."

The young woman gave me the once-over and stepped aside to let me in. For some reason, I felt like I'd passed inspection.

"She's over there." Nose Ring nodded toward the living room, where three people were huddled around their laptops. No one spoke.

With Nose Ring behind me, I walked into the room, unsure where to sit or what to do. Should I wait until Eve acknowledged me, or would it be better to interrupt? I hated to break such intense concentration so opted for silence. Eve continued to type for a few moments before she looked up.

She closed the laptop and stood, gesturing for me to follow her. We walked down a short hallway and into what was originally a bedroom, but now had large pieces of equipment with blinking lights lining the perimeter. There was barely enough room for the table and four chairs that were in the middle. A low hum permeated the stuffy room. Nose Ring closed the door behind us. Eve opened her laptop and turned it to face me, nodding at Nose Ring.

"This is Lady Dedlock. Lady D for short. She'll be working with us on the Pro-Pharma thing."

I was about to ask her why the unusual name when I noticed the words written across the virtual file folder on the screen. *Operation Dirt Bag.*

"Have a seat." Eve pulled out a chair and indicated I should sit. Lady D took the chair next to Eve. "Take a look." She held herself like a Labrador on point and my heart rate kicked up a notch. Had she found the information I was looking for already?

Inside the file folder were several items: documents, webpages, screen shots, even bank statements. I clicked through them and whistled. The words Pro-Pharma or Mick Dobson were on almost every one.

"Damn. You're good."

The comment elicited a smile. "We aim to please."

I studied each page and took notes. When I was finished, a plan had begun to form in my mind.

"Can you hack into his personal computer?"

Eve cocked her head to one side and gave me an amused look. "Where do you think I got the banking information?"

Oh. "Is it really that easy?"

Eve raised an eyebrow. "Once I figured out his IP address and ran a port scan, getting in was a snap. Especially since he never updates his plug-ins."

"This helps. A lot."

"What exactly are you looking for?" she asked.

"A weakness to exploit. I'm hoping to hit him where it's going to hurt the most. His finances. It's the only reasonable explanation for what he did."

"Profits before people from corporate America? How unusual."

Her droll response spoke volumes. It wasn't the first time I wondered what kind of hacking she did. Apparently the look on my face spoke just as loudly as her words.

"I sense that you're curious about our methods."

"You know, it's really none of my business," I said, hastily adding, "No questions asked. I think that's what Angie said."

"Angie assured me that you were no danger to our little community." Eve gave me an enigmatic smile.

"She's right on that count. I'm hardly one to make trouble for you guys. I am interested in why you're helping me, though. It's not like the money I'm paying you is enough if you get caught."

The enigmatic smile made another appearance. "Let's just say that some of us have a vested interest in the outcome."

When I asked what she meant, she changed the subject.

"So, what's the game plan?"

"Is there a way to copy the contents of his computer?" I asked. "I mean everything."

She nodded. "Absolutely. Then what?"

"Then, depending on what I find, we pay Mr. Dobson a visit."

"That's going to be difficult."

"Why?" Surely it would just be a matter of surveilling his house to figure out the best time to break in. "Too much security?"

She waved away my question. "Everything, including the cameras, is wirelessly connected. Taking the teeth out of that will be simple, unless he has dogs or something we haven't anticipated. He's not a computer geek, to put it mildly. Looks like he had someone set up his server and then left it at that."

"Then what's the problem?"

"His house is surrounded by water."

"Like a moat?"

"Like the Strait of Juan de Fuca."

The San Juan Islands are located north of Seattle, an archipelago near Vancouver Island, British Columbia, in the Strait of Juan de Fuca. Over 400 islands populate the area, although some are hardly bigger than large rocks. All are accessible only by boat or floatplane.

Dobson owned one of those rocks, not far from Friday Harbor. Friday Harbor was on one of the four main islands accessible by ferry, the others being Orcas, Lopez, and Shaw Islands. We'd have to first locate his island via satellite, and then make sure he was there before we attempted our plan. Once we'd confirmed his presence, we'd have to sneak onto the island and into his house without being detected. After we were inside, I'd use the information from Angie's enhanced interrogation module to get him to confess, which I'd record and upload to the cloud for safekeeping.

Although the threat to release his and Chacon's recorded confessions would give him a mighty strong incentive to stop selling the dangerous meds, I wasn't convinced we could pull off the plan. There were too many variables that screamed prison if we were caught. On the other hand, if the video was released, Pro-Pharma's stock would tank and he'd lose everything. In a perfect world, he would be held liable and charged with the victims' wrongful deaths.

"But Eve, think about it. This plan has so many holes it's like chicken wire. First, we have to correctly identify the exact rock where his home is among 400 islands. Once we do that, we have to be able to confirm when he's there—alone. If that isn't enough, then we have to sneak onto the island and into his home without anyone knowing. The guy's a CEO for a pharmaceutical company with a lot of discretionary income. He's got security."

The annoyance on Eve's face told me she didn't care about the odds. "All of that can be circumvented." I played devil's advocate for a while longer, but she was adamant.

"Look," she said, as though speaking to a recalcitrant two-year old. "We're doing this with or without you. It's your call. There's too much at stake for us to stop now. Besides, Angie says you'll do whatever it takes. Was she wrong?"

I studied her, trying to figure out if she was bluffing or not, and came to the conclusion that she meant what she said. I knew Angie did. On that point, I was screwed. If Angie wanted me to go with these guys, I would have to go.

"Why are you so eager to do this?" I still wasn't clear on her motivation, and Angie had gone to ground and was unavailable. Again. I couldn't pick her brain about the hackers. "You could go to prison for this. Maybe it's not murder, but breaking into a man's home and blackmailing him after threatening his life isn't going to get you a slap on the wrist."

"That's my business. I will tell you this, though. The deaths from those drugs hit close to home for a lot of us." She leaned back and folded her arms across her chest. "That's all I'm going to say."

Isn't that exactly how I felt? That I wanted revenge for what happened to Lisa? As long as Dobson walked free, the need to make him pay would eat at me. I knew if I didn't act, I'd sentence myself to a lifetime of frustration for letting it go.

"Okay. What about this? I'll work with you in an advisory capacity. I've been a part of successful clandestine operations in the past, and if there's one thing that stuck in my mind, it's that preparation is key. If you don't have a plan, you won't have a chance in hell of achieving your objectives." I had Quinn to thank for that.

"Fair enough. Does that mean you will or won't come with us to the island once we find it?"

"If Angie thinks I need to be there, then I'll go."

"Deal." Eve closed the laptop. "I'm pretty sure Angie will insist that you join us."

"Let's cross that bridge when we come to it."

Locating Dobson's home turned out to be relatively easy, using satellite photos readily available on the internet. His satellite connection had a static IP address, and Eve was able to narrow the search to a manageable area, eventually identifying the estate. The main house was set in a clearing in the center of the island surrounded by a small forest, and was accessible from a dock with stairs leading up a steep rock face. There were also some smaller outbuildings, one of which appeared to be a caretaker's cottage.

Eve discovered the permits and plans for the estate, which detailed an extensive solar array in a clearing to the south, as well as an elaborate cistern running underneath the buildings. Wastewater was filtered through rain gardens and other gravity-fed systems, and sewage was diverted into bio tanks treated with microbes. Two large propane tanks fed his gas stove and three fireplaces. His internet connection was powered by a dedicated satellite feed which bypassed the normal frustrations of the technology like slow loading times and breaks in service.

Tracking his movements was relatively easy, at least for Eve and Lady D. Like many people, Dobson used a smartphone and synced it to his personal laptop. Eve was able to send an innocuous string of code from his computer to his phone that allowed her to take control of both the webcam on his laptop and the audio on his phone without being detected.

We would have to move quickly. Once we tracked him to his house on the island, there was no guarantee that he'd stay there. I suggested watching his movements for a longer period of time, getting a feel for his habits, but Eve and Lady D objected. In the few short days they'd been tracking him, he'd consistently spent the night at a waterfront condominium, one he apparently used while in Seattle. When I proposed that we try for the confession at the condo, both Eve and Lady D shook their heads.

"He's not alone when he's there. Besides, security is tight for the entire building. Neither one of us are comfortable with that or the location."

"How do we know he's going to be alone on the island?"

"We don't, exactly, except for what we can hear on audio or see from the webcam. But we know for a fact he's not alone at the condo. Besides, the condo location has more room for failure, like witnesses and faster emergency response."

Lady D added, "Once he's on the island, we'll have to move the first night he's there. What if he decides to take a trip? We'd have to wait until he got back, and that could be weeks."

"I see your point. But I'm a little uncomfortable just 'storming the castle.' What if there are groundskeepers? Or security guards, or caretakers? I would assume since there's a caretaker cottage on the estate and he's not there all the time that he'd at least have someone keep an eye on things."

Eve shrugged. "No worries there. As long as he's within shouting distance of his computer or phone, which is 99.9 percent of the time, I'll be able to hear most of what he says." She looked pointedly at me. "That means plans he discusses with other people, like his assistant."

"How does he get there? Boat? Helicopter?"

It was Lady D's turn to answer. "He keeps a floatplane at a marina on Lake Washington. I suggest that we get our gear together and be ready to go, so it will just be a matter of grabbing it and heading for the island. Everyone's on call, ready to leave at a moment's notice. All we need to do is wait for Dobson to signal that he's leaving. Once that happens, we can be there with plenty of time to find a way into the house."

"How are we going to get there?" It wouldn't be difficult to rent a motor cruiser, but the less of a paper trail we left, the better.

"We've got it covered."

Two days later, Eve called with the news that Dobson was heading for the island later that afternoon. He'd left instructions for his assistant to let people know he was going to be MIA for a few days in order to get some work done, but to not tell anyone that he was at his estate in the San Juans. He'd also sent a one-line email to someone named Amelia, letting her know he was going to be staying at the island over the weekend.

"He texted his girlfriend and told her he'd call her when he got back," Eve said. "Which means he'll probably be alone in the house, at least for the first night or two."

"Unless he's meeting someone else there. What about the email to Amelia? Do we know who she is?"

"We think that she's his housekeeper here in town, or maybe a standing appointment, like his masseuse. His messages are always terse with very little emotion, like an order. Strictly business, so probably not a second girlfriend."

Eve and I had met earlier in the week and put together everything we thought we'd need, stowing the items in a couple of waterproof duffel bags. We left the bags inside the front door of Eve's apartment, ready to be transferred at a moment's notice. Also earlier in the week, Eve had spoken to Angie, who insisted I be involved with the operation all the way through to completion.

Not that I was surprised. But she dangled the carrot of the damning video in front of me, with assurances that if I joined this one operation, she'd destroy the evidence and we could part ways.

Not that I believed her.

Our ticket onto the island turned out to be a friend of Eve's who was into extreme sports and owned a cabin cruiser, a gift from his wealthy parents. Instead of selling the boat off and using the money, he decided to live aboard, tied up to his parents' dock. By not having to pay a mortgage or rent, he was able to use his money to travel wherever his whims took him. He'd just gotten back the week before from free climbing somewhere in Utah and was on call as needed.

The boat we were going to use had an average cruising speed of twenty-five knots, so it would take us about three hours to reach Dobson's private island. Our plans involved arriving before he did, but training from my time in the Yucatán kicked in, and at my insistence we'd developed a plan B and C in case things went south.

For the last two days, Angie had followed me, showing up at weird moments in places I'd never have expected. Like my mechanic's garage. Or the grocery store I frequented. She even sent me a text to ensure that I arrived at our rendezvous in the quaint town of Edmonds at two o'clock on the afternoon Dobson was scheduled to fly out.

Annoying, to say the least. Like I'd forget she had me on video during the commission of a crime and skip the island tour.

The Asian-inspired waterfront house owned by the guy's parents overlooked the Puget Sound with a fantastic view of the Olympic Mountains. A rolling grass lawn sloped down to a long metal dock boasting two motor cruisers, one larger than the other. I assumed we'd be taking the smaller of the two. I was wrong.

The two waterproof duffel bags we'd packed earlier rested on the dock next to the larger boat. At close to forty feet, the *Olympic Dream* could have been classified as a small yacht. In addition to the cockpit and cabin, the cruiser sported a fly bridge and what appeared to be enough room for at least two forward cabins. An inflatable was tied to the stern.

A guy in his mid twenties with longish brown hair came out of the cabin, hopped onto the deck, and grabbed one of the bags. Hoisting it to his shoulder, he climbed back on the boat and disappeared inside. I walked down the grassy slope and onto the dock, stopping near the stern. I didn't have long to wait. He reappeared a minute later and stopped short when he saw me.

His tall, athletic build and snapping brown eyes reminded me of a much younger Sam, although the latter's calm, thoughtful exterior wasn't in evidence. He jumped off the bow onto the dock and stuck out his hand.

"You must be Kate. Welcome aboard."

I smiled as I shook his hand. "And you are?"

"Luke, at your service."

I handed him my bag and climbed onto the boat. Eve and Lady D were already inside the cabin, stowing their things, along with two other people I hadn't met. When Eve saw me, she gestured to the other two to follow her out to the deck.

"Kitten and Darwin, this is Kate."

We exchanged handshakes. The two were complete opposites. Kitten was a few heads shorter than me, with long, flowing black hair, sultry good looks, and a mischievous glint in her eyes, while Darwin was tall and wiry with flaming red hair and a smattering of freckles across his pale face.

"Kitten is going to hack the security system and loop the video so there's no way to identify us. She's also going to disable the satellite connection, which will disrupt the phone and internet," Eve explained. She put a protective hand on Darwin's shoulder. "Darwin here is our troubleshooter. He'll roam the property, looking for anything out of the ordinary, alerting us if we need to get out of there. He'll also watch the caretaker's cottage in case it's occupied."

Darwin gave me a curt nod. "I'll be using night vision goggles," he said, pointing to a plastic container on one of the aft seats.

"He also brought these." Eve handed everyone a two-way radio about the size of a cell phone, along with an ear mic. Lady D and Luke had finished whatever they'd been doing and joined us on deck.

"I synced the mics to the radios." Darwin turned his radio screen to face the group. "Go into settings and make sure covert mode is selected, if not now, then before we get to the island. That way the display won't light up, and you'll only be able to hear what's going on in your earpiece."

Everyone turned on the radios and checked.

"Be sure to turn them off until you need them. The batteries are rated to last eleven hours, but I don't want to push the envelope."

I turned to Eve. "Is Angie joining us?"

"She surely is, darlin'." Angie emerged from the darkness of the cabin, a drink in her hand and her large tortoiseshell sunglasses perched on her head. Today she wore all black like the rest of us, only she looked much more chic. It must have been the Hermès scarf.

"Angie," I said, by way of greeting.

"Kate, sugar. How nice to see you." Her smile lacked warmth. I was getting used to it.

After Luke gave us a thorough rundown of the *Olympic Dream's* layout and safety precautions, we got under way. I checked my phone. It was five fifteen. The sun wouldn't set until after eight o'clock, leaving us enough daylight to visually locate the island before nightfall. The day was bright and unseasonably warm, at least for May, but the cool breeze off the water made me glad I'd remembered my jacket. Once the sun set, things would turn cold in a hurry.

Sunlight glinted off the calm, slate-blue water, and I relaxed into the gentle rocking of the boat. We followed the coast northwest past Whidbey Island and the Victorian village of Port Townsend, past forests of Douglas fir and western red cedar hugging the shoreline. The trip was so scenic, I found myself almost forgetting our destination. Memories surfaced from years before when I'd been imprisoned on a yacht in the Caribbean by Vincent Anaya's right-hand man, Frank Lanzarotti. Such a long time ago. I wondered how Grace, the island's medicine woman, was doing, whether she was still alive.

Frank wasn't.

Although his death hadn't been unwelcome, the memories still made me nostalgic for the good old days.

And then I snapped out of it. Good old days? Really? I'd been running for my life, hoping my past wouldn't catch up with the people I cared about. This time, things were different. This time, whether I wanted to or not, I was part of the hunting party. Dobson would have to start looking over *his* shoulder.

To say I had mixed feelings was an understatement. I'd have preferred to do things on my own terms, not be blackmailed into it.

Eve stayed inside the cabin and monitored Dobson's phone, listening for any indication that he'd started for the marina and his floatplane. Kitten was stretched out on a chaise, attention riveted on her phone. Lady D was up on the fly bridge with Luke, and Darwin was asleep on a bench nearby. Angie had claimed the captain's cabin, of course, and was nowhere to be seen.

I pulled up a book I'd been reading on my phone, but the beauty surrounding me was more interesting, so I put it back in my bag. A few minutes later, an eagle dipped into the sound and grabbed a fish with its talons before giving a flap of its massive wings and flying off with its prize.

Time passed and the shadows along the shore grew. I must have dozed off with the rocking, because a loud hiss erupted to my right and I jumped to my feet. Heart thudding in my ears, I looked over the side in time to see a pod of three black and white orcas surface just off the stern.

"Whales to starboard," I called, digging my phone out of my purse. Luke glanced behind him and gave me a thumbs- up. The rest of the crew came to my side of the boat to get a better look. Everyone took out their phones and filmed the scene. The pod stuck around for a little while longer before finally swimming away toward the setting sun.

We all stayed on deck, hoping the orcas would come back and give us another show, but everybody eventually returned to their original positions when it was obvious they were gone. All but Darwin, who sat beside me. I scooted over to make room.

"So how do you know Eve?" I asked.

Darwin looked into the distance and paused before answering. "She used to go out with my brother, Sean." He brought his gaze back to mine. "He died a few weeks ago."

"I'm so sorry." I didn't know what to say. The burden of the loss was obvious by the set of his shoulders and the expression on his face.

"That's why I'm here, doing this." His jaw pulsed. "He died of an overdose. There was fentanyl and a bunch of toxic shit in his bloodstream."

Ah. That answered my question regarding motivation for both Eve and Darwin. "My sister Lisa is in a coma because she took a contaminated painkiller manufactured by Pro-Pharma. The last time I spoke to my father, she wasn't doing very well." I let out a long sigh. The excitement of seeing the whales had fallen flat, replaced by claustrophobic worry.

Darwin's expression hardened and he made a fist. "I'm going to make that asshole pay for what he did." His voice was quiet, as though he was speaking to himself.

The memory of Angie killing Chacon—the shock and anger I felt at her taking things into her own hands— rushed back in full technicolor. Darwin's confession had just turned the goal of the trip 180 degrees, and not for the better. Now, instead of just threatening Dobson if he didn't confess to distributing the painkillers, it looked like the group was determined to go even further. I'd hoped the trip wouldn't go sideways, but hope doesn't cut it in horseshoes and blackmail.

Or something like that.

There was no way out of this, not with Angie's video of me in Chacon's house hanging over my head. And Sam's. I was trapped. And just what was Angie's motivation, anyway? Why did she even care about some CEO for Big Pharma?

How far would this band of hackers go?

"What are you going to do?"

"Don't worry. I've got things handled." He glanced at me, a determined look in his eyes. "I want him to hurt like he hurt Sean."

That didn't sound promising. "Does Eve know what you're planning?"

He nodded. "She's good with it." He turned to me, his blue eyes shining with an intensity that hadn't been there before. "I hope you are, too."

A chill spiraled down my back at his words. "Why do you think I'm here?"

My non-answer seemed to placate him. What else could I say? If the rest of the group had decided to hurt or even kill Dobson, there wasn't much I could do without the possibility of the others turning on me. It would be difficult to find my way back to civilization if they left me stranded, and that wasn't even the worst-case scenario. What was Eve's end game? For that matter, what about Angie? Were they going to kill Dobson and then leave me on the island to take the fall? Stranger things had happened. All I had to defend myself from any accusations was the address to the apartment in Seattle and Eve's and Angie's phone numbers, each of which could be changed. Eve most likely had most of my particulars and could make my life a living hell if she thought I had crossed her in any way. Besides, Angie's promise to upload the incriminating video wasn't just a threat. It was a sure thing.

With Angie along for the ride, I had a bad feeling things would not end well for Mick Dobson.

Or me.

TWENTY-EIGHT

WE'D BEEN MOTORING along for the better part of two hours when Eve emerged from the cabin.

"Dobson's headed for the floatplane and the marina. He mentioned picking up supplies before leaving, so our timing's good." She checked her phone. "It's seven twenty now. If everything goes as planned, we should be at the island within the hour. Once he's in the air, it won't take Dobson long to fly there. We need to be set up before he arrives."

"Can I talk to you a sec?"

Eve walked over and sat on the edge of the bench seat. "What's up?"

"Darwin mentioned your connection to his brother."

Eve gave a slow nod. "And?"

"And I think there's more to this trip than you led me to believe. What are you planning to do to Dobson?" I leveled my gaze at her. "You need to be straight with me. I brought this to you. My intent was never murder. I thought we were clear on that."

Conflicting emotions flitted through her eyes. "We are. We're not killers, Kate."

"What about Angie? You do know what she does for a living, right?"

"She's...here to make sure it all runs smoothly."

I almost laughed. "Yeah, you might want to keep an eye on her. Spectator sports aren't really her style."

Eve shook her head. "If she's got other plans, there's not a lot I can do to stop her. We're a democracy here, not a dictatorship."

"You should have a word with Darwin, then. I think he has other plans." I glanced at Eve. "When the reason for your pain is sitting right in front of you, it's hard to pull back. Believe me, I know."

"Dobson *is* the reason for Sean's death. Who else would it be? He knew exactly what would happen. Sean was only trying to stop the pain—" Tears welled in her eyes and she looked away.

"I'm sorry for your loss." I searched her face, hoping for a glimpse of reason. Revenge fueled by hurt and grief and assumed powerlessness was a strong motivator that often masked the real problem. "Lashing out doesn't fill up the hole inside of you." My voice was just loud enough for her to hear over the hum of the boat engine.

She nodded that she understood, but did she really? And, when the time came, would she be able to contain Darwin's thirst for revenge? And what the hell was Angie planning? The way things were going, the evening was headed toward a bloody, horrendous mess. Bile crept up my throat at the thought. I didn't want to be a part of this kind of vigilantism. True, when I broke into Chacon's house, my intention had been to kill him once I'd gotten the information I needed. I'd been naïve. It had become very clear that wasn't the way to rid myself of the pain and anger I felt over what happened to Lisa. The front row seat to Angie killing Chacon had brought it all home. Reality was far different from the imagined scenario. I'd been around enough death and violence to understand that its perpetuation only created more pain. It was obvious to me that Darwin and the others hadn't learned that yet.

And Angie never would.

I gazed across the now-dark water at the deepening shadows. Black, billowing clouds were gathering to the north. Half of me was glad we were almost to the island—it meant the evening would be over soon. The other half kept replaying the fear that we were headed into a seriously bad situation that was quickly growing out of control.

Lost in thought, I didn't notice the abrupt change in weather until the lower pitch of the engine dragged me back to reality. I glanced up at Luke standing at the helm, his back rod-straight, legs canted for stability. I couldn't see his expression, but his tensed shoulders spoke volumes.

"Need any help?" I called. The water had gone from smooth and blue to choppy and black in a matter of minutes. Wind whipped my face as the smell of rain filled the air. The black clouds that had seemed far away were now overhead.

"Thanks, but I got it handled," Luke called back. The boat pitched and I grabbed on to the rail to keep myself from being thrown to the deck. My backpack fell over, sending the contents flying. The ping of coins bouncing onto the deck told me I had forgotten to zip it closed.

Holding on to the gunwales to keep my balance, I retrieved the pack and rounded up the contents littering the deck as a light pattering of rain hit my face. The wind whipped my jacket open, revealing my shoulder holster and gun. I glanced toward the cabin to see if anyone had noticed, but couldn't be sure. I hurriedly zipped the jacket closed. I'd hate to wrestle Darwin or anyone else for it.

"You should probably get inside," Luke yelled. "Looks like we're headed into a squall."

I waved at him and went into the cabin. The rest of the group had taken their positions, with Darwin in the captain's chair, and Eve, Lady D, and Kitten tucked into the built-in seats. I assumed Angie was below in the forward berth. How she could stay there with all the juddering of the boat was anyone's guess. Everyone's attention was riveted on either a phone or a tablet. I marveled at their ability to tune out the storm.

The wind howled and the *Olympic Dream* shuddered as it headed into the chop, slamming down hard with each wave. I staggered over to a vacant seat next to a window and sat down. Spreading my feet wide, I braced myself against the boat's bucking, attempting to stay upright. How were they even able to read?

As the ship rolled and pitched at an alarming angle, I found myself questioning Luke's captaining ability but discarded the thought. The wind had come up suddenly. Squalls were like that. The weather could turn in a minute, especially on the water.

It wasn't long before my stomach started to rebel. Nausea built in my throat and I closed my eyes with a groan.

Bad decision, closing my eyes.

The world started to spin. I opened my eyes and stood. Holding on to whatever was available, I staggered out of the cabin and onto the deck, where I gulped in air and tried not to hurl. The boat was twisting this way and that, tossed on the waves as though it was just a plastic toy in some giant's bathtub. I braved a quick glance to see how Luke was doing, but my hair got in the way and things started to spin again. I raced to the gunwales and leaned over the side.

Experiencing lunch a second time was not pleasant.

At that point, I didn't care what the weather was doing, I just wanted to die. Anything would have been better than living with the misery that was seasickness. I followed the initial barf-fest with several more attempts which proved futile. There was nothing left. Gripping the safety line, I hung my head over the side, my agonized groans lost to the evil wind that had taken over the boat.

What surely must have been a year later, the wind tapered off to a stiff breeze and the space between waves lengthened. Lifting my head, I wiped my mouth with the back of my hand, amazed that I was still coherent. Relief filtered through me, and I leaned back and closed my eyes, glad that the incessant bucking had become less like riding an enraged, psychotic bull and more like a tame pony.

"Land, ho!" Luke's voice drifted down from above. One by one the others emerged from the cabin. Off the port side, a dark, rocky promontory jutted up from the sea. Whitecaps bashed against the base of a bluff, and tall firs spiked across the top edge like a giant Mohawk. The island's sheer granite cliffs formed an impenetrable wall from sea to crest. A deep vertical shadow appeared in the rocks to the left of a lone, stunted madrone clinging precipitously to a ledge. Luke spun the wheel toward the gap in the rock and accelerated. Everyone grabbed hold of the gunwales as the boat rocketed forward.

The nearer we came to the island, the louder the engines echoed against the cliff. Luke pulled back on the throttle, and we drifted past the opening. The dark clouds from the squall were still prevalent, casting the small bay in a murky gray light. A long wooden dock sliced through the steel-colored water like a crooked seam, a covered power boat tied up next to it. The dock joined several stairs leading up a steep cliff. At the top of the rise stood a large structure that reminded me of a north woods lodge where Sam and I had stayed a few months back. Heavy timber marked the peak of the roof, with the front of the house a wall of glass. Little path lights dotted the landscape, illuminating the way up the stairs to the front door.

Luke accelerated and we pushed through the waves past the opening to the far side of the island. He skirted the rocks, looking for a promising spot that he'd found on the satellite photo. Halfway around the island, there it was—a small indentation in the cliff face, marked by a narrow triangle of sand that led to an even narrower crevice further in.

Seeing it now, the climb looked more difficult than it had on the photograph. Luke dropped anchor and joined us on deck. Angie reemerged from below and stood next to him. Her hair was mussed and her complexion had a greenish cast, but otherwise she looked none the worse for wear.

Eve checked her phone one more time. "He's at the marina. That gives us approximately two hours to make it onto the island and get inside the house, depending on whether he takes his time leaving.

"As soon as we have a visual on the house," she continued, "Kitten's going to set up her laptop and hack into the security system. From there we should be able to locate whatever we need to avoid, like cameras and such. Darwin, once Kitten's got that under control, you do your thing. Check to make sure the caretaker house isn't occupied first, and then run a loop of the perimeter. Both of you guys should check in periodically."

Both Kitten and Darwin nodded that they understood.

"Luke will lead us up the cliff to the house," Eve added. "If the place is locked, Kate brought along a set of picks."

"And what's your role, Angie?" I asked drily.

She smiled and shrugged. "I'm just along for the ride, sugar."

Not likely.

Luke walked to the stern and hauled on the rope attached to the inflatable to bring it alongside. "Lady D's staying with the boat, in case the weather turns again."

I followed Darwin into the cabin to retrieve the waterproof bags with our equipment. We handed the bags to Luke and Angie, who were already on board the smaller boat, and they stowed them in the bow. Eve climbed in, followed by Kitten and myself. Darwin jumped in last.

"Don't forget your radios," he said. Everyone slipped on earpieces and took out the radios to turn them on.

Luke started the motor and Darwin pushed off the larger boat using the tip of an oar. Lady D gave us a thumbs-up and disappeared into the cabin. My heart was thumping in time with the outboard engine as I covertly studied everyone on board, wondering what would happen next.

And how I was going to get out of this alive.

TWENTY-NINE

LUKE BROUGHT THE inflatable about and steered toward the tiny patch of sand. His first attempt overshot the mark and we had to use the oars to keep us from running aground on a set of partially submerged rocks. The second try put us on the sand. The six of us climbed out and Eve, Kitten, and I distributed the equipment amongst ourselves while Luke and Darwin dragged the boat further onto the sand. Angie stood to one side, smoking a cigarette and supervising, apparently.

Since Luke was the experienced climber of the bunch, Darwin gave him the night vision goggles and we followed him into the crevice. Angie hung back, staying behind everyone else. I assumed it was so none of us would have a clear shot at her. I wouldn't have tried to kill her, though. Not when I didn't know who was loyal to whom.

Luke was good. He found handholds where I didn't think any existed. To her credit, Angie didn't utter a word of protest, climbing gamely along with the others.

The only sounds were occasional gasps of exertion as we traversed farther onto the island, climbing higher and higher until the terrain flattened. Once we cleared the cliff I sprawled on my back to catch my breath, thankful to have that part of the trip over.

Kitten took out her laptop and booted it up. She typed a few lines and waited. "Got it," she said, referring to Dobson's Wi-Fi. She typed in a line of code and hit enter. "Comin' atcha." Eve checked her phone.

"Password?" Eve asked.

"You're not gonna believe this. It's his birthdate followed by his age." Kitten rolled her eyes at the simple security code. "Dude," she said to the sky as though Dobson could hear her. "Just because your house is in the middle of nowhere doesn't mean you shouldn't have a good password."

Eve typed in Dobson's password and paused for a moment, watching her screen. Then she said, "He's wheels up." She slid the cell back into her jacket and zipped the pocket closed. "The climb took thirty minutes. Pretty good, since we planned on forty-five. From our calculations, it shouldn't take more than twenty minutes to reach the house. That gives us a little more than an hour to get inside and set up."

Luke led the way. We followed him single file through the forest, stopping occasionally to check the GPS on his phone. Far from civilization, the night sky was awash with brilliant stars, tiny pinpoints of light punctuating the deepening indigo blue above. Somewhere an owl hooted. The only other sounds were the footfalls of six people on a mission.

Fifteen minutes later, the lights of the estate winked through the trees. Eve held up her fist, signaling us to stop. She'd been eager to learn hand signals and had been a quick study. Kitten hauled out her laptop once again and walked over to sit on a large rock beneath a big leaf maple. A few minutes later, she'd found her way into Dobson's security.

"I count nine cameras. Looks like a do-it-yourself package."

"Which means?"

Kitten shrugged. "That he's a cheapskate, which isn't unusual for a rich guy. Also, they come with remote access, so he could have someone monitoring the feeds. He's also got motion sensors near the doors and windows, and inside the house. Let me see if I can access that system." Her fingers were a blur as she typed. Soon, a smile lit her face. "Piece of cake. I'll reactivate the alarm as soon as he gets to the front door so he won't be suspicious. Make sure you guys freeze when that happens. We don't want to set off any bells."

"How much time will we have once he's inside?" I asked.

"I'll isolate five-minute loops for all nine cameras, which will run indefinitely, but if someone's monitoring the screens it's possible they could notice after the third or fourth loop. It depends on how closely they're watching." She checked the screens. "There isn't much activity now, but there will be when he gets here. I'll override the decoy loops from the time of his arrival until he goes inside the house. The three of you and Darwin will need to be out of camera view until you hear from me. That way if someone is monitoring the house, then everything will still look normal."

"What's your professional opinion, sugar?" Angie stood behind her, looking at the screen. "Y'all think he's got someone on the outside?"

Kitten frowned and shook her head. "It's not like I do this on a regular basis. But, if he's as relaxed about his home security as he is about his Wi-Fi, then you might have nothing to worry about. Looking at the simplicity of his passwords it's possible he's become complacent because of the estate's location and checks the screens himself when he thinks about it. On the other hand, he could have left the monitoring up to someone else just because he could. He's got enough money to outsource it.

"Worst case scenario, there's someone watching the screens who thinks something's fishy and they call to see if he's all right. If Dobson doesn't answer the phone, it could trigger a call to police. Add in response time to the island and you've got yourself about an hour and a half unless they send out a helicopter, which isn't realistic. Not unless it's obvious there's a crime being committed."

"Let's hope that's enough time."

Eve glanced at Darwin. "You're up."

Luke handed Darwin the NVGs and he slid them on.

"Remember, check the caretaker cottage first," Angie reminded him. "We don't want any surprises."

"Roger that." Darwin gave her a salute and then disappeared into the forest.

"Is there some way to see what's happening in real time?" I asked Kitten. "Or are we stuck with the loops?"

Kitten turned her laptop toward me. On the screen were nine squares showing interior and exterior views. Each of those nine squares had a smaller square in the lower left corner.

"The smaller squares are the loops running in the background and are what anyone monitoring the screens will see. The larger squares are the actual feeds." Just then, a glowing figure moved into one of the larger frames. "There's Darwin."

"So the cameras have night vision capabilities."

"Yep."

Darwin walked along the perimeter and disappeared. A moment later, he showed up in one of the other squares. A majority of the surveillance system monitored the immediate exterior of the house and main interior rooms, like the living room and kitchen. Only three cameras were dedicated to the estate's perimeter, although each of them encompassed a large swath of the grounds.

Eve, Luke, Angie, and I waited until Darwin gave us the all-clear, and we made our way toward the house. I motioned to Luke to watch the front while Eve and I walked up the wide slate steps to the front door. Angie hung back with Luke.

"Are we still good?" I said into the mic.

"Yep." Kitten's soft voice came over the mic. "The loop is on and the alarm's disabled."

With Eve at my back, I tried the handle. It was locked. I pulled on a pair of nitrile gloves, slid out my set of lock picks, and went to work. My right hand shook slightly and my heart thudded in my ears, both of which contributed to my taking longer to open the door than I'd intended. Good thing I wasn't interested in a career of breaking and entering.

After what seemed like much too long, there was a faint click as the lock tumbled open. With a relieved sigh, I pushed the door wide.

"Wait." The edge in Kitten's voice brought me up short. Eve and I froze. "Darwin's acting weird…" There was a pause and then she whispered, "Darwin, what are you *doing*?"

"That's a *good* boy," Darwin said, nervousness lacing his words. "Take it easy, buddy…"

"Shit." Kitten's voice came over the air. "It's a dog. A big one."

Alarmed, I looked at Eve. The whites of her eyes were visible in the amber glow of the patio lights.

"That means…" Eve didn't finish the sentence. We both knew that meant there had to be someone on the island to take care of the dog.

"Yeah." Gravel scattered behind us. I turned in time to see Luke disappear around the side of the house. Angie moved just enough so that she was in deep shadow. "Looks like Luke is headed your way, Darwin," I whispered into the mic.

"That's it, *good* doggy." Darwin's voice had lowered and sounded more like a coo than a desperate attempt at placating an angry canine.

"Seriously?" The disbelief in Kitten's voice would have been comical if the stakes weren't so high. "He's petting the damn dog."

"What?" the rest of us said in unison.

"How the hell did you do that, Darwin?" Kitten demanded.

A soft chuckle floated across the mic. "I remembered what Kate told us about being chased by dogs at that drug dealer's place and thought it couldn't hurt to bring along some treats."

"What are you going to do once the dog's done with those treats?" I asked. "You need to get out of there, now."

"No worries. In a minute, this puppy's gonna be taking a nice, long nap. I added a couple of doggy downers to the snacks."

Eve and I glanced at each other, and I shook my head in disbelief. "You need to go find the dog's handler.

Have you got anything like that for humans?" I said it as a joke, not expecting a response.

"Isn't that what guns are for?" he replied.

"You're kidding, right, Darwin?"

There was a little too long of a pause before he answered. "Of course I am. What do you think I'm going to do? Kill the caretaker?"

I glanced back at Angie, barely noticeable in the darkness except for the gleam of her eyes.

At that point, all bets were off.

THIRTY

LUKE JOINED US in the foyer a few minutes later. He and Darwin had carried the dog to a gazebo at the edge of the property and left him sleeping under a bench. Darwin continued his reconnaissance, insisting that he would keep to the shadows so as not to raise suspicions if someone was in the caretaker's cottage.

"Do you believe him?" Eve asked Luke, off mic.

He shrugged. "I'm not sure, to be honest. He seemed whacked. He smeared mud on his face and had a scarf tied around his head like in that old Stallone movie."

"You mean *Rambo?*" I asked.

"That's the one."

"That can't be good."

"I've known Darwin a long time," Eve insisted. "He's never been interested in action movies or guns, or anything like that. I can't believe he's going to turn into some vigilante."

"I think we need to talk," I said. Angie hovered nearby as I pulled Eve aside and recounted the conversation Darwin and I had on the boat, and that he thought she was good with his decision. After the initial shock, she still didn't believe he'd be a problem.

"Darwin's about as dangerous as a puppy. He might think he's capable of taking revenge for Sean, but he's never killed anyone. I don't think he's going to start now."

Angie cleared her throat. Eve and I looked at her, waiting for her input. "All this talkin' about killin' is fine and dandy, but can we get this show on the road? Time's a wastin'."

Eve glanced at her phone. "She's right. Dobson will be here soon. Let's get on with it."

Using the Maglite from my backpack to light the way, we moved through the house. Dobson's taste ran to midcentury modern—a pair of Eames chairs and matching sofa had pride of place in the living room, accompanied by a low oval coffee table and floor lamps with Jetson-style shades. There was even a vintage orange metal cone fireplace in one corner.

Angie stopped to admire the paintings in the living room and foyer. I recognized a Rothko and a Pollock, two of my favorite modernists. One, with a white background, had what looked like a bunch of colorful amoebas on it. I squinted at the distinct signature in the lower right corner. Miró. It looked like Dobson had invested heavily in some very valuable art.

The open-concept kitchen was a Michelin chef's dream. I counted three ovens and two large Sub-Zero refrigerators, with an eight-burner gas stove. The eat-in counter seated twelve, lit by expensive-looking pendant lamps.

We continued down another hallway, this one quite a bit longer, past a bathroom that could host the Academy

Awards and an office with a curved flat-screen television and an elegant pool table. The master bedroom was similar to the living area. It was like standing in a fifties time warp, with every stick of furniture a midcentury modern masterpiece.

Luke went to work securing a video camera to a mini tripod, which he then placed on the dresser across from the bed. He angled it toward a chair that Eve had placed next to the window. Eve sat in the chair while Luke adjusted the picture. Angie did what she did best: stand nearby and supervise.

I looked over Eve's shoulder at the small screen. She checked the remote connection on her phone, zooming in and out to test the framing.

"Mary had a little lamb."

As she spoke, a colorful graphic displayed her voice's audio level. Satisfied, she pocketed the phone while Luke rearranged a few items on the dresser in order to obscure the camera. He then stowed the bag holding everything needed to restrain Dobson. All we had to do now was wait.

"We have incoming." The edge was back in Kitten's voice.

Startled, I asked, "Dobson's here?" I hadn't heard the floatplane approach.

"No. It's someone else. A woman. I don't know where she came from. She just appeared from the woods."

"Where's Darwin?" Eve asked.

Before Kitten could answer, there was a loud crash, followed by a scream. I was out the bedroom door in a second, headed for the front entrance. Just past the kitchen, I skidded to a halt. Darwin had a young woman in a stranglehold. Her face white, she whimpered and squeezed her eyes shut, her hands wrapped around his forearm.

"Darwin. Let her go." I put as much steel as I could into my voice. The woman tried to look at me, but Darwin jerked her head back with a vicious twist of his arm.

"I can't." He shook his head, his eyes dark. "She's going to ruin everything."

"Darwin," I said and took a step toward him, my voice calm, acutely aware of Angie's and Luke's presence behind me as well as the gun in my holster. "She won't ruin anything. We're not here to hurt anyone, remember?"

Darwin swiveled until the woman was between us.

"Stop." He nodded at me. "Don't come any closer." He glanced down at the woman he held in his grip. "Who are you?" he demanded.

The woman whimpered again and shook her head, tears streaming down her face. "What have you done to Brutus?" she cried. Darwin choked her words short. I winced, hoping the pressure of his forearm didn't damage her windpipe. Or worse.

"Shut up. Or you'll end up like the dog." His face now a dark red, Darwin clamped his mouth closed, making his jaw flex. Dried mud flaked from his cheeks onto the tile floor. The woman fell silent. Angie slid her hand underneath her jacket. She was going for her gun. I'd have to think of something, quick, or both Darwin and the young woman would be dead.

"Darwin." Eve's voice floated through the earpiece. "You don't have to do this. Sean wouldn't want you to."

Darwin closed his eyes for a moment. "Yes he would. He'd want to avenge all of the people who died because of Dobson."

"But not with an innocent life," she countered, walking into the kitchen so he could see her. "If you kill this woman, you're no better than Dobson."

Darwin stared at the back of the woman's head, and I held my breath, unable to guess what would happen next. Seconds ticked by. The tension in the room was palpable. Angie's gaze never left the two of them.

Finally, Darwin let go of the woman and stepped back. A collective sigh of relief rippled through the kitchen. Angie's shoulders lowered a fraction, and her hand dropped to her side. I hurried to where the woman was hunched over and rubbing her throat, gasping for air.

"Are you all right?"

She nodded and slowly straightened, wariness evident in her eyes.

"Who are you people?" She smoothed her hair back with a shaky hand. "And where's Brutus?"

"The dog is fine. He's been given a sedative to keep him quiet." I led her into the living room and lowered her onto the couch. "As for who we are, the less you know the better."

"You'll never get away with whatever it is you're doing. There are security cameras everywhere." A look of fear crossed her features and she stared at me. "Unless you're here to…" The question hung heavy between us.

"We're not here to kill anyone."

"Then what?"

"Let's just say we want a confession."

"A confession." She frowned and shook her head. "From Mick?" A moment passed before the spark of understanding lit her eyes. She sighed. "I really liked this job," she said, her voice quiet.

"I'm afraid we're going to have to keep you out of sight. At least until we're finished here." I stepped back, giving her room. She stood and smoothed her hands down the front of her jeans.

"He'll wonder why certain things haven't been done."

"Like what?"

"Like turning on the exterior lights and the lights to the dock."

"Good to know." I studied her face. "What's your name?"

"Amelia."

The name on the terse emails Dobson sent. "Well, Amelia, is there anything else we should do?"

She nodded.

"I usually have a snack waiting for him on the kitchen counter."

That didn't sound unusual. She could use this as an opportunity to signal to Dobson that something was wrong, though. "Okay. Why don't you go ahead and prepare whatever it is you usually fix for him, and then we'll head back to one of the other rooms where we can keep an eye on things."

Amelia nodded and walked into the kitchen, where she set out a small dish of olives and cheese from the fridge, along with a box of crackers, a chilled bottle of white wine, and a wineglass. Angie and Eve watched her closely, while Luke and Darwin disappeared down the hall. I walked to the opposite side of the room and flicked on the lights for the front of the house.

"Where do I turn on the dock lights?"

Amelia pointed to a set of light switches to the right of the door. "Second one in," she said. I flicked the switch and two floodlights blinked on below the house, illuminating the dock and dark water beyond.

"Is that it?" I asked again.

She nodded. I joined her in the kitchen, and we followed the others to the back of the house. I was surprised that she wasn't more protective of her employer and said so. She appeared to think over my observation and then stopped in the hallway.

"Can I ask you something?"

I nodded.

"Does this have anything to do with the overdoses in Seattle?"

The answer must have showed on my face, because she hurriedly explained. "One day when I was cleaning his study, I ran across a bunch of clippings from the news. Every one of them was an article or post about the fentanyl overdoses, and how no one could figure out the source of the contaminated supply." She shrugged. "At the time, I didn't really think anything of it. I just assumed he was interested in the story because that's the business he's in. But now..." She looked at me, the unasked question in her eyes.

"I can tell you that the plan is not to kill him, or you. I can also tell you that by the time we're finished here, you'll understand."

My answer must have satisfied her, because she allowed me to lead her down the hall to the guest bedroom.

"Luke, could you bring some rope and the roll of duct tape to the guest bedroom?"

"Be there in a flash."

After securing Amelia to the bed, I turned on the TV that was attached to the wall and slipped a pair of noise-canceling headphones over her ears so she could watch TV in peace. The headphones would also make sure she couldn't hear anything if they got rough with Dobson.

I hoped it wouldn't come to that.

A piece of duct tape over her mouth ensured she wouldn't call out to warn Dobson. Shutting the door behind me, I crossed the hall to the master bedroom to join Luke, Angie, and Eve, who were all waiting in the gigantic master bath. I had hoped Eve would send Darwin away from the house and back to the forest to keep Kitten company.

No such luck.

Darwin was curled up in the oval bathtub, his back to the room. I glanced at Eve. She motioned for me to follow her into the bedroom.

"I wanted to keep an eye on him. It doesn't feel right to let him loose out there," she said.

"Good point. We're still on the same page, right?" I watched her carefully, alert for signs of deception. "No murder, just get him on video confessing to releasing the drugs, whatever that takes."

Eve nodded. "Yeah. Of course. I don't want to be an accessory to murder and have that hanging over my head for the rest of my life. I've asked Luke to watch him while we're dealing with Dobson."

"That's good, because as long as he's part of this crew he's going to be a liability."

"I know. And he knows we know. He'll be fine, I'm sure of it. He's still hurting about Sean. We all are."

"There's hurting and then there's wanting to strike out at what's hurting. I have a feeling that Darwin is firmly in the latter camp."

"Maybe. But I have a feeling that Angie is…"

"Angie's what?" Angie asked, walking in the door. Her look said she wasn't very happy that she caught us talking about her. Eve opened her mouth to reply but was interrupted by the sound of Kitten's voice over the radio.

"Dobson's here." The faint sound of a low-flying plane could be heard echoing off the rocks in the tiny harbor.

The three of us went back into the bathroom and closed the door.

"We're in position," Eve said into the mic.

"Got it. I'll let you know when he's inside the house."

THIRTY-ONE

WE WAITED IN silence as Kitten gave us a play-by-play of Dobson's movements.

"He's at the door. Looks like he's got a bag of groceries in his hand."

"Taking out his key."

"He's inside, next to the alarm."

There was the faint sound of an alarm beeping, and then it stopped. The front door slammed.

"I restarted the loops."

"What about the wine and food on the counter?" I asked. "If someone's monitoring, the counter will be empty."

"Oops. Yep. No problem. I'll reset it now."

We waited in silence while she worked.

"Okay. Got it." There was a pause. "He set the groceries on the kitchen counter. Now he's pouring himself a glass of wine. You guys are free to move about the cabin."

"Let's go," Eve said and eased the door open.

We moved through the bedroom into the hall. Luke and Darwin went first, then Eve, then me. Angie came last, as usual. The gun I was wearing reminded me that I had the element of surprise in case things got out of hand.

I followed them into the hallway next to the kitchen. Luke and Darwin stepped into the room.

"Wha—who the hell are you?" The surprise in Dobson's voice sounded more like outrage than fear. I nodded at Eve and we joined the guys. Angie stayed behind, out of sight. Wide-eyed, Dobson looked from one to the other of us. He wore a white button-down Oxford shirt, and his narrow shoulders sloped to a rounded belly that spilled over a pair of baggy jeans, ending with nubby socks and leather sandals. It was kind of a letdown. For some reason, my imagination had painted him as more sinister.

At least more fit.

"Who the hell are you?" When he didn't get a fast enough answer, he added, "I'm calling the police." He started to reach into his front pocket.

Angie rounded the corner, a .45 in her hand, and cleared her throat.

His gaze fell to the barrel of the gun aimed at his chest and he blinked twice, as though hoping the scene would disappear. He pulled his hand back empty and raised them both in the air. Beads of sweat broke out on his forehead. "Look, I've got money. Take what you want." With a panicked expression, his gaze shifted around the room, landing first on a sculpture, then a glass bowl, and last on the paintings.

"We don't want your money." Darwin's narrowed eyes and clenched fists gave the impression he was having a hard time controlling his anger. Luke took a step closer to him.

"Then what are you doing here?" He glanced behind us. "What have you done with Brutus? And Amelia?"

"Don't worry about them. Worry about yourself, murderer."

Eve shot Darwin a sharp look and he clamped his lips closed. "Luke, tie him up," she said.

Luke walked around to the other side of the counter and pulled Dobson's hands behind his back, securing his wrists with a zip tie. Dobson didn't struggle.

"Listen, whatever it is you want, and I mean anything, just tell me. We can work this out. Obviously, I'm a very rich man."

"Well, darlin', that's somethin' we might discuss later, if you cooperate," Angie drawled.

Luke pushed him toward the hallway, with Darwin close behind. As he passed by me, a flicker of hope sprang into his eyes.

"You people will never get away with this. You know that this is illegal and you'll go to jail, right? Tell them. Tell them now." He jutted his chin at his captors like a bulldog.

When I didn't reply, he searched each of our faces, looking for an ally.

He didn't find one.

Luke and Darwin led him into the master bedroom and ordered him into the chair by the window. He sat down, his eyes filled with conflicting emotions. Disbelief. Fear. Hope. Anger. Luke and Darwin strapped him in with more zip ties and then stepped away.

Eve walked over to the bed, picked up a large envelope, and stood in front of him. He winced at her expression. She removed the contents, which turned out to be large color photographs. She rifled through them before she decided on one, which she flipped around to show him. His gaze trailed from her face to the photograph. Confusion filled his eyes.

"Why are you showing me this?"

Without replying, Eve shuffled the photographs and showed him another one. He gave it a quick glance and looked away. She did the same again. This time, Dobson refused to look.

"Look at the picture, dammit." Eve's voice shook. She took a step closer and shoved the photo in his face. He resolutely stared past the image, refusing to see it. "Look." She ground out the word. When he didn't respond, she slapped him hard across the face. The sharp crack of her palm hitting his cheek split through the room. He glared at her. With a frustrated cry, she threw the envelope and its contents to the floor. I glanced at the top picture.

It showed a man lying on a gurney, eyes closed, skin as white as the sheet underneath his head. Vomit ran down the side of his face, staining the pillow.

"That's Sean," she said, her voice quivering with emotion. "Sean was amazing. He was talented, handsome, kind, and he loved people." Tears slid down her face as she looked at the ceiling and wiped her eyes. I glanced at Darwin. He stared into space, repetitively bumping his fist against his thigh, his jaw flexing.

"And you know what happened to Sean? Loving, generous, talented Sean? Hmm?" She grabbed him by the chin, forcing him to look at her. "*You killed him*, that's what."

Disgusted, Eve let go and bent down to pick up one of the photographs. She held it in her hands and stared at it, grief playing across her face. Slowly raising her head, she looked up at Dobson. "He died because he took your drug. The one your company created. He died because he passed out and no one was there to roll him over onto his side—" Tears streamed down her face. "No one was there to help him. He suffocated on his own vomit." Her voice trailed off and she started to sob. My heart went out to her. It was a horrifying way to die.

Dobson had the grace to look ashamed. At least, that's what I thought.

I was wrong.

"There's no evidence that I or Pro-Pharma did anything wrong. So a couple of the pills ended up on the streets of Seattle and a few junkies died. Big fucking deal. The majority of the batch went to the Democratic Republic of Congo, not the US."

Startled by his callous confession, I stared at Dobson. "And how is that even remotely acceptable?"

Dobson leveled his gaze at me. "That's what junkies do." His tone suggested he was speaking to a three-year-old. "They overdose. Survival of the fittest. As for shipping the drugs overseas, it's a win-win. They get cheap drugs, and Pro-Pharma recoups part of their investment. The board was all for it when I explained how much they'd make from an essentially worthless shipment." When I didn't say anything, he frowned and narrowed his eyes. "Obviously, you don't get how the world actually works. What the hell are you? Some liberal, pansy ass political group upset because Big Pharma made a little money off some worthless junkies?" The derisive sneer on his face was enough reason to pistol-whip him.

I restrained the impulse.

"I'll bet you guys fancy yourselves as some kind of vigilante squad, am I right?" he continued, digging himself an even deeper hole. "What are you going to do, save the world from the big, bad corporations? Some kind of wannabe Anonymous group?"

My anger got the better of me. I checked to make sure I wasn't in view of the camera.

"Now, Mick," I began. "Can I call you Mick?" I smiled, all friendly-like. "I know quite a bit about how the cartels in Mexico work, spent a lot of time with them, actually. And what I'm hearing from you is pretty gosh-darn similar. They don't care squat about their customers except to hook them. You've heard about the power of free, right?" I raised my eyebrows. "Well, of course you have. Your company is most generous when it comes to giving out free samples to doctors." I shook my head in mock concern. "The cartels took a page out of Big Pharma's playbook. They send the subgrade stuff to third world countries, keeping the higher-grade drugs for their US customers. Although, from what I understand, even that's changing."

"You can't compare what my company does to a criminal enterprise." Dobson was getting angry. His face a deep red, he strained forward in his chair.

"Actually, I can. The people in this room have lost someone they loved, your so-called junkies, to the toxic painkillers your company created." Everyone except Angie. I looked for her, but she was nowhere in sight. I returned my attention to Dobson. "Whether you intended the drugs to end up on the streets of Seattle or not, you're still liable for the deaths. You didn't destroy the contaminated painkillers. I'm not sure, but I think Pro-Pharma's image as a caring, progressive corporation will suffer when we tell the world your company thinks nothing of sending dangerous, toxic drugs to unwitting patients in Africa."

"You won't. We'll sic our lawyers on you for libel so fast, the speed of light will seem slow. You'll be buried in paperwork for a decade. Not to mention the enormous legal fees. I see bankruptcy followed by a long prison term in your future. In all of your futures." He nodded at everyone in the room. Then he looked back at me with a look that said *top that.*

"Maybe so, but I think you've already implicated yourself and your company enough to initiate an investigation."

"You idiots are dreaming." Dobson rolled his eyes. "No one will believe a violent vigilante force against one of the top CEOs in the Northwest. Shit, with the FDA stretched as thin as it is, I could probably distribute arsenic as some kind of fucking miracle cure, and no one would be the wiser."

Eve stepped forward and turned her phone so he could see it. Dobson's voice came over the speaker.

"There's no evidence that I or Pro-Pharma did anything wrong. So a couple of the pills ended up on the streets of Seattle and a few junkies died. Big fucking deal. The majority of the batch went to the Democratic Republic of Congo, not the US."

Dobson's eyes widened and he stared at Eve.

"We have the rest on video. What was it you said? *That's what junkies do. They die.*" She shook her head in mock sympathy.

"What are you going to do with that?" he asked, staring at the phone. His voice had a slight tremor.

Eve shrugged. "That depends on you."

"What do you want?"

Quite the change in attitude. I was surprised he didn't get whiplash.

"For starters, you will resign as CEO of Pro-Pharma, but before you do, you will recall the drugs from the

Democratic Republic of the Congo and convince the board to earmark a percentage of earned profits to go to the victims and their families. If the board disagrees, then you will pay the survivors out of pocket."

"Or what?"

"Or we make the video available online. I guarantee with our connections it'll go viral." Eve smiled. This time, it was her look that said *top that*.

"Fuck you. It won't work. No one will believe you. Pro-Pharma has the best reputation in the business. It took years of public relations to build it. You won't be able to destroy my company that easily. Even with a video."

"He's right. It won't be enough." His jaw set, Darwin circled behind Dobson, fists clenched. Luke moved to restrain him, but Darwin shook him off. He reached inside his jacket and pulled out a knife. Before anyone could stop him, Darwin grabbed Dobson by the hair and held the knife to his neck.

Eve's sharp intake of breath told me she hadn't known he had a weapon. With everyone's attention on Darwin and Dobson, I unzipped my coat to make it easier to get to my gun, but hesitated. From where I stood there was no clear shot, and I didn't trust myself to "wing" him. I didn't want to shoot either one. I understood Darwin's anguish and didn't think he deserved to die. My preference to see Dobson alive was entirely selfish. I wanted him to live long enough to pay for his sins.

"Darwin." Luke's voice cut through the tension in the room. "Give me the knife. You don't want to do this." He took a step closer to him and held out his hand for the knife. Darwin shook his head.

"No, Luke. I can't. I can't let this asshole live a second longer. Not after what he did to Sean."

"Baby, Sean's gone—there's nothing we can do about that." Eve softened her voice, but stayed where she was. "He wouldn't want this."

Darwin shook his head again, the agony of loss clear on his face. Tears and confusion filled his eyes.

No one moved. The knife shook in Darwin's trembling hand. It looked like he might have been rethinking his decision, but I couldn't be sure. I moved to get into a better position when there was a disturbance near the doorway. A loud popping sound followed.

A small dark hole appeared on Darwin's forehead. The knife fell from his hand as his eyes glazed over and he crumpled to the ground.

Thirty-Two

NO!" EVE AND Luke both lunged for Darwin. A trickle of blood oozed from the bullet wound. I whirled to see Angie with a silenced gun in her hand, a pissed-off expression on her face. Amelia was behind her, a stunned look on her face.

"You killed him," Eve cried. She cradled Darwin's head in her lap as tears coursed down her cheeks. Luke felt his neck for a pulse. Evidently not finding one, he closed his eyes and hung his head.

"He was a loose end," Angie snapped. "I told you I would do whatever was necessary to keep this plan moving forward. Luke, get the knife and give it to me." Moving slowly, Luke did as he was told. His hand shook as he gave it to her. She slid the knife into her coat pocket and turned her attention to Dobson. "Now where the fuck is the Picasso?"

Dobson's poker face barely cracked. The only indication of fear were the beads of sweat rolling down his face and the stains at his armpits.

His gaze flickered, landing on Amelia. "Amelia. What—"

"Don't say another word," Amelia said. She visibly stiffened and glared at him.

"Look, if this is about vacation time—"

"Fuck you." Amelia advanced, her fists clenched tight. "This was *never* about vacation days. This is about you sitting on your flabby white ass while the people around you work themselves to death trying to keep their jobs." She took another step closer, her breath coming in explosive bursts.

"This is about you not giving a shit who your mistakes hurt, just as long as you can have your precious art, and your expensive wines, and your—"

A knowing look filled Dobson's eyes. "You're jealous," he mused. "And you feel entitled. That's it, isn't it?"

Amelia frowned. "What? No."

"Fucking Millennials. Always thinking they're entitled to everything. Well, I've got news for you. You have to work for shit. Get it? It isn't just going to drop out of the sky and fall into your waiting arms." He snorted. "And sure as hell nobody's going to give it to you just because you think you deserve it. Special little snowflake, my ass. I worked hard for this house, the art. My wine. And here you are, Miss Crybaby, upset because your life hasn't turned out like you planned. Waah." Dobson screwed his face into a pitiful rendition of a baby squalling.

"You're one to talk. You didn't work hard for any of this." Amelia gestured at the surroundings, her voice ratcheting up a notch. "You fucked people to get your money, that's what you did."

Dobson's face turned crimson. "And you're not doing that now? The woman with the gun over there just asked me where the Picasso was. Isn't that why you let these criminals in?"

"I didn't let them in. But I did make a deal with her." She nodded at Angie. "For my life. I'm not taking the painting."

Angie raised her gun and aimed it at Dobson.

"No, darlin'. *I'm* the one who's gonna take the paintin' just as soon as you tell me where it is."

Dobson leaned back in his chair, apparently too arrogant to be afraid. I wanted to grab him by the shoulders and shake some sense into him. Did he think Angie wouldn't kill him? Darwin was just the appetizer, as far as she was concerned.

"Fine." Angie pointed the gun at his foot and fired. Dobson's screams filled the room as he rocked back in his chair. With everyone's attention on Dobson, it was now or never. I reached for my pistol.

"Hurts, doesn't it?" She turned her head and smiled sweetly at me. "Someone taught me that little maneuver a few years back."

I froze, my hand halfway to the gun.

Angie refocused her attention on Dobson, who was now gripping the arms of the chair and hyperventilating, eyes squeezed shut to block out the pain. I let my arm drop to my side.

There'd be another opportunity.

There had to be.

"Now where's the Picasso?"

Breathing hard, Dobson opened his eyes and stared down at his bloody foot, pain and alarm obvious on his face. "I'm bleeding. Sweet Jesus, I'm bleeding." His voice was one beat shy of hysterics.

Angie's look of distaste brought him up short.

"My goodness. Men surely are sissified in this part of the country." She took a deep breath and let it go with a quick glance at the ceiling as though some supreme deity would suddenly appear from the heavens and rescue her from this unmanly place. She refocused and aimed at his other foot. "Where. Is. The. Picasso."

Dobson winced in anticipation of the bullet. His voice cracking, the words came out in a jumble. "A secret door in the guest bedroom. Use the keypad on the thermostat. Five-two-three-four."

A smile curved Angie's lips. "Perfect." She glanced at Amelia. "Sugar, would you mind goin' and tryin' to access his li'l hidin' place?"

Without looking at Dobson, Amelia nodded and walked out of the room.

Angie waggled the gun barrel for emphasis. "We'll just wait here until Miss Amelia gets back. Luke, would you be a doll and make sure she actually does what I asked?"

Luke turned from staring at Dobson's bloody foot and focused on Angie. His eyes were glazed, like he was in shock.

"Be quick now, hon."

The look on his face told me he knew enough not to argue. He started for the door.

Still holding Darwin's head in her lap, Eve glared at Angie, mistrust in her eyes.

"You don't have to do what she says, Luke."

The corners of Angie's mouth twitched in an apparent attempt at suppressing a smile. "Oh, now darlin', I do believe he *does*." She jiggled the gun. "What is it they say? He, or she, as the case may be, who holds the gun, holds the power."

Eve glanced at Luke. He paused for a moment, but then walked out the door.

When Luke had gone, Angie moved further back against the dresser so she had a full view of the room and everyone in it. Keeping her eyes on us, she grabbed the cell phone off the tripod and slid it into her pocket. My mind raced for a way to either disarm Angie or put her out of commission, but another opportunity didn't present itself. Her sharp gaze roamed the space, flitting from Dobson to Eve to me and back again. I wasn't certain of her plans, but I didn't want to give her another reason to kill me.

I had a feeling I knew what she was going to do, and that feeling wasn't good.

Everyone there was a witness to the art theft, not to mention Darwin's murder. No way would she allow nonessential personnel to survive. I calculated how many of us she'd need to get the paintings off the island and came up with one.

Luke.

Once the frames had been discarded, two people could easily carry the canvases to the inflatable and then transfer them to the cabin cruiser. With his knowledge of the boat and the waterways, Luke was all she'd need to get back to Seattle.

That meant the rest of us were expendable. Eve, Amelia, Kitten, myself, and Lady D were all in danger. There had to be a way to let everyone know. But how?

It was then I realized I hadn't heard from Kitten in a while. I checked my radio. The battery was still charged. Why didn't she say something when Angie shot Darwin? Was she aware of Angie's plans? Part of the deal?

I tried to catch Eve's eye, but Angie noticed and turned her attention on me.

"You doin' all right there, darlin'?"

"Jus' fine, honey child," I replied, smiling at the way my mocking tone pissed her off.

"Then why don't you just hand over the li'l ol' gun you have in that shoulder holster, hmm?"

"The what?" My heart sank into my stomach. I'd blown my only chance. She knew I'd been reaching for my gun.

"The gun." She wiggled the fingers of one hand while aiming the .45 at me with the other. "Now."

Reluctantly, I reached for my weapon. Fantasies of getting off a shot before she could respond warred with reality. There was no way I could out-shoot her. Especially since she was right there and in position.

I handed her my gun. "Did you expect me to be unarmed?"

"Of course not." She slid the Beretta into her coat pocket. "I'd have been disappointed if you weren't."

"Then why take it? I thought we were in this together."

She was about to reply when Amelia and Luke walked back into the room. Amelia's eyes were wide with excitement and her cheeks were flushed.

"We found it," she said breathlessly. "The Picasso's there."

"Yeah, along with about thirty other paintings," Luke added.

A slow smile spread across Angie's face. "Well, that's just swell, isn't it?" She turned to Dobson. "Looks like it's your lucky day."

Dobson grimaced at his foot and then looked at Angie. "What do you mean? You put a fucking bullet in my foot."

"I'm not gonna torture you, hon." Angie raised her gun and shot him. Twice. Two perfectly placed rounds in the center of his chest. Dobson slumped forward.

Damn. Two down. Five to go. She was systematically picking off anyone who had no value to her. Dobson had outlived his usefulness now that she knew where she could find the prize she sought.

Where was Kitten?

I wasn't sure how long Angie had been absent from the room when Eve was interrogating Dobson. Kitten had outlived her usefulness as soon as Dobson had entered the house and she'd restarted the video feed. Had she killed her, too?

Angie wasn't leaving anything to chance. Lady D's death was likely once Angie and Luke were on board the *Olympic Dream*. That left Eve, Amelia, and me.

Instead of seeking revenge as a vigilante group, by the end of this evening we'd all be dead.

Luke would just live a few hours longer.

Amelia started forward, but then stopped. "You— you…" She sank to her knees at the sight of her now-dead employer.

Angie looked expectantly at Amelia, waiting for her to continue. "I what? Promised not to kill him?" She shrugged. "Well, golly, I guess I lied, then, didn't I?" She shook her hair back and gestured for her to get up. "Time's a wastin'. We really do need to move this li'l operation along."

By the look on Amelia's face, the same realization I'd had was dawning on her—that she'd essentially made a deal with the devil. Would Angie make good on any arrangement she made with her? Knowing the assassin's track record, it was highly doubtful, and Amelia was obviously just now figuring that out. She slowly climbed to her feet. Luke remained in the background, uncertainty obvious in his eyes. Angie gave Eve a sharp look.

"You too, darlin'."

Eve gently laid Darwin's head on the floor. With one last look at her dead friend, she stood, a wary look in her eyes. Dark blood from Darwin's gunshot wound soaked her pants.

"Come along, now. Let's all go see this secret room, shall we?"

Thirty-Three

WITH LUKE IN the lead and Angie at the rear, the five of us filed out of the master bedroom and down the hall to the room where Amelia had been. The television was still on, although there was no sound. The headphones lay forgotten on the bedspread.

A narrow opening in the wall next to the closet revealed a set of stairs leading to a lower level. At Angie's prompting, we descended into a large room lit by strategically placed track lights. A large river rock fireplace with gas logs took up a portion of one wall. Two leather wingback chairs with side tables flanked the fireplace, positioned to get the maximum view of the artwork. The room temperature was cool, telling me that no one had been down here for a while.

There were at least thirty paintings on the walls, each with a spotlight aimed at it, perfectly illuminating the modern masterpieces. I recognized the signatures of artists from an art history class I'd taken. The thought that after tonight I would never get to see another painting flashed through my mind.

Angie let out a low whistle as she perused the art. Her eyes bright, she turned to Amelia. "And you're absolutely certain these aren't forgeries?"

"Mick wouldn't have allowed it," Amelia said woodenly. Judging by her expression, she was in shock.

"Excellent. Luke, you take them down, and Amelia will bring them here." She walked over to the far corner of the room, beckoning us to join her. "Eve, you and Kate remove the canvases and put them in a pile here on the floor. Carefully, of course."

As Eve and I waited for the first of the paintings, I systematically went through my options. Angie had her gun, my gun, and a knife, which put the rest of us at an obvious disadvantage. Escaping up the stairs wouldn't work. Angie would shoot anyone attempting to escape, and then probably shoot whoever else she didn't ultimately need. Right now it was convenient to have us do the drudge work.

Which meant there wasn't much time.

There weren't any windows or a back door, leaving the stairs as the only way out. I'd have to create a diversion so that Angie would be focused on something other than me or the stairs.

When Luke had a hard time removing a large de Kooning, Angie took off her jacket and draped it over the back of one of the chairs and went to help. The hilt of Darwin's knife poked out from one of the pockets.

"You know Angie only needs Luke to get off this island, right?" I whispered to Eve, making sure Angie couldn't hear our conversation.

She nodded. "What can we do?" she mouthed. "No gun."

I nodded toward Angie's coat and the knife. Eve shook her head. "Too risky."

Amelia picked up a midsize painting and started toward us.

"We need a distraction. Think we can trust Amelia?"

Eve glanced at Angie, who was helping Luke lower the painting to the floor.

"Maybe."

Amelia leaned the painting she was carrying against a nearby wall and turned to go back for the de Kooning when I touched her arm.

She hesitated a moment.

In a low voice I said, "We need you to distract Angie."

Without turning she gave a quick nod and walked back to where Angie and Luke had successfully lowered the larger painting to the floor. I kept an eye on the three of them, waiting for her to do something as Eve and I worked on the canvas.

I didn't have to wait long.

Amelia had almost made it to where Angie and Luke were standing when she tripped and fell. Her arms flailed as she grabbed for something to steady herself. That something was the de Kooning. Both she and the priceless painting crashed to the floor. Angie's cry of horror and subsequent leap forward to try to save the painting was my cue to move. With Angie's back to me, I quickly crossed the room to the fireplace, searching the firebox for the gas valve. A flat metal handle jutted out from the ceramic logs on the right side. I didn't see the telltale flame of a pilot light, which I assumed was powered by a wall thermostat. I grabbed hold of the valve and twisted it wide open. The stench of garlic-laced propane hit me and began to fill the room.

I glanced at Angie who was inspecting the de Kooning for damage, and started back to join Eve. Angie's coat lay enticingly close, but I didn't dare take the time to grab the knife.

Good thing I didn't.

"What are you doing, Kate, honey?"

I froze, halfway across the room, heart pounding in my chest.

"I—I thought you might need help, but I see now that you've got it under control." I continued back to my spot next to Eve and turned to look at her. She narrowed her eyes in suspicion and cut a glance to her coat, then my hands. Unaware that I'd been clenching my fists, I flexed my fingers to show her I wasn't carrying anything. She frowned but appeared to let it slide. Relieved, I knelt to help Eve remove the backing of the painting she was working on.

"Whatever you do, don't turn on or off any lights, and be ready to move," I murmured. Eve nodded and we bent to our task.

A short time later, Angie stopped what she was doing, lifted her head, and sniffed the air.

"What the hell—?"

I did the same and was rewarded with the distinct odor of garlic-scented propane. The gas, at first heavier than the available oxygen, had filled the room and was now obvious. Angie's eyebrows disappeared into her hairline as she searched the room, her gaze landing on the fireplace.

"Shit." Her face a mask of cold fury, she started for the stairs. "Grab as many paintings as you can," she snapped at Luke. She elbowed her way past Amelia, who dropped the artwork she'd been holding. Angie whirled on her, pulling out her .45. Amelia shrank back at the sight of the semiauto.

"Don't shoot!" I was on my feet in a flash, holding my hands out in an attempt to stop her from discharging her gun. "One shot and the room blows," I said as I edged closer to the stairway. Eve followed my lead.

Angie gave me a look that could freeze a nuclear blast. "Well, isn't that just dandy?" She turned back to Amelia. "Looks like you get to live a few more minutes." She pushed Amelia backward onto the floor, then grabbed her coat off the chair and shoved her gun into Luke's back.

"You first," she said. His face pale, Luke started toward the exit.

I'd almost made it to the top of the steps. Eve raced past me and through the door as I turned to block Angie and Luke's way, my hand on the light switch. Angie scowled but paused on the stair, the .45 aimed at Luke's head.

"Give me the gun, Angie."

"What are you going to do? If I don't pass, then neither does Luke or Amelia. You don't want to be responsible for their deaths, do you?"

"Give. Me. The. Gun," I repeated, and held out my hand.

"Or what?"

"Or I'll flip the light switch and blow the room."

She gave me a look that said either she didn't believe I'd go through with it, or she didn't think flipping the switch would work.

I wasn't exactly sure, either. In theory, the sparks from the contacts in the light switch could set off the propane now filling the stairwell. Hell, sparks from the static cling of a polyester shirt had been known to set it off. All I needed was for her to think there might be a possibility that the spark from the contacts in the switch would be enough to ignite the propane.

"Now, Kate. After all the time we spent together don't you think I know you? You'd rather die than be responsible for ending an innocent life. Last time I checked," she nodded at Luke and then at Amelia, who stood on the stairs behind her, "these two didn't do anything wrong, other than being accessories to a little breaking and entering."

When I didn't respond, she turned as though to look behind her and then swung back with the coat in her hand. I punched at the fabric as Angie shoved Luke away from her and into me. I lost my balance, and Luke and I landed hard on the stairs. Luke rolled off of me just as Angie reared back, her leg raised for a kick, but I moved in time and she hit air. I grabbed her ankle and gave her foot a fierce twist.

Arms flailing, Angie slammed against the wall with a grunt, but recovered and launched herself past me. I flipped onto my hands and knees, grabbed her leg, and yanked her backward. She fell face first onto the stairs but immediately raised herself onto her elbows. With a vicious kick, she freed her leg from my grasp and sprang up the stairs. As I started up the steps to go after her, something cold and hard pressed into my palm.

Darwin's knife. I glanced behind me. Luke had Angie's coat. He'd found the dagger in her coat pocket and put it in my hand. I closed my fingers around the hilt.

Angie was ready for me. As I neared her position at the top of the stairs, she pivoted and her hand crashed down on my wrist in an iron grip, numbing the nerve running from elbow to hand. I might have let go of the knife if I hadn't expected the move. Angie had shown it to me in module six.

She tried to wrest the weapon free, but I countered with my other hand, just the way she'd taught me, grabbing the knife as close to the hilt as I could, and wrenched it from her grasp. The sting of the cut and slickness of the blood on the inside of my palm barely registered. Without thinking, I thrust the knife at her, aiming for the waist. The first try glanced off her ribcage. She twisted her torso to get out of reach. I lunged forward, and the second try scored a softer target. I buried the blade as deep as it would go. Angie grunted in pain as she pummeled me, trying to loosen my grip in an attempt to pull it out. When it was obvious that wouldn't work, she headbutted me and knocked me backward. I staggered down the stairwell before Amelia stopped my descent and pushed me back up the stairs.

Moments later I burst through the open doorway and raced through the guest bedroom as Angie's slender form disappeared down the hallway. The stench of gas was strong. We needed to get far away from the house or there wouldn't be anything left to ID the bodies.

"Everybody—run!" I yelled.

The farther we got from the gas leak, the more likely it was that Angie would use her gun. I checked my pace and followed the intermittent blood spatters on the floor. Eve was waiting in the kitchen. Amelia and Luke were steps behind.

"Did you see her?" I asked, breathless from running. The blood trail ended abruptly outside the kitchen.

Eve shook her head. "No sign of her, and I was here the whole time."

I was about to say something when there was movement in my periphery. Angie stepped from the shadows in the living room, the gun in her hand. She pointed the weapon up and away from her, toward the hall ceiling.

"Get down!" I screamed, and dropped to the floor. The gun discharged and the hall light exploded. Everything went dark as a loud *whooshing* noise swept through the house.

And the world exploded.

THIRTY-FOUR

I CAME TO slowly, the ringing in my ears the first indication I was still alive. Opening my eyes, I rolled to one side and almost coughed up a lung. Dust was thick in the air.

Once I finished hacking, I took stock of my body parts, making sure everything was still intact. Aside from a sharp pain in my right side and confused, foggy thoughts, I was in one piece. I groped for the cool stone surface of the kitchen island and hoisted myself to my feet. The pain in my side lanced deeper and I froze, trying to catch my breath. Afraid to look at the wound, I leaned on the counter for a moment, trying to ignore the pain while I regrouped.

The back half of the kitchen near the hallway had been demolished. There was a gaping hole where the Sub Zero refrigerator had been, revealing broken interior wall framing. The path of destruction created by the fridge's trajectory ended at the far wall, where the huge metal box was now dented as though a giant stomped on it and kicked it out of the way. Liquid puddled on the floor below. The kitchen lights flickered, and here and there a few small fires crackled.

I pivoted in place, scanning the hallway. My breath caught at the sight of a delicate wrist and loosely curled fingers poking out from a pile of debris.

Forgetting my pain, I stumbled to the wreckage and started digging. Once I'd cleared away enough of the drywall and other broken pieces, I grabbed the wrist to check for a pulse.

There was none.

Someone groaned behind me and I whirled around.

Covered in a fine white dust, Eve lay on the floor just past the kitchen. A gaping hole in the ceiling explained the pieces of drywall scattered around her. She appeared disoriented and tried to roll over onto her side to prop herself up. Relieved that she was alive, I realized that meant the body beneath the pile of rubble had to be Amelia. Shoving aside my feelings for the time being, I frantically searched the room for Angie, but didn't see her. She'd been standing in front of the still intact fireplace at the time of the explosion.

Which meant she probably survived the blast.

Unable to help Amelia, I picked my way through the demolished kitchen toward Eve. Kneeling beside her, I helped her to a sitting position. She winced with the effort but otherwise seemed all right. Other than a few cuts on her face, there was no blood visible.

"Are you okay?" My voice sounded muted to my own ears, and I had to yell so she could hear me. It was as though I was underwater listening to grains of sand rolling across the seabed with a backdrop of faint ringing.

Eve nodded. "I think so." I watched her lips to get the gist of what she said.

"We need to go. Now." When I tried to help her to her feet, a razor-sharp stitch flashed across my ribs, stealing my breath. With a frown of concern, Eve stood the rest of the way on her own. Unable to ignore it any longer, I opened my jacket and glanced at my side. Blood saturated the fabric of my pullover, staining the dark material darker. Wincing, I pulled the fabric free and looked. A dark gash sliced across my midriff. Blood oozed over the waistband of my jeans.

Eve held up one finger, indicating I should wait, and picked her way back into the kitchen. She returned a few minutes later carrying a kitchen towel and a roll of duct tape. Gritting my teeth against the pain, I held the towel in place as she wrapped the duct tape tightly around my torso.

The ringing in my ears had begun to lessen. With the towel firmly in place, I figured things were as good as they were going to get.

"We need to find out what happened to Luke," I said.

"Over here."

Eve and I turned toward the raspy voice. From the dim glow of the patio lights, I could barely make out the hand waving from under a door that had been blown off its hinges farther down the hallway.

We made our way over to him and heaved the door to one side. Eve joined me as I dug through the debris covering his legs, careful to avoid the shards of glass from paintings thrown to the floor in the blast.

"Am I glad to see you guys."

We each took a side and hoisted him to a standing position. His leg buckled and he slumped toward the floor. Blood from my injury oozed through the towel from the strain of holding him up, but I ignored it.

"I think my leg is broken." Luke winced as he attempted to put weight on his right foot. He shook his head. "No way I can walk out of here under my own steam."

"We'll help you," I said. "We need to get moving. It won't be long before somebody comes by the island to see what happened, and I'd like to be gone before then."

"What about my phone?" he asked. "Angie grabbed it before we went downstairs."

"But it's a burner, right?" Eve had cautioned everyone to bring phones with no identifying information. "And you live-streamed the video to an account in the cloud?" Meaning the video bypassed the phone's memory altogether.

"Yeah, but the account information is still in memory. I didn't have time to delete it."

"Do you still have your phone?" I asked Eve. "Couldn't you transfer the video to another account and disable Luke's?"

She went through her coat pockets. "I put it away when we went to the underground room." Relief flooded her face. "It's here." She squinted as she hit the on button. "It's not working. The screen is cracked. I must have fallen on it."

"Then you'll have to do it as soon as we get back." As long as we didn't run into Angie on the way to the boat, we should be all right.

The three of us staggered through the living room toward the front door like three-legged race participants. Eve was the only one who hadn't been severely injured, although the explosion had done a number on her equilibrium. She was having a hard time walking in a straight line and had to continually self-correct.

"You might want to have a doctor take a look at your inner ear," I said. "A blast like that can screw things up." Memories of surviving an explosion in the Yucatán jungle flashed through my mind. It had taken me days to get back to normal.

Understanding flitted across her face. "That's why it's so hard to walk."

"And here I thought it was me." Luke's grimace looked like it was supposed to be a grin.

"Well, there's that, too."

Although my main concern was getting us to the boat quickly, I was worried about Angie finding her way off the island. The knife in her side could easily be a mortal wound. There was a good possibility she'd bleed out before long. Hopefully before she reached the cove. Even if she did make it back to the boat, she'd have a hard time finding her way to Seattle without running into some serious trouble. Navigating at night through the islands was difficult, even if you knew what you were doing. Out of the remaining crew, only Luke had the knowledge and skill to bring the *Olympic Dream* home safely.

Angie still had the video of me at Chacon's house, which didn't give me the warm fuzzies. Sam was still in danger of being linked to my stupidity. I could, however, meet Angie's attempt at blackmail with my own, as long as Eve gave me access to the recording of Dobson's murder. It was also possible that Eve would be able to help me locate Angie's files—she'd mentioned earlier that she'd hacked the cloud before, and that it wasn't really that hard depending on the user's tech savviness. Like Eve, Angie used an iPhone. I assumed that she automatically saved photos and video to the cloud, as well. If Eve was able to get into her files, I'd have to be sure she deleted all copies, and hope Angie hadn't uploaded more.

We continued out the door and around to the back of the structure, now a smoking, twisted wreck. The cold, damp air seeped through the open collar of my jacket, and I shivered. I zipped up the rest of the way and tugged on my hood.

Most of the windows had blown out from the back of the house. Gleaming shards of glass littered the grounds. The eeriness of the landscape added to my anxiety, and I stepped up our pace.

Twenty-five minutes later, we reached the spot where we'd left Kitten. Using my flashlight, I was the first to spot her. She was propped against a tree, staring sightlessly into the darkness, a gaping wound across her throat. A dark stain covered the front of her jacket where the blood had streamed from the gash. Her computer lay in pieces around her. We stood for a moment, taking in the grisly sight.

"Angie." A chill slid down my back at the grim proof of her survival.

"Kitten deserved better." Eve's words came out dry and brittle. With a quiet sniff, she wiped her nose on the sleeve of her jacket and took a deep breath. Tears glistened in her eyes, illuminated by the dusky blue moonlight. "Wait here." She left Luke and me standing in the darkness as she walked to her friend and gently closed her eyes. Then she started sifting through the pieces of Kitten's laptop.

"We don't have a lot of time, Eve. Once the police figure out what happened here, we won't be able to leave the island without being seen."

"She got the SD card, but not this." She rejoined us, holding up the laptop's hard drive, which she slipped into her coat pocket. "At least it's something."

We resumed our trek to the cove where we'd left the inflatable, vigilant for signs of the wounded assassin.

It took us over two hours to retrace our steps through the narrow canyon and back to the cove. Luke had picked up a fallen tree branch to use as a crude crutch, which came in handy during our climb down the rocky face. I tied our jackets together to form a makeshift sling, which Eve and I used to lower Luke down the steepest sections of the cliff.

The inflatable was where we'd left it. The beach had doubled in size from the outgoing tide, and pushing the boat back into the water would take some effort. Thankfully, it wasn't as heavy as one made of wood or fiberglass. There was no sign of Angie, and I began to relax. I didn't think she'd be able to make the climb down to the beach with the depth of the knife wound she had. I'd been careful with my own injury when navigating the rocks, and the pain still took my breath away.

Although exhausted from the hike and our descent to the beach, we put our backs into pushing the boat over the sand and rocks toward the water. Luke helped as much as he could, hopping on one foot and leaning his weight against the bow. When the stern hit water, the three of us stopped to rest, breathing hard from the effort.

I reached inside the boat and grabbed three hermetically sealed packets of survival water from the bow locker. I gave one to Eve and handed the other to Luke. A voice in the darkness stopped me cold.

"Did you forget about *moi*?"

The breath caught in my throat at the sound of Angie's southern twang. I slowly turned around. Illuminated in a beam of ghostly moonlight, the assassin stood behind me, gun in one hand, the other clutching her side. She'd lost some of her ever-present bravado—stooped over and in obvious pain, the weapon trembled in her hand. Luke looked ready to charge, broken leg or not, but I shook my head and he stood down. Eve remained motionless. I knew from experience that if I moved now, Angie would track me with her gun like a hunter tracking prey.

Or, shoot me on the spot. This time there was no possibility of an explosion to stop her from discharging her gun.

"Look, Angie," I said, my tone conversational through sheer force of will. "There's no reason to kill any of us. You've got me by the shorthairs with that video you took of Chacon, and the two phones we were using to record Dobson were destroyed in the explosion." I hoped she didn't know Eve and Luke had live-streamed the confession. "And, you disabled Kitten's laptop and took the memory card, so there's nothing tying you to the shitstorm back at Dobson's house." A sharp flame of anger flared at the thought of Kitten's lifeless body propped against a tree.

Don't let her know you're angry, Kate. You need to stay calm.

"True. But think of the satisfaction I'll have when I finally complete the contract originally taken out on you." She winced as she closed the distance between us, gun aimed at the center of my chest. "I'll be back on top, baby."

She was going to shoot me, and probably Eve. I had to keep her talking. My mind raced through the moves I'd learned from both Sam and Angie, finally settling on one. It was a long shot.

Could I pull it off?

"I thought you said it didn't matter, now that there was no money involved."

A thin smile stretched her lips. "I lied."

With those last two words I raised the Maglite and shined it in her eyes. At the same time I hurled my packet of water into her face and stepped forward, slapping the gun barrel away with as much force as I could. The .45 discharged with a bang before it flew from her grip and landed in the water with a splash. Her slowed reactions were likely a side effect of losing so much blood and gave me an advantage I otherwise wouldn't have had. Without giving her time to react, I lowered my head and charged. I caught her at the waist and shoved her to the ground, landing on top of her. We both grunted in pain.

And then it was like someone flipped a switch—she was all nails and teeth and flailing arms, seemingly oblivious to the pain that had stopped her only two seconds before. I did my best to fight back, but she soon had the edge and the next thing I knew she was on top of me with her hands at my throat. I bucked and thrashed, but she held me in an iron grip. My vision tunneled. I opened my mouth, desperate for air. Someone yelled. Angie's head snapped back, and the vice-grip around my throat loosened.

Gasping, I rolled onto an elbow and raised my head. Eve was clinging to Angie's back, her hands wound tight around the assassin's neck as Angie whirled in place, attempting to throw Eve off.

I climbed to my feet with a grunt of pain and staggered toward them.

"Kate!" Luke called. I turned as he heaved the branch he'd been using as a crutch toward me. It landed on the ground less than a foot away. Lightheaded, I took a deep breath and bent over to retrieve it, ignoring the black spots sparking in my periphery. I hefted the pseudo crutch in my hands, turned toward the whirling dervishes, and took a batter's stance. With Angie and Eve's backs to me, I had no target except Angie's legs. I was about to swing for the back of her knees when Angie pivoted.

With the assassin gripped in a headlock, Eve glanced over Angie's shoulder at me. Her gaze zeroed in on the branch and a look of understanding lit her eyes. She let go and stumbled back. Angie leaned over and clawed at her throat, gasping for air. Powered by fear and rage and the pent-up emotions of the past few weeks, I swung for all I was worth. A splintering, cracking, sickening thud fractured the air as the heavy wood connected with Angie's temple. Her head snapped sideways, body paused for a millisecond in midair, and dropped like a stone.

Breathing hard, I staggered toward Eve.

"Cover me," I rasped, and handed her the branch.

I made my way back to Angie and bent over to check for a pulse.

"Nothing." I straightened and took a deep breath, wincing at the pain in my side.

Eve stared at the blood on my hand and blinked.

Luke called from the inflatable. "Is she dead?"

I nodded, the adrenaline still pushing my heart rate to the moon. "Yeah. She's dead." I took the branch from Eve, wiped the end off in the sand, and brought it back to Luke. "Check her pockets for her phone, keys, anything that might be useful," I called behind me.

Eve did as I asked while I shoved aside the thought that I'd eliminated another threat from my past. Her death was a hollow victory. Angie might be gone, but I'd still lost Sam. It didn't matter what happened next. Luis was the only threat left. I shouldn't have any trouble sidestepping him, if he was even looking for me. I touched my side and my hand came away wet. The wound was bleeding again. I had to get on board the *Olympic Dream* where I had access to medical supplies.

Eve straightened. "I got Luke's phone and the SD card, but that's it."

"Should we do something with the body?" Luke asked. "I wish we could have had time to bury Darwin and Kitten."

"I've got a better idea. Can I use that anchor?" I nodded at the one we'd used to keep the inflatable in the cove in case a storm came up while we were on the island.

"What are you thinking?" Eve asked.

"Burial at sea."

THIRTY-FIVE

N HOUR LATER, we were onboard the *Olympic Dream*. After hearing the muted sounds of the explosion on the other side of the island, Lady D had been relieved beyond measure to see us, but broke down in tears at the news of Darwin's and Kitten's deaths. The anger in Eve's eyes and set of her jaw told me that Dobson's death probably wouldn't be enough.

Thankfully, Luke kept a well-stocked first aid kit on the boat and I was able to dress my wound. Next, we set his leg using duct tape and an oar as a splint. He suggested I go below decks and try to get some rest, so I took his advice. Angie had left her purse in a locked compartment in the forward berth, which was where I found her phone after getting the extra key from Luke. Her screen was password protected, so I put it in my pocket to give to Eve.

Luke secured himself to the captain's chair, and using a combination of the radio, charts, GPS, and the depth finder expertly steered us through the islands back to his parents' house in Edmonds. Lady D, Eve, and I helped tie up to the dock and then went our separate ways, with Eve promising to look for Angie's files after I gave her the phone. I told her about Chacon's murder and how I was on the video, but that I hadn't been the one to kill him. She took the admission in stride, letting me know she would delete the evidence once she found it.

"I'm still angry that we weren't able to go through with our plan to make Dobson pay the victims." Eve narrowed her eyes and shook her head. "Some of the families lost their main income earner. A payout would have meant so much to them."

"You know, there is one thing you could do."

Eve gave me a sharp glance.

"Upload that video of Dobson confessing and wait until Pro-Pharma's stock crashes."

"I don't get it. How would that get money to the families?"

"Ever hear of shorting a stock?"

I made it to my hotel just as Seattle was waking up for the day. The din of traffic from the early morning commute rang hollow in my overly sensitive ears, and I was happy to step through the glass doors into the hushed atmosphere of the hotel lobby. As I waited for the elevator to my room, the smell of coffee wafting toward me from the restaurant was almost overwhelming. I decided caffeine would interrupt the sleep I so desperately needed and opted out.

I slept all day, waking in time to catch the local news. The lead story screamed "Explosion in the San Juans," and at first attributed the explosion to faulty propane tanks. Aerial views from the King 5 helicopter showed the damage to the home. A German shepherd ran excitedly from one side of the yard to the other, barking at the chopper. The reporter speculated on whether the CEO for Pro-Pharma might still be inside.

Later on, during the same newscast, the reporter broke in live to report that Dobson's body had been found tied to a chair in the master bedroom, victim of a gunshot wound. There was a brief mention of three additional bodies—two in the house and one on the grounds—but no other identifying information was given. I waited for news of the discovery of another dead body on the other side of the island, tied to an anchor near a narrow spit of sand, but none came.

I calculated the hours since our departure from the island and figured the beach had disappeared under high tide, leaving Angie even deeper than where we'd left her.

I turned off the television and walked into the bathroom. A small amount of blood had soaked through the bandage and the wound still throbbed, but other than that things were manageable. I splashed cool water on my face and stared at my reflection.

A stranger looked back at me.

The old Kate had disappeared leaving a new, not necessarily improved Kate in her place. My emotions were raw, with emptiness the only definable feeling. I thought about texting my father to find out how Lisa was doing but couldn't summon the energy to walk out of the bathroom to pick up my phone. I leaned forward with both hands on either side of the sink and looked into my eyes, searching for a remnant of something familiar.

I thought back to the events leading to this moment. Lisa's overdose. Jason Whitmore's death and his family's need for closure. My stubborn refusal to wait for the DEA to do what they were paid to do while I tried to mete out my own justice. Training with Angie. Chacon's murder. Losing Sam.

And now this.

True, Dobson was dead, had paid for his transgressions with his life. But that one fact hadn't filled the hole created by Lisa's overdose, or losing my family and Sam.

What do I do now?

I turned from the mirror and walked back into the room. Suddenly restless, the thought of being alone spurred me into action. I threw on a pair of jeans and a shirt, grabbed my coat and bag, and took the elevator to the lobby, intending to walk to a nearby restaurant for dinner. The elevator doors pinged open and I walked out onto the marble landing, stepping to the side when someone brushed past me.

"Sorry," I muttered, and looked up to see who I'd stumbled into.

"Kate."

Sam's deep brown eyes stared into mine, and I stopped short, my heart fluttering in surprise. With an impatient snort, the man who had been behind me in the elevator shouldered his way past us to the lobby.

"What are you doing here?" My heart filled with hope, but a second later came crashing down to earth. My bad girl returned with a vengeance to tell me not to get my hopes up, to remember what I'd done.

Sam pulled me aside and walked me over to a nearby sofa, where we both had a seat.

"I came as soon as I heard about Dobson." He lifted my chin with his hand and held my gaze. "You had something to do with it, didn't you?"

I closed my eyes and nodded. He let his hand drop.

"But it's not what you think." I opened my eyes and searched his, hoping to find a hint of understanding, or at least a willingness to hear me out.

"I'm listening."

I took a deep breath and recounted everything that had happened since we'd split up. How I couldn't figure out a way to ditch Angie, since she still had the Chacon video. How she'd blackmailed me into going along with the hacker's plan to exact vengeance from Dobson, and her real plan to steal the artwork, kill everyone except Luke, and leave me on the island to take the blame. I told him I stabbed her in the side but she'd reappeared, and how I'd killed her with the branch. I then explained how Eve had recorded both Darwin's and Dobson's murders with her phone but didn't get Angie in the frame until she'd killed Dobson.

Sam let out a breath and his shoulders relaxed. "I'm glad Angie can't hurt us anymore."

I was about to reply when it hit me. He'd said us. A tiny flicker of hope blossomed inside of me at the word, but again, Bad Kate warned me not to get my hopes up.

"At least I think so. She could have a dead man's switch set up in the event of her death, although I don't know if that's her style. She was arrogant enough to think she wasn't going to die. Not at my hands."

"How did Angie survive the blast?"

"She was near the front door when she shot out the light. The propane hadn't spread that far."

He nodded. "What did you do with the body?"

"Eve and I tied her to an anchor and dragged her into the water as far as we could. It was low tide," I added, by way of explanation.

Sam studied me for a long moment. "You're different. Like a part of the Kate I used to know isn't there anymore."

I sighed. "I've been giving things a lot of thought."

"And?"

A woman with a teacup poodle in her purse walked by, distracting me from answering. Sam put his hand on my arm. "And?" he repeated, his tone gentle.

I turned to look at him. "I know that we're through, and I understand why. But I want to apologize. My anger made me foolish, and my actions put us both in danger."

Sam crossed his arms and leaned back.

"I want you to know—" I cleared my throat. "How much I loved you. You were my home."

Sam shook his head. "So what you're saying is—"

"What I'm saying is, through this entire ordeal, I finally realized that you were right." I watched people hurry past through the lobby, wondering if I could make Sam understand what I myself could hardly put into words. I took another deep breath and turned to face him.

"Look. I was filled with anger and hurt and guilt at what happened to Lisa. Then, when my family told me to leave them alone, that I shouldn't have anything to do with them, it was more than I could take. I felt adrift, rudderless. I had to grab on to something concrete that I could do, something other than sitting idly by, waiting for whichever agency to make their move. I thought it was up to me to make Chacon and Dobson pay." I stared into space. "I was wrong. Vengeance doesn't make the pain go away. It makes things so much worse. By the time I figured that out, Angie already had her hooks in me and I didn't know how to get out."

Sam's silence spoke volumes. He didn't understand. The dead feeling returned, and I stood to leave. He took hold of my wrist.

"What?" I asked, looking into his eyes.

The expression on his face was unreadable. Pure Sam. He never showed emotion. I could count on one hand the times I'd actually been able to read his thoughts. I sank back onto the settee and waited.

"You spoke in the past tense. Are you telling me you don't love me anymore?"

"I'll always love you, Sam. Please believe that." I moved to leave. His hand tightened on my wrist.

"Where are you going?"

"Don't make this harder than it already is, okay?" Tears sprang to my eyes, and I blinked them back.

"Does this new you mean that I won't have to worry about you running out and getting yourself killed every time somebody does something that pisses you off?"

My cheeks heated from the pulse of hope rushing through me. Maybe he'd be willing to try again. "Probably not." The corners of my mouth twitched. "But it does mean that I won't try to kill the bastards myself."

Sam's mask slipped for a moment, and a look of relief swept over his face. He leaned forward and wrapped his arms around me, burying his face in my neck.

"That's all I needed to hear."

And that was all I needed, too.

Thirty-Six

TWO WEEKS LATER, Pro-Pharma's stock took a nosedive over rumors of illegal activities. Someone hacked into one of the national news sites and uploaded the video with Mick Dobson's confession. When asked for a comment, the acting CEO of Pro-Pharma issued a brief statement of denial accusing Mick Dobson of skimming off the top and distributing subpar meds to an illegal drug network, headed by the now-deceased Andrew Chacon.

The public outcry far exceeded the company's ability to spin the problem of shipping deadly pharmaceuticals to foreign countries under the guise of "helpful commerce," and Pro-Pharma's stock tanked even further. The Food and Drug Administration was in the process of building a case against them, and the Department of Justice had opened an inquiry.

A few days after Pro-Pharma's collapse, I walked into the kitchen to see what Sam was making for dinner. Onions and garlic and all sorts of wonderful smells were emanating from a pan on the stove. Sam dipped a spoon into the mixture and held it up for me to taste.

"Oh, that's good. When's dinner ready?"

Sam smiled and turned back to the pan. "About twenty."

At that moment, my phone chimed, indicating a text. I checked the sender. The screen said anonymous.

```
Vigilante Kate. Check your bank
account. Thanks for the idea.
```

Puzzled, I pulled up my banking app.

"Holy crap."

Sam glanced at me and then at the phone. "What?"

"Take a look."

He came over to join me, and I turned the screen toward him.

"Whose account is that?"

"Mine."

He gave a low whistle. "Seven and a half million? That's some serious bank. What did you do?" He stepped back and raised his hands. "Wait. Don't tell me. I don't want to know."

I swatted at him. "Don't be silly. It has to be a mistake." I checked the deposit. It looked legit—the funds had been wired into my account that morning. I replied to the anonymous number and asked who it was, but I had my suspicions. The reply came back instantly:

```
An art lover.
```

I texted back with a simple *Thank you.* Shaking my head in disbelief, I set the phone on the counter.

"She actually did it."

"Who, and what?"

"Shorted Pro-Pharma's stock. I mentioned it to Eve the last time we spoke." Laughter bubbled up inside of me, and I couldn't hold back any longer. Apparently it was catching because pretty soon Sam had a big grin across his face.

"I'm betting that there are some mighty grateful families who recently lost a loved one to an overdose."

"Yeah. Seven and a half million will go a long way toward providing high quality care for Lisa." I'd set up an account as soon as I finished breakfast and give my dad access. "Knowing Eve, she covered her tracks and the tracks of everyone involved so there won't be any question of insider trading."

"Now that's my kind of vigilante."

I nodded. "Vigilante Kate. What do you think? That's a good moniker, right?" I walked over to the cupboard to grab a couple of plates for dinner.

"Definitely better than Vigilante Dead."

I smiled at his play on words. *Yes. Yes it is.*

THE END

ACKNOWLEDGEMENTS

I'd like to thank the following people for their help and support in writing *Vigilante Dead*. First and foremost, Mark Lindstrom for your unconditional support, fabulous dinners, and wicked sense of humor; my amazing editor, Laurie Boris—I consider myself lucky to work with you; my writing group: Ali Mosa, Jenni Conner, Darlene Panzera; Mistress of Mayhem, Ruth M. Ross-Saucier; early readers Michelle and Brian Yelland, and Bev and Larry Van Berkom. Special thanks to the stellar ARTeam (you guys know who you are ;-), and as ever, TSODA134 (a.k.a. Special Forces Dude)—your detailed input adds an element of realism to my novels that I wouldn't be able to achieve without your help.

Writing is never a solitary endeavor.

ABOUT THE AUTHOR

 **DV Berkom** is the USA Today bestselling author of two action-packed thriller series featuring strong female leads **(Leine Basso** and **Kate Jones**). Her love of creating resilient, kick-ass women characters stems from a lifelong addiction to reading spy novels, mysteries, and thrillers, and longing to find the female equivalent within those pages.

Raised in the Midwest, she earned a BA in political science from the University of Minnesota and promptly moved to Mexico to live on a sailboat. Several years and adventures later, she wrote her first novel and was hooked. ***Bad Spirits,*** the first Kate Jones thriller, was published as an online serial in 2010 and was immediately popular with eBook fans. ***Dead of Winter, Death Rites***, and ***Touring for Death*** soon followed before she began the far grittier Leine Basso series in early 2012 with ***Serial Date***.

D.V. currently lives in the Pacific Northwest with her husband, Mark, and several imaginary characters who like to tell her what to do. Her most recent books include ***Shadow of the Jaguar, Dakota Burn, Absolution, Dark Return, The Last Deception, Vigilante Dead, A Killing Truth,*** and ***A One Way Ticket to Dead.*** She's currently at work on her next thriller.

For more information, please visit her website at www.dvberkom.com.

NOTE FROM THE AUTHOR:

Thank you for reading **VIGILANTE DEAD**. I hope you enjoyed it. If you would like to find out more about Kate or my other novels, see the links below:
Facebook: facebook.com/DvBerkomAuthor
Twitter: twitter.com/dvberkom
Website: dvberkom.com

***Sign up for my Readers' List to be the first to find out about new releases and subscriber-only offers: **http://bit.ly/DVB_RL**

Other books by D.V. Berkom
Kate Jones Thriller Series:
Kate Jones Thriller Series Vol. 1 (#1-4)
(Bad Spirits, Dead of Winter, Death Rites, Touring for Death)
Cruising for Death (#5)
Yucatán Dead (#6)
A One Way Ticket to Dead (#7)

Leine Basso Crime Thriller Series
A Killing Truth
Serial Date
Bad Traffick
The Body Market
Cargo
The Last Deception
Dark Return
Absolution
Dakota Burn
Shadow of the Jaguar